Killer Getaway

By Amy Korman

Killer Getaway

Killer WASPs

Killer Getaway

A
KILLER WASPS
MYSTERY

AMY KORMAN

WITNESS
IMPULSE
An Imprint of HarperCollins*Publishers*

EPub Edition MARCH 2015 ISBN: 9780062357861
Print Edition ISBN: 9780062357885

10 9 8 7 6 5 4 3 2 1

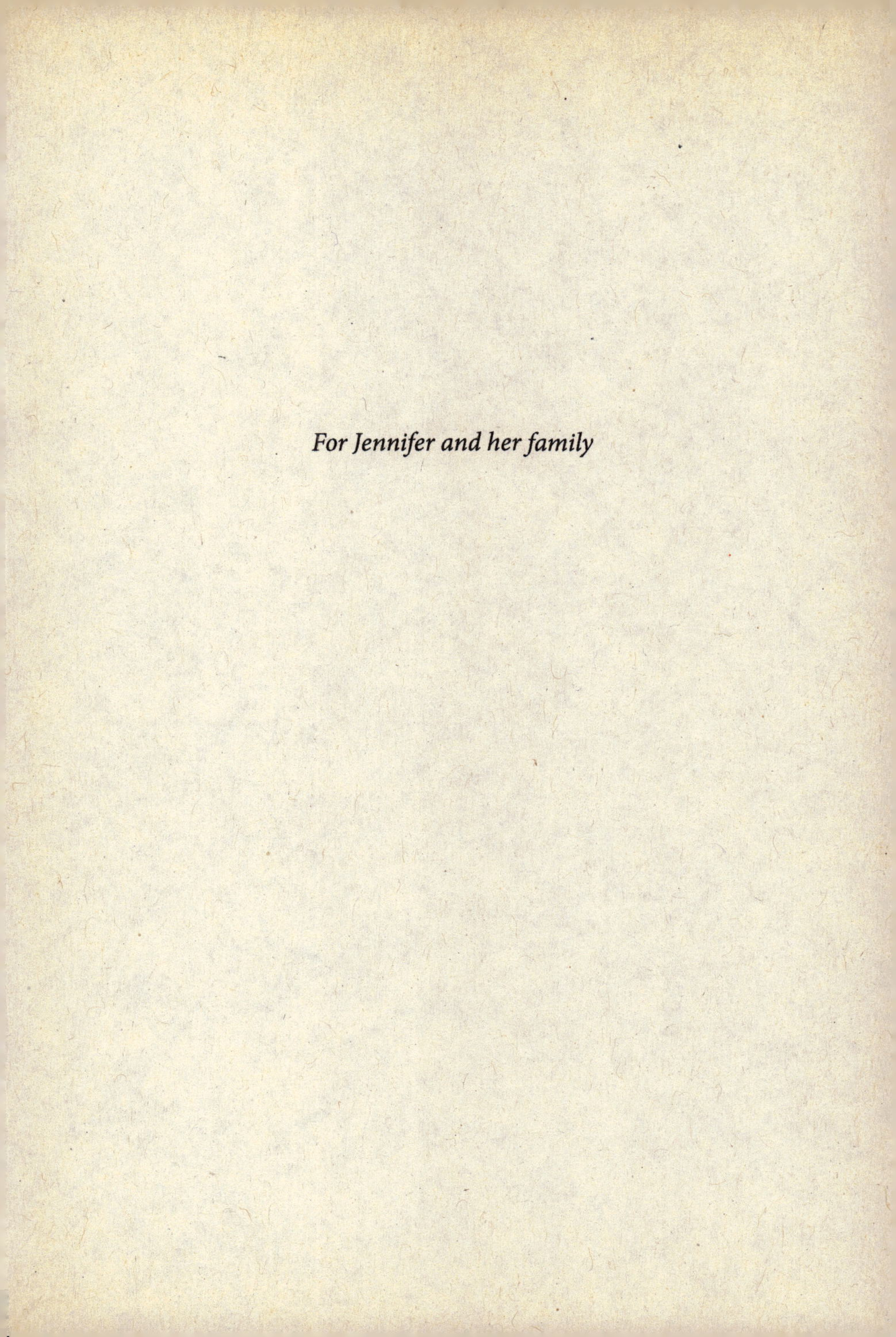

For Jennifer and her family

Chapter 1

"CHAMPAGNE?" ASKED A handsome, dark-haired waiter as a jazzy bossa nova percolated through Vicino, Magnolia Beach's newest and hottest restaurant, at 8:30 on a jasmine-scented Florida night.

"Abso-freakin'-lutely!" shrieked Sophie Shields, a tiny blond woman in purple Versace seated to my right on Vicino's corner banquette. She held her glass up for the young waiter to top up her Moët.

"Ever since we got to Florida three weeks ago, it's been nothing but champagne and moonlit nights," Sophie told me. "This place is so darn romantic, it just puts me in the mood to get some lovin'!"

Well-dressed couples had turned to gaze askance at our table of five. The word "Abso-freakin'-lutely" isn't screamed regularly at Magnolia Beach restaurants, a South Florida enclave where many of the patrons are over seventy and are clad exclusively in Ralph Lauren outfits 24/7.

"And we eat here at Vicino pretty much every night, where—and this is sort of a secret—I own forty-five percent of the restaurant!" added Sophie.

"I don't think it's a secret anymore," observed Joe Delafield, my friend of more than fifteen years. He was seated to Sophie's right, her hand possessively clutching his blue-blazer-clad arm. "You've announced that you're the co-owner of Vicino at every party and every store we've entered since we set foot on this island," Joe told his girlfriend.

Sophie, the estranged wife of a former mafia-connected real estate developer, and Joe, a preppy thirty-something interior designer, have been dating for seven months. They're complete opposites, but they seem happy together, much to everyone's shock, including Joe's.

"Yeah, I started out as a silent partner, but it turns out I don't really do silent," Sophie noted, shrugging.

Holly Jones and Bootsie McElvoy, the remaining members of our party, merely rolled their eyes. Holly and Bootsie went to high school with me in our hometown outside Philadelphia, where in January the weather is slushy, sludgy, gray, and freezing. Holly, who possesses virtually unlimited funds, had decided on New Year's Day that she was relocating to Magnolia Beach to wait out the rest of winter, and Sophie and Joe had followed suit.

Since my own funds are limited—in fact, I barely scrape by at The Striped Awning, the antiques store I run in our village of Bryn Mawr—Bootsie and I were staying with Holly at a house she'd rented. Picture tall palm trees around a pool, a vast living room that opens out to said pool, and white linen sofas everywhere, and you get the idea of the place.

"Can I get a margarita, Patron, extra salt, please?" Bootsie asked our waiter, who was busily uncorking the next bottle of bubbly. "And a double order of the grilled shrimp? And two of the wood-fired pizzas? And . . ." Bootsie consulted the left side of the menu. "Actually, let's have all the appetizers. The oysters, the figs in prosciutto, the scallops, the crab risotto. Just keep them coming."

Bootsie, who's six feet tall and plays a lot of tennis, can eat like an NFL player.

"Ya got a good appetite!" said Sophie admiringly to Bootsie.

"Seventeen hours in a car can make you a little hungry," Bootsie told her, while I swigged some champagne, shuddering at her words. I'd spent all seventeen of those hours today with Bootsie in her black Range Rover as she'd sped down I-95 from Philly toward this tropical paradise. It had been a white-knuckler, with Bootsie speeding, honking, and cutting off 18-wheelers during her stint as driver, then yelling at me to go faster when I'd taken the wheel in South Carolina.

Truth be told, and I say this with all due affection for Bootsie, who's a good person and loyal in her own interfering, nosy way, I've envisioned permanently ending our friendship—and possibly ending Bootsie's life—several times since we left Pennsylvania in the predawn hours.

Just then, though, the grilled shrimp arrived, and they were so delicious that I thought maybe the trip had been worth it. A breeze through the restaurant's open French doors wafted the fragrance of camellias our way, and my mood skyrocketed.

"Thank you so much, Holly, for convincing us to come down here! This is perfection."

Holly and Joe exchanged a meaningful glance, and a tingle portending bad news crept down my spine.

"Perfection might be slightly overstating how things are going on this little boondoggle," Joe told me.

"There is one small detail I left out," Holly said, "about what's been going on since we got to Magnolia Beach."

"Small detail?" said Joe skeptically. "You mean the part when you were almost murdered on Tuesday?"

Chapter 2

UNTIL THE PREVIOUS spring, murder, attempted murder, or crime of any kind was never a topic of conversation among my friends, unless you count that time Bootsie toilet-papered the gates to Bryn Mawr Prep during Senior Week back in the late '90s. We'd lived a protected, peaceful existence in our leafy, tranquil Pennsylvania town, where Bootsie works at the local *Bryn Mawr Gazette*, Joe runs his interior design business, and Holly—well, Holly does whatever it is that heiresses to poultry fortunes do all day.

Then we met Sophie Shields. And her soon-to-be-ex-husband, Barclay Shields, who'd been knocked on the head and left for dead under a hydrangea bush across the street from my house. From that moment on, a crime spree erupted around Bryn Mawr, complete with mafia guys in leather sport coats visiting our polo-shirt-loving town.

As I looked at Holly, who was nibbling a stalk of celery (she doesn't consume much in the way of solid food, which explains her willowy frame), I knew she and Joe were telling the truth: If

hie who'd claimed she was almost murdered, I'd
tful, but Holly and Joe didn't make this stuff up.
ights ago," Holly told Bootsie and me. "I was leaving here around ten, and Jessica and I were heading out to our cars, since these two"—Holly indicated Sophie and Joe with a tanned, slim hand—"had already left."

"Cause I needed to get some time alone with my Snuggle Bunny!" Sophie informed us helpfully, adding a meaningful wink. "If ya know what I mean."

"Whatever," Holly continued. She explained that she and Jessica, the skinny blond manager of Vicino, had stood chatting near Jessica's car in the side street outside Vicino for a few minutes. Channing, Vicino's Armani-model-looking chef, had been inside finishing up his work for the night.

We all knew Channing and Jessica, who had lived in Bryn Mawr until moving to Florida last summer to open the restaurant in which we now sat. Channing had been sous-chef to a star restaurateur named Gianni Brunello, which was how he'd met Jessica—Gianni's former girlfriend.

Jessica and Channing had started an affair right under Gianni's nose, and soon afterward they had fled the Northeast. That had been a wise move, because Gianni, who's known for his temper, hadn't been all that happy about the steamy fling his girlfriend and sous-chef had been carrying on all over Bryn Mawr, including in the walk-in fridge in his restaurant. When the two had decided to open Vicino, both Holly and Sophie had signed on as silent partners—Sophie, of course, not staying too silent about her investment in the restaurant.

"So on Tuesday night, all of a sudden, this car—it was a small dark red car, maybe a Chevy—tore down the alley," Holly told us, her sky-blue, almond-shaped eyes wide with remembered fright. "It was aiming right for the two of us, tires screaming, and was literally inches away when Channing opened the kitchen door and grabbed both me and Jessica, one in each arm, and hurdled us over the trash bins."

"Channing's like a superhero!" Sophie contributed. "I mean, I wasn't there, because Joe and I were home getting some nooky, but it sounds like Channing saved Holly and Jessica's lives! But not their outfits. Holly had on this cotton Prada number, and it got, like, old cocktail sauce all over it," Sophie added. "It's ruined. Oh, and Jessica sprained her wrist."

"Maybe the car was being driven by some drunk senior citizen on the loose," offered Bootsie. "Just look at this crowd. They're plastered!" We looked around at the convivial scene, where the wealthy older diners were knocking back vodka and gin with abandon.

"I don't think so," Holly told her. "Because the car squealed back around the corner, then turned around and came after us again, but Channing yanked us all inside just as the car took out the trash cans. One more second, and we would have been flattened to death in the alley."

I felt terrified for Holly, as well as Jessica. Memories from last spring came flooding back; as I'd been trying to help solve the almost-murders of Barclay and Chef Gianni, I'd come within minutes of being killed by a psychotic, country-clubbing matron. As beautiful as Magnolia Beach was, if there was a crazed would-be killer driving around town, I wasn't eager to stick around. "This doesn't sound so good," I told Holly. "I mean, look what happened last May in Bryn Mawr—we could have all been killed. If someone came after you once, don't you think they'll try again?" I paused and looked around the table. "We should go home!" I urged.

"Are you crazy?" shouted Bootsie. "There's thirteen inches of snow on the ground in Bryn Mawr. We're staying down here until we figure out who almost ran down Holly and Jessica."

"What do you think?" I asked Holly. "And what did Howard say when you told him about the alley incident?" Howard is Holly's husband, a waste-removal mogul who owns a lot of trucking companies which keep him too busy to spend the winter in Magnolia Beach.

Holly looks fragile with her thin frame, blond hair, and closet full of two-thousand-dollar dresses, but she has a surprisingly steely core. "I'm not telling Howard, because he'll make a big deal about it and try to get me to go home." She squared her shoulders. "I refuse to be intimidated," she said bravely. "Plus," she added with a practical air, "I've prepaid the rent on the house until April, and it's thirty thousand dollars a month. If I get run over, at least I'll die in warm weather!"

ELEVEN HOURS LATER, I woke up in the guesthouse of Holly's rented Florida villa, blinked, and looked over at my dog, Waffles, who was slumbering next to me, his portly, sausage-shaped, brown and white body snuggled into the 700-thread-count duvet. Sun was pouring in through long white curtains, and I couldn't help jumping out of bed and doing a little happy dance around the room. I momentarily shelved the disturbing story of Holly almost getting run down near the trash cans a few nights earlier, and marveled that I was actually here in Magnolia Beach, sun pouring through the windows and a gentle tropical breeze ruffling the fuchsia bougainvillea just outside.

Magnolia Beach is a small island just off the coast of Florida, adjacent to Palm Beach, with a village-y setting and beautiful oceanfront houses from the 1920s and '30s. There's a causeway to the mainland and a shopping street that rivals Worth Avenue, which is just across the inlet. I'm not sure how both islands can support Hermès, Gucci, and Lanvin stores, but that's because I shop mostly at Target and Old Navy. When Bootsie and I arrived in Magnolia Beach last night, the sun was setting over a bank of pink clouds, the air was scented with namesake magnolia trees, and the crazy drive with Bootsie suddenly seemed worth it.

Honestly, two days ago, as I'd unlocked the doors to The Striped Awning back home in Bryn Mawr after a quick chicken salad run to the luncheonette, I'd pretty much given up hope of ever seeing the sun again. My jeans had been soaked with snow and sleet, and my puffer jacket felt like a wet sleeping bag. The vitamin D levels within my freezing frame had hit an all-time low, and I'd lost all sensation in my toes three weeks before when the temperature had dipped below eighteen degrees and stayed there. I couldn't have imagined I'd be enjoying a view of the indigo pool and white chaise lounges that I could see through the French doors just outside the guesthouse.

Then again, I'd reminded myself that I had a lot to be thankful for, despite the dismal weather in Bryn Mawr in January. While The Striped Awning wasn't too busy this time of year, I had a part-time job helping oversee the renovations on Sophie Shields's new (well, old, since it had been built in 1913, but new to her) farmhouse while Sophie and Joe were out of town. And my friends, who are family to me, were all happy and in love. Holly, who'd been separated from her husband Howard last year, had happily reunited with him. Sophie was almost done settling her mega-divorce from her shady-businessman ex, and was spending all her free time with Joe.

Bootsie, who's been married almost ten years, was as stable as ever with her husband, Will. Her J. Crew catalog–style family, including two toddler boys and two yellow Labs, embodies preppy, sporty perfection. Then again, I don't see much of Will or the kids, because Bootsie—while devoted to her family, not to mention the Labs—well, Bootsie kind of does her own thing. Somehow, despite her job covering real estate and social events for the *Bryn Mawr Gazette* (she mostly writes about gossip), Bootsie seems to have a ton of free time to play tennis, including in the winter, when she's always on the indoor courts at the country club. The rest of the time, she's gathering information in the bar at the club, at the luncheonette, at the liquor store and post office.

I should be happy, I'd told myself as I'd shaken off the snow from my coat and given Waffles a couple of Beggin' Strips for lunch: Everyone was stable and settled.

I mean, just because Holly and Joe had taken off for balmy seventy-eight-degree days and left me behind all by myself in an arctic zone, there had been no reason for the pity party I'd been hosting for myself.

I mean—and here I couldn't help smiling—hadn't *I* been dating an amazing guy for seven months? This was something of a miracle. I'd met John Hall, a handsome, tall, and good-natured veterinarian, in line at the buffet at a party for the Symphony Women's Board that Sophie had hosted the previous spring. John and I had bumped into each other again at Bryn Mawr Country Club the next day, and sparks had flown—surprising me, because not only did John have great blue eyes, lean arms, and a nice tan from all the work he does with animals at farms outside of Philly but he's also a normal, dependable guy. He played tennis, had four dogs, and jogged. Unlike most of the guys I'd fallen for in the past,

John had never once let me down, stood me up, or disappeared to Australia without saying good-bye in the time we'd been dating. We grilled steaks and went to flea markets together. We drove to the beach with Waffles and John's pack of motley mutts. We'd even gone on a trip to Tuscany in August, getting together with Holly and Howard and Joe and Sophie.

Of course, there was that one issue with John's divorce—John had been married to a beautiful tennis-playing WASP named Lilly Merriwether, but they had amicably split almost a year before I met him. Unfortunately, Lilly's mother, Mariellen Merriwether, one of Bryn Mawr's leading doyennes, hadn't been happy about the breakup of her daughter's marriage. Mariellen, it turned out, had had something of a psychotic break about a *lot* of changes going on around Bryn Mawr, and had been the unlikely criminal behind the attack on Sophie's soon-to-be ex, Barclay Shields, and had also pushed Chef Gianni off a balcony.

Mariellen had almost succeeded in shooting me, Waffles, and my elderly neighbors, Jimmy and Hugh Best, but we'd been saved when Lilly had come home early from a tennis match and convinced Mariellen to hand over a gun she'd been holding on us. So these days, Mariellen was being cared for in an upscale mental-health facility in Connecticut, where she's allowed to garden, play bridge, and ride her beloved chestnut horse, Norman . . . all under supervision, of course, in case she gets any homicidal urges again. Even better, Lilly moved up to Connecticut, too, where she's dating a tennis pro. Who needs their boyfriend's gorgeous ex-wife, especially when said gorgeous ex has fabulous tennis-honed legs, wandering around town? Not me.

But for the past two weeks, John had been out of town doing a residency in bovine medicine at Sacramento State University, and he wasn't due back for another month. I'd sighed, my pity party starting up again as I'd cranked my balky radiator, which had responded with . . . nothing. The ancient heater had seemed to be stuck at fifty-eight degrees, and belched a blast of lukewarm air about twice a week. Just then, the store phone had jingled.

"Kristin, you need to close up that mausoleum of a shop and get down to Florida," Holly had informed me. "We just saw the weather guy on CNN get blown off the steps of the Philly art museum. Enough's enough."

She'd gone on to describe the layout at her rented mega-house on Bahama Lane in Magnolia Beach, mentioning breakfasts of fresh sliced mangoes every day and dinners of grilled lobster at Vicino every night.

"So you're saying I'll have a guesthouse . . . all to myself?" I'd said, as I'd looked around my chilly shop on the main street of Bryn Mawr, miserably spritzing some Windex at my front window as snow and sleet had gusted by outside. Why bother? There hadn't been a soul out shopping that day.

"It's completely separate from the main house, adjoins the pool, and has its own kitchen, fully stocked wine fridge, and a garden with lemon and avocado trees," Holly had confirmed. "Also, I've been shopping a lot down here, and I'm too busy to return all the stuff I decided I don't want. I have a ton of Milly dresses and Trina Turk pants in the guesthouse closet that I'm positive will fit you."

I'd thrown aside the Windex, startling Waffles, who'd been licking sleet from his paws and looking dispirited. *A closet full of designer clothes in Magnolia Beach!* Since I rarely cook and usually can only afford to buy Progresso soup, I can somehow wriggle into most of Holly's fancy dresses.

Gosh, this was tempting. I mean, business was terrible right now. . . .

"Give me the phone," I'd heard Joe demand in the background. "Listen, Kristin," he'd said. "This isn't even a question. The contractor's shutting down the job at Sophie's house for two weeks anyway—all the electricians left town for a Game of Thrones theme cruise to Cancun." He'd paused to suck something on a straw. It had sounded like a frozen drink.

"You're going to be the only person left in all of Bryn Mawr," Joe had told me. "They'll probably find you and that mutt of yours frozen and dead in your bed when the town thaws out in April."

Inwardly, I'd been ninety percent there. Just the name of the street—*Bahama Lane!*—conjured images of frosty rum drinks, coconut palms, steel drum music, and suntans.

Then I'd remembered—I wasn't an heiress or successful decorator or the wealthy almost-ex of Barclay Shields. I am, to put it bluntly, pretty much penniless. It's all my friends who have the money. What if The Striped Awning suddenly got a rush of customers who were dying to buy 1940s vanities and crystal chandeliers circa 1920, and I wasn't there?

"Er . . . let me think about this for a couple of hours," I'd told Joe. "I'll call you back."

I could close the store for a week, I'd thought hopefully as I'd ended the call. I mean, how much money would I lose during the current dead retail season?

Since it had already been close to 4:00 p.m. but as dark as midnight outside, I'd decided to lock up for a few minutes and take a walk down the block to the Bryn Mawr Pub. A glass of pinot noir would enable me to make a much better decision.

"Come on, Waffles!" I'd sung out at the back door, jingling his leash. "Time for a bathroom break!" Two Beggin' Strips later, he'd gone out and done what he needed to do, getting sleeted on in the process and giving me an accusatory glance as he'd galloped back inside and made for his dog bed. I'd sighed. I'd been pretty sure Waffles had the winter blues, too.

"OF COURSE WE'RE going to Magnolia Beach!" said Bootsie. She was the first person I saw when I walked into the pub seven minutes later. As soon as I told her about Holly's call, somehow the trip now included her, too. And Bootsie's really fun on a trip. Her margarita gene kicks in and she always finds the bar with the best drinks and most fun crowd, something she has a sixth sense for.

"Don't you need to check with Will? And shouldn't you make sure your nanny can watch the twins?" I hazarded, gulping a bit of pinot noir. I wondered if I needed to text Holly and Joe, since they hadn't mentioned Bootsie coming along to Florida. Then again, this was the same woman who barged into parties from Center City all the way to Nantucket with a wave of her press pass. And they know Bootsie—they probably figured she'd show up eventually.

"They're fine!" said Bootsie with a dismissive wave of her muscular, tennis-callused hand. "Will and the sitters have everything under control."

I sipped my drink as I considered the most responsible course of action. I had pretty much no income from the shop in January, but my situation wasn't quite as dire as it had been last spring. Plus, I knew the trip to Florida would cost me nothing more than airfare, because Holly's incredibly generous.

The real reason I couldn't go to Magnolia Beach was just down the block: seventy-five pounds of chubby basset, snoring on an L.L.Bean dog bed. I mean, leave Waffles for a week? He'd be clinically depressed if I stuck him in the kennel.

"Well, I should probably go see the twins, since we'll be in Magnolia Beach for at least a few weeks!" said Bootsie, ignoring my reverie and plunking down a ten-dollar bill as she gathered up her phone and tote bag.

"I need to think this over, Bootsie," I told her. "I mean, closing the store is kind of irresponsible. And Magnolia Beach is really expensive. The airfare alone probably costs a fortune.

"And," I added miserably, aware that Bootsie, though fond of her yellow Labs, wouldn't understand how anyone would forgo such a great freebie because of a dog, "I can't leave Waffles. I mean, I could ask my neighbors to watch him, but the Best brothers are old, and they drink so much they'd probably forget to feed him!"

"That's the dumbest argument I've ever heard," Bootsie told me. She drained her drink and zipped up her Lands' End parka. "I'll *drive* us to Magnolia Beach in less than one day. You can bring that mutt, too.

"I'm going home to pack my Lilly Pulitzer," she said, her eyes lighting up happily. Bootsie loves nothing more than a flowered frock, or a pair of shorts embroidered with turtles. "And you know Holly didn't rent some dump. I mean, she even took Martha with her. Just think about the homemade scones and omelets!"

Fear gripped my gut as I pictured barreling down all of the East Coast with Bootsie in an SUV. I started to argue that I don't like freeloading from Holly, but Bootsie—who's an inveterate house guest, and has no problem accepting gratis accommodations, drinks, and food—was on the move, flinging the words "Let's leave tomorrow; I'll pick you up at three" over her shoulder.

"I haven't decided about this trip!" I called, the pub's front door slamming on my doubts as Bootsie took off to ransack her closets and pack a suitcase full of lime-green and fuchsia shift dresses.

I was still staring at the door when someone approached the bar and I felt a warm, strong hand close over my wrist. An involuntary rush of excitement shot up my spine. Even before I looked down and saw a tanned, muscular forearm, I knew who it was.

"Heading out of town?" asked Mike Woodford.

I'D MANAGED TO avoid Mike all through the fall and winter. This had taken some effort, since Mike lives right across the street from me. Then again, Mike's cottage is in the middle of a rambling, historic estate belonging to his aunt, Honey Potts. Mike takes care of the cows that roam the gorgeous property, and I'd briefly—okay, not that briefly—had a massive crush on him the previous spring. This was right before I'd met stable, handsome John Hall and switched my crush over to him.

I'd even pretty much succeeded in a self-imposed ban on thinking about Mike—when I didn't see him, that is. Every time I laid eyes on his dark scruff, torn jeans, and dark eyes, I immediately flashed back to a spectacular barn make out session with Mike the previous May, and had a sudden urge to rip off his shirt. So you can imagine how hard I tried to not bump into him around town.

"Bootsie and I might be going to Florida," I told him, feeling nervous. I started rustling in my bag to find a crumpled five-dollar bill and some ones, which I handed over to the bartender. I needed to get out of the pub, pick up Waffles, and go home, pronto.

"Well, I'd better go!" I said, making a move toward the door. "It's supposed to start snowing again."

"I'll walk you to The Striped Awning," offered Mike, seeming not to notice my mad dash away from him. Forty seconds later, I unlocked the back door to the shop and watched Waffles greet Mike.

Why did Waffles like Mike so much? I mean, Mike was really handsome, smelled great, and had animal magnetism. But I'd dated enough guys like him to know—he was not relationship material. He was way too independent, and he was a bit of a loner. I was pretty sure he loved cows more than people.

Just then, as I snapped Waffles's leash on and turned out the store lights, ready to head toward my car, Mike leaned over to where I stood, next to a rack of cleaning supplies, and kissed me. "Still dating your veterinarian?" he asked.

"Of course," I assured him. "In fact, everything's going great with John."

I could see Mike smiling in the dark. "Well, call me if you decide not to go to Florida."

"I'm *going* to Florida!" I grabbed Waffles's leash and my keys and bag, and unceremoniously ushered us all out the back door, whereupon I locked up. "See you in the spring!" I told Mike, jumping in the car after loading Waffles in and speeding away. Well, as much as it was possible to speed, given that it was snowing like a scene from *Frozen* and I could barely see through the slapping windshield wipers.

Five minutes later, I was home in my drafty but charming house, angry at myself for picturing Mike in his masculine cottage, which I happen to know has a massive stone fireplace. I could be in front of said fireplace with Mike, putting my January soggy blues behind me.

Then again, John had been an incredible boyfriend for the past seven months! What kind of person was I, anyway?

I had a feeling I was the kind of person who would be over at Mike Woodford's within twenty-four hours if I didn't take immediate preventive measures. Just then, fresh sleet started hammering the windows of my house. "Don't worry, this is going to be great!" I told Waffles, who wagged his tail from his end of the sofa as I dialed Bootsie.

"I'm in," I told her.

"Great!" she said. I could hear a suitcase being snapped open and garments whooshing into it as we spoke. "See you at three tomorrow! In fact, let's make it two-thirty."

"Isn't that a little late to leave?" I asked, starting to formulate a list of everything I needed to do between now and then. "Maybe we should leave in the morning."

"We *are* leaving in the morning. That's 2:30 *a.m.*, not p.m.," Bootsie informed me airily.

My next call was to Holly.

"You arrive when?" she answered. I heard a tropical bird chirp in the background, and I think I heard the sound of a gorgeous pink sun setting.

"Tomorrow around seven p.m.," I confirmed, having calculated the distance on Google Maps and subtracting an hour and a half from its ETA, given the fact that Bootsie speeds like a NASCAR driver. "I have a couple of, um, extra items coming with me, if that's okay?"

"Let me guess," she sighed. "Is one of them short, overweight, and sheds all over everything?"

"That's the first one," I confirmed. "The other one is six feet tall and obsessed with tennis."

Chapter 3

So HERE WE were, fourteen hundred miles away from the cold and sleet, and a safe distance from Mike Woodford. Who needed Mike and his muscular arms and sexy beard scruff, anyway? Waffles and I were officially commencing our first full day in Paradise, and thanks to Holly—and thanks to Bootsie's insane end run down I-95—we were now residents of Bahama Lane! At least, we were for the next six days.

I did a few more seconds of my Happy Dance, made even happier by the fact that Bootsie was staying in the guest room of Holly's main house, not out here with me and Waffles. I threw open the French doors, blinking in the bright sunlight, and stifled a small shriek of delight at the sight of swaying palm trees and gorgeous white chaise lounges surrounding the fantastic pool, which was set in a flower-filled courtyard between the main house and the guesthouse.

After I jumped in the shower and got dressed (Gap Outlet dress, $24.99 from last summer), I sent John Hall a quick e-mail, giving him the highlights of the ride down with Bootsie and Waffles. While I waited for Waffles to wake up—he logs about twelve hours of sleep per night, plus an additional eight hours a day of naptime—I aimed a blow-dryer at my wavy hair and took a good look around the guesthouse in the sunny light of day. It was even better than I'd thought the previous night: The walls, chairs, and sofa were bright white, softened with pink pillows, a Lucite coffee table, modern glass lamps, and a sisal carpet. There was a tiny kitchenette and fully boozed-up bar at one end of the living room, where coffee was currently brewing and the cabinets and mini fridge had been thoughtfully filled with all my favorite snacks, fresh fruit, kibbles and Beggin' Strips—Waffles's all-time favorite snack—and Havarti cheese. The bedroom was similarly all white, but with huge European pillows on the bed, embroidered with a sunny yellow Greek key pattern, and a huge mirror with an intricate yellow-and-white inlaid frame. There was also a large closet—*stocked with Holly's never-worn impulse buys!*—and the white marble bathroom, in which I'd just enjoyed a steam shower, that was glossier than any hotel bathroom I'd ever seen in a magazine or on the Travel Channel. I almost cried with joy when I noticed a fluffy white terrycloth robe hanging on the back of the door, which I'd missed earlier. I mean, what screams relaxation more than a white terry robe?

"That mutt doesn't look right down here," Joe said three minutes later, when Waffles and I wandered outside and found Joe sucking down coffee at a long, island-style wooden dining table and inhaling a plate of scrambled eggs. He gave my dog a critical once-over as Waffles wagged at him, then headed toward a small group of hibiscus bushes at the side of the yard to conduct his morning business.

"He's too fat for Florida," pronounced Joe. "He looks more like he belongs in a ski lodge. He's not the tropical type."

"Waffles loves sunbathing," I told him, trying not to be insulted. "He's all about warm weather. Trust me, he's ready for Florida."

"Maybe he'd be okay in Key West," Joe said dubiously. "Magnolia Beach, definitely not. They don't do drool here."

"I'm not so sure about that," Holly said, emerging from the main house in a white caftan over a beige Chanel bikini and towering Prada wedges, enormous sunglasses pushed atop her blond hair. "There's a couple that's been coming into Vicino every night this week. He's about a hundred and ten years old, and she's thirty-five. He drools, but then again, I'm not sure he's actually awake during dinner."

Waffles came back from the hibiscus hedge looking relieved, and he sat, wagging, next to Holly, who ignored him.

"So, what's everyone doing this morning?" I asked, wondering if I'd have time to jump in the pool at some point. Not surprisingly, the pool had the look of one that's never actually seen any swimming. Crisp blue-and-white towels were rolled in perfect hotel-like conformity on the shelves of a British Colonial–style dark wood cabinet, on top of which was arranged the aforementioned coffee service, a pitcher of juice, a bowl of sliced papaya and mango, and a full bar.

"I'm going to my workout class at The Breakers," Holly said, glancing at her watch. The Breakers, just across the bridge in Palm Beach, is South Florida's most imposing, grand place to stay, and it's an absolutely beautiful 1930s structure that houses magnificent public spaces, restaurants, and a beach club, along with several hundred luxury suites. Holly had decided to make the place her personal hangout for the duration of the winter, and she was already on intimate terms with the concierges, the salon staff, the personal trainers, and the staff who served food and drinks at the beach and pool.

She'd been tipping them like crazy, which seems to work well for her. "The class is amazing: It's called the Glutenator. It's for people who are gluten-free, which obviously everyone is in Florida, and who want to have amazing glutes. You should see these women. Not one is under seventy, and they have the thighs of Cameron Diaz!"

"And after that?" asked Joe, an unusually stern note in his voice as he pushed away his empty plate and stared meaningfully at Holly. "You won't be going anywhere near Palm Avenue, right?"

"Of course not!" Holly said, her almond-shaped blue eyes darting around a bit. She rose and headed toward the house.

"You won't be going into Gucci? Or Hermès? Or stopping at that antiques place with the forty-seven-thousand-dollar Chippendale sideboards?" Joe barked at her.

"I'm going to be late for class," Holly said, ignoring him and heading into the house. "The Glutenator fills up in the first twenty seconds after they open the door. After that, I'm going to Vicino to help Jessica meet with a landscaper. We've decided to add a grove of orange trees out on the patio, and Jessica isn't sure if we should do these two-thousand-dollar French planters, or some cheapo four-hundred-dollar ones she saw at Restoration Hardware, which obviously is a terrible idea. I'll probably be gone all day." With that, the French doors into the living room of the main house slammed shut, and she was gone, while I pondered the fact that anyone could consider four-hundred-dollar planters "cheapos."

Clearly, Holly was mid manic shopping episode, since Joe would never have questioned her normal spending, which is obscene by most people's standards. I'd find out more from Joe as soon as I could. I quickly fed Waffles, who inhaled his kibbles, downed a bowl of water, and returned to the air-conditioned guesthouse. Through the French doors, I could see that he'd hurtled himself back onto the vast white expanse of bed in the yellow and white bedroom and was asleep again, snoring.

"Where's Bootsie?" I asked Joe. It's not like Bootsie to miss a gathering, especially if there's potential information being downloaded, not to mention food being served.

"She left twenty minutes ago," Joe said. "She took off for some tennis tournament down in Delray Beach. And Sophie's got conference calls and Skype sessions all morning with her divorce lawyers.

"Which leaves you free to come along and help me with my new client!" Joe told me. "Let's go."

"So, WHO IS this mysterious new client?" I asked Joe as he steered his rented beige Cadillac convertible down South Ocean Boulevard. Joe had informed me that the Caddy embodied "retro cool." Plus, it had a ding in the door, so the rental agent had given it to him for a hundred bucks a week.

"Adelia Earle," Joe told me, a jaunty straw hat tipped back off his forehead. "She's absolutely adorable! Dresses impeccably. Lots of hats and jewels. You know the type, somewhere between sixty-five and eighty-five, but with a youthful spirit. She has this old gazebo thing in her backyard that she wants to turn into an outdoor dining room."

"She sounds like fun," I said. "Is she a native Magnolia Beacher?"

"Virginia tobacco money," Joe told me. "Look, there's the old Woolworth estate," he added, pointing to a low, elegant old house that sat right on the ocean. "Anyway, Adelia's a Stokes by birth. You know the old cigarette ads: 'Stokes Makes the Best Smokes'? Adelia even appeared in some of their ad campaigns when she was Debutante of the Year. She's a little vague about her age, so I'm not clear on when she was this celebrity deb, but I think it was sometime in the late fifties."

"I've seen Stokes cigarettes ads in old magazines," I nodded, thinking of the vintage *Vogue* and *Town & Country* issues from the '50s and '60s I sometimes pick up at flea markets and stock at The Striped Awning. "Very stylish!"

"Think *Gone With the Wind* meets *Mad Men*," Joe told me. "That's Adelia. More Vivien Leigh than Elisabeth Moss, though."

Across the inlet I could see The Breakers, its grand main structure facing a long, palm-lined drive. I could easily picture Holly frantically working out in order to stave off the urge to shop. We drove through the center of town, where busboys were cleaning the sidewalks outside Vicino, then swung past some upscale shops and rode through a district of mansions, each more beautiful than the next.

Tall ficus hedges were clipped to perfection. The town had looked beautiful the night before, but now, in the sunshine, I realized I'd never seen a place so perfect in all my life: The hibiscus flowers on all the bushes were bigger and a more vivid crimson, the bluebirds flying past the Cadillac were bluer, and the blond girls walking down Palm Avenue were blonder. It was like the movie *Pleasantville*, where the rest of the world was in black and white, and Magnolia Beach was in stunning color.

Joe told me that Adelia lived south of Palm Avenue, and as we drove, he pointed out various houses that he'd seen in *Elle Decor*. There were hotel-sized, newly built, Moroccan-style palaces with minarets and towers. There were vintage Addison Mizner Mediterranean castles and French-style manors with shingled mansard roofs. I felt my mood skyrocket as I took in the velvet lawns, meticulous gravel driveways, and expanse of gorgeous ocean at our left.

"Just a heads-up about Adelia," Joe told me casually as he hung a right onto a tiny street called Bougainvillea Way. He pulled into a circular driveway paved with white stones, which sat at the foot of a Colonial-style house that would have looked right at home in Pennsylvania, except for the hibiscus hedges and hot-pink shutters.

"She, uh, drinks a little."

SINCE JOE IS no slouch himself when it comes to rum and vodka, and given that the annual consumption of alcohol in the five-county Philly region rivals that of Siberia and the Ukraine combined, Mrs. Earle must have been a truly epic consumer of cocktails, I thought to myself, digesting this information and putting it into context as we walked up a white-coral stone walkway toward Adelia's house. At the country club, unless someone falls down the stairs or drives into the giant oak at the end of the driveway, which happens about once a summer, drinking isn't really mentioned. It's just assumed that there will be a festive drinking at the club, accompanied by secondary pursuits including golf, tennis, and food.

As Joe rang a doorbell that played the refrain of "Dixie," I admired Adelia's lawn: Well-clipped lime trees lined the walkway, their shiny fruit gleaming, and elegant Chinese porcelain planters bursting with orchids flanked the bright-green-lacquered double front doors.

"What's her drink of choice?" I whispered to Joe.

Just then, the door was opened by a gray-haired man in a white shirt, long white apron, and yellow trousers. Close on his heels was a bejeweled person in a glittery green caftan.

"Margaritas for everyone!" hooted a silvery, Southern-tinged voice from inside the caftan, answering my question.

"Adelia, this is my friend Kristin Clark," Joe told her as the guy in the yellow pants closed the door. I extended my hand and shook Mrs. Earle's, which was tiny and warm. She had red hair, wore a lot of makeup, and had a sweet smile beneath a pair of giant Chanel sunglasses. A faint waft of Joy perfume floated my way, along with a whiff of tequila.

"Where's your other gal today?" Adelia asked Joe with a slightly tipsy wink from behind her vast sunglasses. "Sophie, isn't that her name?" She paused to assess Joe approvingly. "Do you have *two* girlfriends? I love it!"

"We're just friends," I assured Ms. Earle. "Sophie is Joe's girlfriend, but she has a call scheduled with her lawyers this morning."

"A likely story!" hooted Adelia, winking at Joe. "I knew I liked you, you old bird-doggin' decorator. Well, let's have a little drink, and then look at the pavilion."

Adelia's house was anchored by a fifteen-foot-wide, gallery-style central hallway that ran nearly seventy-five feet in length. We followed her and her butler past doors to a dining room, a library, various sitting rooms, and a fantastic paneled bar as we traversed the corridor, which went right into a green-and-white, chintz-filled living room with a nonexistent back wall: The living room was essentially a fabulous twenty-five-by-forty-foot covered space open to the pool, with adorable seating areas, a grand piano, and a handsomely carved fireplace. Big-band music played jauntily over speakers hidden somewhere in the room, and despite the fact that the room was open to the outdoors, an arctic blast of air conditioning was gusting overhead.

The man in the yellow pants immediately began squeezing limes and crunching ice into an enormous Waterford pitcher, glugging in most of the contents of a fat bottle of Patrón Silver. I took a quick look at my watch: 10:00 a.m. I shrugged to myself and followed Joe's lead, accepting an icy crystal rocks glass from a silver tray.

"Thank you!" I said to Adelia and the butler-guy.

"That's Osbourne, my house manager," Adelia told me. "We call him Ozzy. Would you like some toast, or maybe some egg salad, dear?"

"Um, no, thank you," I said, sipping my drink, which was delicious.

"All my friends are so jealous that I found Joe!" Adelia told me as we sat down on poufy chintz sofas. "He's the perfect extra man at any party!" She sipped delicately at her drink but somehow drained it by a third in about four seconds. "If I'm not careful, all the gals in Magnolia Beach are going to hire him, too, and I won't be able to get my dining pavilion finished!"

I could see Joe's eyes light up at the thought of Adelia's friends as he gulped down his drink, and I had to stifle a laugh. Joe's dream is working with ladies of a certain age. He's big on lunching and dinner-ing with this kind of clientele, who love him and who always end up hiring him for months at a time and taking him on all-expenses-paid antiquing excursions in places like Provence and Umbria.

"Maybe we could schedule a lunch with some of the ladies," he suggested hopefully, pouring Adelia a refill from the Waterford pitcher Ozzy had thoughtfully left on the coffee table in front of us. "As soon as we finish your project, of course," he added hastily, noticing that Adelia didn't look all that pleased at his suggestion.

"Have you ever seen my advertisements?" sang out Adelia brightly, changing the subject. Next to the handsome Chinese Chippendale gilt mirrors were beautifully framed black-and-white magazine layouts of a fragile-looking girl in a white ball gown, leaning back dramatically and puffing a delicate pouf of smoke from a Stokes cigarette.

"C'est moi from my debutante days!" she said in her Virginia drawl. "We just love the cigarettes, darlin', because they're payin' for that new dining pavilion. I don't smoke anymore, but we have boxes of the things all over the dang place! Do you smoke?" she asked me, indicating a vast porcelain box heaped with Stokes cigarettes.

"Not usually, but I could try to light one up if I drink enough," I told her. The smoking on top of morning drinking didn't seem like a great idea, but Osbourne mixed a mean margarita.

"Let's visit that marvelous gazebo of yours, Adelia!" suggested Joe, giving me a meaningful glance toward the pool and backyard as he rose from the sofa and politely offered Adelia his arm. I was enjoying myself, honestly, and could have spent the day with Mrs. Earle in a pleasant haze of tequila, but Joe seemed to be ready to get moving on his project, no doubt calculating how much money he could make once he finished up with Adelia and got working on similar projects with all her friends.

Trailed by Ozzy, we cruised out to the pool, bordered by an L-shaped wing of the house, which, I could see, included a dated-looking kitchen and butler's pantry.

"Here's the gun room," Adelia said tipsily, pausing at a locked white door just past the pool. "Have I shown you this yet, Joe, honey?"

"Oh, yes, Mrs. Earle," Joe said grimly. "Twice."

"Ozzy, unlock this door, please," she said to Osbourne, who whipped out a ring of keys and had the door open in a jiffy. Shotguns, rifles, and pistols were arranged in neat rows in racks along the walls. I sighed through my slight tequila haze. What is it with rich older ladies and guns, anyway? Having been on the wrong end of Mariellen Merriwether's pistol not seven months ago, I really didn't want to see Adelia's collection of firearms. Of course, Adelia seemed like a sweet person, completely unlike the evil Mariellen, but Adelia did have a lot of Patrón coursing through her veins.

Joe and I exchanged scared glances as Adelia picked up a three-foot-long Remington and brandished it in the direction of a hedge separating her property from the stunning estate next door. "No bullets," Mr. Osbourne mouthed to us.

"I love to do target practice at night when my neighbor is having cocktails by the pool!" Adelia said happily, making a few practice squeezes on the trigger of the Remington. "Scooter Simmons. He's a lawyer and advisor to the Magnolia Beach Town Council." She hooted. "Back in Virginia we'd have called him a professional bottom-feeder. I like to whiz a few bullets right past his ear as he's mixing up a vodka tonic."

"I'm dying to see that pavilion!" I said, which appeared to refocus Mrs. Earle. She put down the gun, Ozzy quickly locked up the little room, and we made for a structure that was centered in her perfectly cut back lawn. Adelia's octagonal gazebo was open to the elements, with adorable Victorian-style woodwork revealing a charming interior—or what once was probably very charming. In contrast to the rest of her perfectly maintained property, the gazebo was a complete wreck. The woodwork was rotting, the paint was peeling, and the interior contained nothing but two falling-apart old pool chairs.

"I've got my ladies poker club coming here the Wednesday after next, and I promised them we'd be having our crab salad right here!" Adelia said brightly, turning to Joe. "So what do you think? Can y'all get this little shack up and running in nine days?"

Chapter 4

"NINE DAYS," MOANED Joe at Vicino that evening, where we were sitting with Bootsie, Holly, and Sophie on the same corner banquette. Joe hadn't stopped complaining since we'd left Adelia's house six hours earlier, but I couldn't blame him, given the fact that the gazebo was more like a six-week job. "I know Adelia was drinking, but when she says nine days, she means it. I mean, she has guns. A *lot* of guns."

"Don't worry, Honey Bunny!" Sophie told him. "People hardly ever get killed over gazebos. I mean, if you fucked up her living room, she might shoot you, but she's not gonna do that over some dumb pool house."

"That's so comforting," Joe told her. "How did I ever manage stress before you came into my life?"

"I don't know!" Sophie told him, throwing her arms around him and giving him a big smack on the lips. "But you don't have to worry about that, 'cause I ain't going anywhere. You're stuck with me!"

"Is there any Scotch in this joint?" Joe whispered. "How much

Xanax do you have left?" he asked Holly, who stocks up on anxiety meds but mostly ends up giving them to Joe. He hailed a passing waiter, who took notice of Joe's desperate expression and immediately returned with a glass of Glenfiddich.

"Let's dial down the meds for tonight," Holly told Joe. "Your pupils are the size of quarters."

"Definitely!" I agreed, since Joe's head was beginning to droop dangerously close to his chilled cantaloupe wrapped in prosciutto. "So, do you three eat here every night?" I asked Holly, trying to change the subject. "Not that that's a bad thing!" I added hastily, thinking of my cabinets at home, which held a lonely can of tomato soup, as waiters arrived with several delicious-looking thin-crust pizzas topped with fresh mozzarella and basil leaves.

"Absolutely. We drink at other establishments, though," Holly told me.

"We usually have lunch at The Breakers, or sometimes at Tiki Joe's!" Sophie added. "Have ya heard of it? It's the cutest restaurant. Everyone goes there!"

"Very retro and cool," Joe confirmed. "Think sixties Hollywood lounge meets pu-pu platter." Then his expression darkened. "That's where I first encountered Adelia. She was sitting next to us at the bar when we stopped in for a drink on my first night here. She seemed so innocent that night." He noisily sucked down his Glenfiddich.

"I love Tiki Joe's!" said Bootsie, tanned from her day of watching tennis. She crunched some pizza, then grabbed an oyster from a platter Joe had ordered but was now too drunk to eat. "I once met Lilly Pulitzer there, which was on my bucket list."

We all stopped to take in Bootsie's outfit for a moment, which was a Lilly P. maxi dress in a vivid pink floral print. It was actually pretty fashion-forward for Bootsie, who usually goes for a more tailored silhouette.

"If only you'd been able to meet the actual L. L. Bean," offered Joe.

"Believe me, I've looked into it," Bootsie said, chewing. "He died in 1967."

"I would've wanted to meet either one of them!" piped up Sophie, as the waiter popped open some Moët and poured it for everyone. "I love designers!"

"Sophie, L. L. Bean invented the waterproof hunting boot," Joe told her. "The company he founded makes thirty-eight-dollar tote bags, not two-thousand-dollar handbags."

"Oh, right," said Sophie, undaunted as usual. "I guess I was thinking of someone else. Well, just so you know, Honey Bunch, my bucket list consists of one item: Meeting Donatella Versace! Or Lady Gaga. Either one would be awesome."

"What about Kelly Ripa?" Bootsie asked. "I thought you had an obsession with her, too."

"I forgot about her!" shrieked Sophie. "She's on the list!"

"Where's Channing?" I whispered to Holly. "Why isn't he out here working the room?" I'm no restaurant expert, but given the fact that Channing resembles a genetic blend of David Beckham, the guy in the Eternity perfume ads, and any of the hot guys who portray vampires on the WB Network, it wouldn't hurt for him to work the dining room a little. Then again, chefs are supposed to actually cook, so I could understand why we hadn't seen him the night before.

"I told him the same thing," Holly replied, looking annoyed. "Last night he had some glitch with the veal chops, which is why we didn't see him or Jessica. We need him out here, front and center."

"Hey, guys," a smooth, charming male voice murmured just then.

Channing! His deep voice was almost as good as the package it emanated from. Our heads swiveled as one to gaze upon the chef, who stood there in a tight white T-shirt and dark jeans, over which he wore a manly looking long chef's apron.

Channing really is ridiculously handsome: He's somewhere in his late twenties, with a soap-opera actor's perfectly muscled arms, glossy blue eyes, and square jaw. His smile could star in a tooth-whitening commercial, and he unleashes his irresistible grin quite frequently. Six months in Florida had somehow made him even better-looking, which I didn't think possible.

Honestly, Channing had never really fit in when he'd lived in Bryn Mawr, but he appeared to have been made for Magnolia Beach. His skin had a golden glow now (maybe I would take Holly up on the spray tan she insisted I needed), and he had the confidence of the newly minted entrepreneur, now that he helmed his own restaurant. Even if he only owned ten percent of it.

Though Holly had dropped the subject, I hadn't forgotten her tale of almost being run down by the speeding car in the back alley with Jessica the other night. Had the driver been after Holly—who, as far as I know, has no enemies? I mean, Holly doesn't really do anything much except shop and throw the occasional party.

Had Jessica made an enemy in Magnolia Beach during the time they'd been down here? It didn't seem like the kind of place where enemies would abound, unless someone stole your parking spot or bought the mansion you'd been eyeing. It was too perfect a place to create dissension among its lucky ranks.

As per usual, women at every single table in the restaurant were staring at the hunky chef, and anyone who had the bad luck to be seated outside was straining to get him in her sightline. This was impressive, since most of the women were over sixty-five, but the beefcake that is Channing crosses all age lines. Men were staring, too: This wasn't surprising, since even in Bryn Mawr, where people tend to be pretty restrained, everyone, whether straight or gay, had a crush on Channing. Here in South Florida, with palm trees rustling and fresh-squeezed cocktails on every table, he looked even hotter.

I noticed that Bootsie's mouth was hanging open as she took in the sight of Channing, who she's always had the hots for. Sophie, meanwhile, actually caressed the chef's left bicep as she squeaked, "Hiya, Channing!"

"Hi," added a second, somewhat bored-sounding girlish voice from behind Channing.

Jessica, the restaurant manager and Channing's girlfriend, had teetered out to say hello to us, which was about all she usually says. She's not exactly unfriendly, Jessica, but she's not the effusive type, either. Her pedicured feet were shod in her ever-present Louboutins, this time a pair of teetery, glossy black patent sandals, and she wore white jeans and a silver tank top on her skinny frame. Her injured wrist had a small bandage wrapped around it, but she appeared the same as usual: beautiful and somewhat sour.

Jessica's permanent expression is one of mild contempt for all of humanity, unless she's looking at Channing, who brings out a sunnier side to her personality. She also seems to like Holly and Joe, and from what I'd observed of her design skills and work ethic, Jessica's actually a pretty determined person.

"I hope you guys are enjoying yourselves," Channing said. "How's the pizza? We had the oven specially constructed in Naples and installed by Neapolitan stonemasons. It hits eleven hundred degrees no problem."

"The pizza looks really good," Holly told him. "If I ate carbs, I'm sure I'd love it."

"It *is* really good," said Bootsie, back to chewing.

"Everything's awesome," Sophie agreed. She adopted a stern, scolding tone, which was at odds with her outfit: a cropped pink silk top and matching miniskirt, plus a large gold Versace necklace. "But Channing, seriously, I got two hundred grand sunk in this place, and I need you out here in the dining room, schmoozing. No one gives a crap about the food! They just want to see your hot bod!

"Sorry, Jessica," she added to the bored-looking girl, who shrugged, unperturbed. "But we need Channing to get his flirt on with these older gals. And you could be a little friendlier yourself to the husbands, Jessica. I mean, smile once in a while! Maybe you need some Saint-John's-wort or something! Because people spend more when you butter them up. When I worked in the concrete biz, I used to . . ."

Then, all of a sudden, Sophie paused, clasped her tiny cocktail ringed hand to her mouth, pointed dramatically toward the front doors of the restaurant, and squeaked, "Look!"

"*Sì*, I HAVE arrived in Florida!" shouted a tall, thin bald guy in parachute pants, Crocs, and a white chef's jacket, who'd just entered Vicino and now stood in the foyer. Gold earrings gleamed in each earlobe.

"Gianni has come to show this town what a real restaurant is!" added Chef Gianni Brunello, famed (at least in Philadelphia) Italian restaurateur, and the previous employer of both Channing and Jessica. Holly, Joe, and I exchanged horrified glances.

"Am I hallucinating from the Xanax?" Joe whispered. "Chef Gianni's in *Magnolia Beach*?" Next to Gianni stood a tall, slim girl in a clingy black dress, her long dark hair in a perfect ponytail. I assumed this was his new girlfriend, since she rolled her eyes at his pronouncement, opened her small handbag, and began texting.

Gianni has always been able to get beautiful girls—such as Jessica and the willowy, dark-haired model type he'd just arrived with— to go out with him, but they seem to tire quickly of his frequent outbursts and tantrums. On the plus side, Gianni's always going somewhere like Rome or St. Bart's to check out hot new restaurants, so there's some travel involved in dating him.

"I get sick of winter and decide to come see what Channing has done down here," Gianni continued with typical lack of modesty, shouting over the music as curious heads swiveled at every table to take in his entrance.

"Plus, I want to see what my backstabbing bitch ex-girlfriend's up to!" He aimed this last comment at Jessica, who had frozen like a Popsicle at the sight of her ex.

"Hey, Chef, take it easy," said Channing politely, attempting to defuse the situation, since Gianni's face was turning purple with rage. "Can I get you a drink?"

Jessica, for her part, came back to life and disappeared through swinging doors into the kitchen.

"No, I just look around," Gianni responded, appearing to calm down a little as he eyed the convivial long bar, the mosaic floors, the warm orange walls and comfortable upholstered banquettes. He looked up at the charming antique chandeliers and out at the lantern-lit patio. Every table and bar stool was filled, and waiters were buzzing by with plates of grilled meats and seafood and inviting cocktails. The scent of jasmine votive candles and huge arrangements of orange blossoms added to the exotic appeal. To me, the place emanated fun, glamour, and Florida chic.

Apparently, Gianni didn't agree.

"Poof!" said Gianni finally, kissing his fingers in what I took to be a dismissive gesture. "Channing, your place looks like something for the fast food! I mean, you got orange walls like a hamburger joint!"

Just then, Chef Gianni noticed Holly. He loves Holly: Not only is she gorgeous but she always hires him to cater her parties at home, since Gianni is undeniably a fantastic talent in the kitchen. His mood improved immediately.

"Holleeee Jones!" he screamed. "And Sophie Shields! Two of my favorite ladies!" Gianni paused to do some dramatic fawning over Sophie and Holly, while his dark-haired new girlfriend found a seat at the bar and ordered what appeared to be a shot of Jägermeister. I felt for her—it had to be embarrassing and uncomfortable to see her boyfriend scream at Jessica, whose exit to South Florida he clearly hadn't gotten over.

"And is perfect timing I see you two girls," he told Holly and Sophie, rudely ignoring the rest of our table. "Because I got big news. Look through the window, right over there!"

Gianni, heedless of the fact that he was impeding passing waiters, stood in the middle of the dining room and pointed dramatically through the open French doors toward a building situated directly across Ocean Boulevard.

In the large front window, a huge white banner had been hung, with a spotlight illuminating words that proclaimed in navy script "Opening this Sunday: Ristorante Gianni Mare!"

Chapter 5

At 8:30 a.m. the next morning, we convened a poolside meeting at the house on Bahama Lane to download and dissect the appearance of Chef Gianni in Magnolia Beach.

The reaction among our group wasn't too positive. Gianni's a genius with seafood and pasta, but he wouldn't receive four stars on a Yelp review as someone you wanted to spend your vacation with.

"When did Gianni get here?" Bootsie asked, buttering a homemade carrot muffin. "Because if he's been down for a few days, it was probably him behind the wheel of the Death Chevy the other night. He definitely hates Jessica enough to run her down in an alley."

"Gianni loves me!" protested Holly, who was wearing yoga pants and a tank top, stretching in anticipation of a 10:00 a.m. workout class. "I spent seventeen thousand dollars on one dinner he catered last summer. He wouldn't run me over with a Chevy."

She paused for a second. "Well, maybe he would."

"He'd kill you in five seconds if you were standing in the way when he was going after Jessica," Joe told her, forking into a fluffy spinach and Manchego omelette that Martha had customized for him. He'd arrived with Sophie ten minutes before, dressed in impeccable khakis and a crisp lavender shirt, but with slightly bloodshot eyes, courtesy of his Scotch-and-Xanax hangover. The omelette seemed to be having an invigorating effect, though, and his hands were no longer trembling as he forked in the awesome egg dish.

"Gianni told me last night that he only got to Magnolia Beach yesterday," Holly shrugged. "So he couldn't have been the one who almost ran us over. Though, obviously, he could be lying."

Holly took one for the team the night before when she invited Gianni and his dark-haired companion to go out for drinks at Tiki Joe's while the rest of us finished dinner at Vicino. This gave Holly time to pump the Italian chef for information about his new restaurant, and it also got Gianni out of Vicino before he caused even more of a scene.

During the two-block stroll to Tiki Joe's, and, subsequently, over a couple of rums at its convivial bar, Gianni told Holly that he and his new girlfriend, whose name was Olivia and who was an aspiring model/actress/singer, were staying at The Breakers, along with a small entourage of staff and decorators who were installing the interior of his new Magnolia Beach restaurant.

"It's going to be mostly seafood—that's the *mare* part—and some pastas and grilled meats. The space was the old Peacock restaurant, which closed a couple months ago, so it has a full kitchen already, and should be easy to get up and running quickly.

"And of course, Gianni's a hundred percent sure he can charm the Lilly Pulitzer pants off the Magnolia Beach crowd," Holly told us, sipping black coffee.

We all nodded, knowing that Gianni can in fact be incredibly charismatic.

It's hard to explain, but his muscles, tattoos, and trademark gold earrings somehow take on a sexy bad-boy vibe when Gianni turns his attention on women and gushes over them. At age thirty-nine, with a bunch of "Best New Chef" honors in the world of foodie magazines, the guy has star quality.

"The crazy part is," Holly added, "Gianni's calling his new place a pop-up restaurant, since that guarantees a lot of media coverage. And he's got a deal with HGTV to feature Gianni Mare on *Restaurant in a Weekend*!"

AT THIS NEWS, Joe choked on a bit of spinach, Sophie pounded his back with tiny be-ringed fists to try to dislodge the offending veggie, and we handed him glasses of water. We all avoided eye contact with Joe, who—once he finally gulped down the wayward bite of omelet—looked like he'd be reaching for the anxiety meds again any minute.

Restaurant in a Weekend is a show in which a team completely overhauls, remodels, and installs a new eatery in about twenty-two minutes. At least, that's how it looks when you watch the show, and it seemed—given the fact that Gianni's sign had announced he was opening his new place tomorrow night—that the turnaround really was incredibly quick.

I mean, there had been a restaurant on the site of Gianni Mare before, so it wasn't a total makeover, but this was still a bold move and a PR coup for Gianni.

HGTV's a subject no one brings up around Joe, because a couple of years ago, he'd submitted a casting tape to the network and had been told that unless he was a super-hunky contractor in a tight T-shirt and ripped jeans (preferably with an identical twin or equally hot brother), or a gorgeous girl who had a working knowledge of carpentry, he could forget about getting a decorating show. Joe doesn't really work out, is an only child, and he would never wear ripped jeans, so that had been the end of his HGTV dreams.

Clearly, though, some bitterness lingered.

"That's the tackiest thing I've ever heard!" Joe said, pushing aside his breakfast. "Cheap publicity stunt."

"I've gotta call my editor," Bootsie said, standing up and punching at her iPhone. "Gianni's pop-up thingy sounds like a Page One story for the *Bryn Mawr Gazette*."

Her eyes took on a happy gleam. "I'm going to get him to reimburse me for the four tanks of gas I used getting down here—just as soon as I get some more eggs!" She got up and made for the kitchen.

"What's really important, though, is if Gianni's the one who tried to run over Jessica and Holly the other night," I pointed out as Bootsie reemerged from the house and sat down again.

"You know, at first, I figured that Chevy had to have been after Jessica, since she's not that likable," Bootsie told us. "But a theory came to me while I watched Martha dish out these eggs. The death car could have been actually going after *Holly*," she pointed out, loading a piece of toast with butter.

From her spot on a yoga mat, Holly's eyes widened, taking on the expression of a frightened fawn.

"I don't have any enemies!" she told Bootsie. "One lady at the Glutenator class got mad when I tried to pay her to give me her spot near the instructor the other day, but usually people like me. Especially salespeople. I mean, I've tipped everyone in town! The people at both Hermès and Lanvin are my new best friends!"

"That's true," Joe nodded. "And you've been spending *a lot* lately." He gave me a significant glance indicating that we needed to talk over the Holly spending situation, which worried me.

"Yeah, Holly's a walking ATM—no one's gonna want her dead," Sophie added. "I'm thinking it probably was some drunk in that car. Magnolia Beach just isn't the kind of place where people flatten people in alleys. Maybe it was just a fluke!"

"Not to change the subject from Holly being about to get killed, but I'm heading to the tennis tournament down in Delray Beach," Bootsie told us, forgetting her theory about Holly's would-be killer and grabbing her tote and keys. As usual, her attention span rivaled that of a gnat. "There are some hot guys playing today."

"I'll meet you down there," Holly told her, "if I'm still alive by lunchtime." She paused for a minute as she scrambled up from her yoga mat. "Maybe I should hire a bodyguard! Everyone in Miami has one."

"That reminds me," piped up Sophie, slurping foam from her cappuccino, "did I ever tell ya about the time in South Beach when my ex invited a whole bunch of girls he met at the pool at the Fontainebleau back to our suite at the Setai? I came back from shopping at Saks, and one of them had gotten a bellboy naked, and was about to—"

"See you this afternoon!" Holly said, thankfully interrupting Sophie's reminiscences. "Also, I'll ask around at The Breakers and find out when Gianni checked in. Maybe he got down here by Tuesday, and he *was* the hit-and-run driver!"

"I need to skip the tennis til later. I gotta go home and do more lawyer stuff," Sophie told us sadly, forgetting her story about the bellboy as she gathered up a giant Gucci handbag. "This frickin' divorce is more work than my old job selling concrete."

"I'll drop you back at your place, Sophie," Bootsie announced.

As Joe and I climbed into the Caddy, I heard Bootsie ask her passenger, "Whatever happened to that bellboy at the Setai?"

Chapter 6

"Is SHE THE one from the Spice Girls?" asked Adelia a bit tipsily. She was in a pink caftan today and an equally large pair of sunglasses. It was 10:00 a.m. chez Earle, where we sat at an outdoor table shaded by an umbrella and a ficus hedge. Ozzy the butler was holding Adelia's drink on a little silver tray as she looked over Joe's sketches and magazine tear sheets, one featuring a party hosted by David and Victoria Beckham and held under a vast and very opulent canopy lit by about seven thousand dangling lanterns.

The magazine clippings were supposed to help Joe sell Mrs. Earle on his idea for a custom tented ceiling design for her pool hut, which he'd seen in *Coastal Living.* This was the specialty of a West Palm Beach design house called, naturally, La Tente.

"Absolutely!" Joe assured his client. "This Beckham party? Tented by La Tente. That royal wedding a couple of years ago in Monaco? They tented it. The firm is owned by a French couple who can tent the crap out of anything," he told Adelia. "Tenting is huge right now."

I'd have suggested he use slightly older celebrities to convince

Adelia, more along the lines of classic Hollywood stars like Sophia Loren, who'd probably tented something at one point in her fabulous life, but Joe hadn't asked for my input. Instead, he peremptorily ordered me to go through his tote bag and find La Tente's estimate, which he'd printed out but hadn't had a chance to review yet.

I'd somehow been dragooned into a job as Joe's temporary Florida assistant, which I wasn't sure I'd agreed to, and felt a bit grumpy about. But I had to hand it to Joe: Galvanized by his nine-day design deadline (now down to eight days), he arrived at Adelia's with a tote bag of fabric samples, magazine tear sheets, and sketches at the ready.

It was Saturday, but Frank, a carpenter Channing and Jessica had recommended after working with him on Vicino, was already at the gazebo, measuring to replace the exterior woodwork and install bench seating within the structure.

"The tenting sounds nice," Adelia said, gazing with mild interest at the photos Joe had placed in front of her. "What do you think, Ozzy?"

"Beautiful," replied her houseman patiently. Mr. Osbourne seemed to be an especially sweet-tempered guy. Adelia was a genial lady, but the constant margaritas and the guns had to be a bit wearing on a day-to-day basis.

I found the paperwork from La Tente, glanced at the total, and my vision got blurry and I had to sit down. The tenting, including fabric and labor, would cost thirty-six thousand dollars.

"For the pavilion, I'm thinking we'll go with a blue and white theme, and do the ceiling in a gorgeous blue and white stripe," Joe told her. "Think Grace Kelly at the beach club in *To Catch a Thief*."

I discreetly handed him the estimate for this blue and white striped masterpiece. He took one look, swallowed hard, and stuffed it back in the tote, apparently deciding to nail Adelia with the hefty price tag at a later date.

"That all sounds real cute," Adelia told Joe. "Just remember, sugar, you got eight days to finish this job. I know decorators. Getting you to finish a job is like nailin' Jell-O to a tree."

"Frank's got his circular saw set up in your driveway, Adelia, and he thinks he'll have most of the woodwork done by Tuesday at noon," Joe assured her. "Then we'll start with the new floor, the lighting, the painting, and, obviously, the tenting. Tell those poker ladies to get ready for a pool house that'll knock them on their asses!"

"I CAN'T BELIEVE I'm saying this after my toes were in Stage One frostbite for the last six weeks . . . but it's really hot!" I told Bootsie an hour later as I fanned myself with a printed program featuring photos of Rafael Nadal and Maria Sharapova. We were sitting in the stands of the Delray Beach Tennis Center, which turned out to be a small stadium in the center of an adorable beach town.

"And," I added, looking at the scene in the tennis stadium and the palm-tree-lined street beyond it, "this town is kind of awesome!"

Delray Beach, though only twenty-five minutes south of the serene and peerless shops of Palm Avenue, felt like a funky village in the Florida Keys. Reggae and Cuban music poured from speakers along Atlantic Avenue, its café-lined main street, and cool couples, both gay and straight, sipped coffee at shaded tables. Colorful pillows lined outdoor banquettes on the patios of restaurants. Shops and boutiques offered everything from cute dresses to ornately decorated cupcakes to vintage furniture. And though it was only 11:00 am, a festive island air percolated through the whole town.

I loved the formal precision and manicured hedges in Magnolia Beach, but I felt my shoulders instantly relax as soon as we drove into Delray Beach. If Magnolia Beach was the incarnation of a black-tie ball, then Delray was the fun backyard barbecue where everyone got tipsy on mojitos under strings of party lights, and ate quesadillas and guacamole. It was amazing to have two such diametrically different places just miles apart on the coastline.

I texted a few quick photos of the scene to John Hall in California, giving him a quick update on Adelia, Gianni, and Waffles. John's a really sweet and polite guy, so he always says he likes to hear what my dysfunctional posse is up to, even if he's likely more interested in things like bovine breeding trends.

"Delray is where my parents had their honeymoon," Bootsie told me, her eyes on the court where two handsome tennis players, one from China and the other Australia, were battling out for a third set in the already steamy sunshine. "Look at that serve!"

I tried to follow the guys and the rocketing tennis balls on the court, but frankly, other than the fact that they were both cute and tan, I couldn't muster up much enthusiasm about the actual game.

"My brother Chip was conceived right down the street at Crane's Hotel," Bootsie continued. "Mummy said she had no idea what was coming her way after the wedding, but boom! One night at Crane's, and she was knocked up."

"What a beautiful story," said Joe, climbing into the seat next to us, followed by Holly. While everyone else in the stadium was in shorts, T-shirts, or workout clothes, Holly had on a crisp striped sundress and flat Hermès sandals. She wasn't even sweating. "I might need to visit this Crane's place just so I can fully envision Chip's conception."

"When does Javier Guzman-Ferrara play?" Holly asked, pushing up her sunglasses to scan the sidelines. "He's the only reason I'm here." She pointed at a gorgeous dark-haired guy in his early thirties doing some stretches by the main court. "I'll just go say hi to him," she said, getting up again. "I sat next to him once on a plane."

"Javier Guzman-Ferrara?" shouted Bootsie, swiveling her attention away from the action on the court to ogle the handsome guy Holly had indicated. "The dark-haired, muscular Spanish guy who once beat Rafael Nadal? I'll come with you!"

"Okay," said Holly, not sounding all that thrilled about Bootsie accompanying her. "If you really want to."

"Is Sophie going to join us?" I asked Joe, as Holly and Bootsie took off toward the hot tennis player.

"She's still Skyping with her lawyers," he said gloomily, flagging down a passing drinks seller for a Diet Coke. "She thinks Barclay's really dragging his feet getting the divorce finalized. And it seems like he's out of town, because it takes about forty-eight hours to get the simplest question answered. We've been waiting since last Monday to find out if he wants his cashmere sock collection returned, which somehow ended up in a chest of drawers at Sophie's new house back in Bryn Mawr."

"If they're negotiating socks, they must be close to being done with this settlement, right?" I asked.

"You'd think so," confirmed Joe. "I mean, cashmere socks are pricey, but at six hundred and fifty an hour, fighting over footwear doesn't seem like the greatest use of time for the top two divorce firms in Philly."

"I hate to bring up the obvious, but once Sophie is officially single again, isn't she going to want to make things legal with you?" I asked Joe, unable to resist a slightly evil impulse to torture him by raising the topic of getting hitched. I'm pretty sure Sophie's already been pushing for him to propose as soon as she's divorced, and I'm equally positive Joe's scared to death of getting married. He froze, Diet Coke sloshing onto his loafers.

"I mean, you two seem so happy together, and you could have a big wedding at Sophie's new house," I said merrily, enjoying a bit of revenge for having been forced into the role of Joe's new design assistant. "Since Sophie's mere weeks away from being legally free to walk down the aisle again, you could start looking at wedding tuxedos anytime now. . . ."

I paused for a second, my eye catching on a familiar figure seated in the stands just above where Holly stood.

"Look!" I gasped to Joe.

"What, you mean Holly flirting with the tennis guy?" said Joe, following my gaze. "Holly always flirts when she's mad at Howard. Last year, it was the golf pro at the club, the one from Scotland who looked like Tom Brady in a cable-knit sweater. She doesn't actually fool around with them or anything."

I know it's rude to point, but I couldn't help extending my finger to indicate the familiar face—above a set of incredibly muscular female shoulders—I'd just spotted in the Delray tennis stands. "Not Holly. Four rows up from where Holly and Bootsie are standing. Blond. Braids like Heidi. In a black track suit."

Joe stiffened, and a look of fear gripped him.

"I see her," Joe moaned. I noticed that below us, Bootsie had just picked out the same woman in the crowd, seated mere feet from where she and Holly were chatting with Javier.

Bootsie's jaw dropped, and she turned to stare at me as I nodded a grim confirmation to her that I'd noticed the braid-wearing spectator as well.

"Gerda," moaned Joe, burying his face in his hands. "How the hell did she end up in Florida?"

"MR. SHIELDS FLEW me down," Gerda told us a few minutes later.

"Barclay's here?" Joe said, blanching.

Joe did his best to keep the fact that he was dating Sophie on the lowest possible profile. Sophie, however, wasn't quite as discreet, posting gushy Facebook missives to her "Honey-Bunny Joe."

She lovingly depicted on Instagram every meal and movie night they shared, tweeting descriptions of how much fun she and Joe were having together, how he rocked her world and reminded her of the Nicki Minaj song "Anaconda."

Meanwhile, Barclay had made it clear in regular drunk-texts to Sophie that he wasn't exactly happy that his soon-to-be ex was dating at all—and he was especially mad it was Joe, her interior decorator. Barclay, a developer of new homes all around the Philadelphia area, hadn't been all that complimentary about Joe's design work, either. This was because Joe had renovated the enormous house Barclay now inhabited in Bryn Mawr—back when Sophie was living in it, post-split.

Gerda, an Austrian-born Pilates instructor, once saved Sophie's life, and when she showed up on Sophie and Barclay's doorstep several years ago, the softhearted mafia wife didn't have the heart to ask Gerda to leave.

Sophie initially kept their marital domicile—and Gerda—when she and Barclay split, he relocating to a condo over in Haverford. When Holly, Joe, and I met Sophie last spring, her house—a Disney-castle-style edifice—featured Swarovski crystals on every possible surface and a lot of tables featuring carved cherubs. Joe tried to give the house a make-under, removing much of the gold plating and smoked glass in favor of tasteful wainscoting and soothing oyster wall colors. But the house still retained the feeling of a Vegas high-roller suite. As much as Joe tried, it just couldn't be un-glitzed.

Finally, Joe convinced Sophie to just give the house back to

Barclay in the divorce and start over, which is when Sophie bought her current charming, rambling farmhouse.

Barclay, meanwhile, was furious that Joe stripped a lot of the glitzy elements from the casino-style house, and was having the whole place painted purple again, with the floors done in a jazzy white and purple mosaic featuring his initials in the front hallway. He was doubly pissed at Joe: first, for dating his estranged wife, and second, for all the money he was spending to re-glitz the house.

To make matters worse for Barclay, his doctors had ordered him to go on a strict diet for the entire fall and winter.

This worked out fantastically for Joe, because Sophie—using the time-honored tradition of reverse psychology—had gotten Barclay to hire Gerda to oversee his weight-loss program.

When Gerda lived with Sophie, she was always nagging both Sophie and Joe to do things like eat kale and give up vodka. As Joe told us, if there's anything that kills romance, it's having a live-in Pilates teacher from Austria in the next room.

"Mr. Shields rented a house," clarified Gerda. "In Magnolia Beach."

"What!" Joe groaned. "I've gotta call Sophie. I can't believe Barclay followed us here! What a stalker."

"I might get in trouble with Mr. Shields if Sophie find out he's here in Florida," said Gerda, looking as nervous as I'd ever seen her, which wasn't all that nervous. Gerda is nothing if not stoic, and doesn't fluster easily. She once fell flat on her face from atop the bar at the Bryn Mawr Pub and emerged totally unscathed.

"Mr. Shields, he said he tired of cold weather, and he not going to tell Sophie he's staying two blocks away from her," Gerda elaborated. "His lawyers told him stay away from Sophie—no stalking. I think maybe we keep it secret that you know he's here in Florida. Okay?"

We all considered this. No one wanted to see Barclay. No one wanted Sophie to have to deal with him. And Joe looked terrified. Barclay is a little scary, given his onetime mafia ties and also because of his sheer physical bulk. Even down sixty pounds, Barclay's still roughly twice the size of Joe. We agreed to make sure Sophie didn't throw a tantrum about her ex being in town.

"How's Barclay planning to hide out in Magnolia Beach?" Joe asked. "It's not that big a town."

"We mostly stay home. Me, I'm not supposed to be here at the tennis match," Gerda admitted. "I told Barclay I take taxi to the Delray farmers' market. He has business meeting at the house, so he said it was okay, but he told me to keep low profile."

"Don't worry about it," Holly told her. "We'll tell Sophie that she can't let her ex know that *she* knows he's here. Just don't mention to Barclay that you saw *us*."

"Not on your life," Gerda agreed.

Holly gazed thoughtfully at Gerda. "I wonder why Barclay came to Magnolia Beach, though, if he didn't want to run into Sophie. There are a million other towns in Florida."

Gerda perked up a little. "I have information about that. He has business down here, he's working on some kind of secret deal. Plus, he gets a lot of calls from that chef."

"Chef Gianni?" Joe asked.

"Yeah, that one," Gerda confirmed.

"Gerda, this is huge, because we think Gianni might have tried to run me over with a Chevy the other night, plus kill the manager of a restaurant that Sophie and I have personally sunk a fortune in," Holly told her. "And the fact that Barclay's down here *too* seems like too much of a coincidence."

"Yeah," Gerda said. "When did you almost get nailed?"

"Tuesday night, around ten," Holly told her.

"I hate to tell you this, but Barclay got a rented Chevy at the house!" Gerda informed us. "I don't think he drive much, though. He has Town Cars with tinted windows pick him up so he can go around and not be seen." She paused to think for a second. "But it could have been Barclay who run you down," Gerda said grimly. "We got to rented house in afternoon on Tuesday, and I went to bed at nine and had to take sleeping pill because I hear a lot of weird cricket noises. We don't have this in Austria."

"I guess Barclay *could* be trying to get back at Sophie by killing Jessica, which would definitely put Vicino out of business," mused Bootsie. "Although wouldn't it make more sense if he just hired a hit man to run over *Sophie*? Doesn't Barclay farm out this kind of hit-and-run work?

"Wait a minute," she added. "Gerda, aren't you some kind of computer genius? Can't you read all Barclay's e-mail, and then give us the four-one-one on what he's up to?"

This was true: In addition to her fitness acumen, Gerda dabbles in forensic computer snooping and is quite good at hacking into online bank accounts and personal e-mails. It isn't that Gerda steals from people; she just enjoys gathering potentially embarrassing information.

"Yeah, I'm pretty awesome at computer hacking," Gerda said, a note of pride in her voice. "I gave up snooping as New Year's resolution, but since Sophie needs help, I do it for her.

"Plus, I can tell Mr. Shields up to something—he gets a special smile. He looks super happy this week, so I know he's about to screw somebody over."

We gave our cell phone numbers to Gerda, who said she would hit the farmers' market for some kohlrabi, then head home to start reading Barclay's e-mail. She promised to call us within the hour, after printing out whatever seemed suspicious.

"Tell you the truth, I miss Sophie," Gerda told us, surprising me with this admission of a human emotion. "She always sneak the bad food and champagne when I tell her not to. But Sophie is nice person. Barclay, he is asshole."

"So true. Well, I've got to make a quick stop on the way home," Holly breezily told us. "Bye, Gerda. Good to see you," she added, turning on the heel of her pricey sandal and heading for the stadium exit.

"I leave, too," said Gerda, heading off in the direction of another egress from the stadium, which led toward Delray's town square, where the aforementioned farmers' market was in full swing.

"What's that all about?" Joe asked suspiciously, staring at Holly's trim and perfect form disappearing out of the arched entrance. "Where do you think she's going?"

I had a pretty good idea Holly was off to make some lucky salesperson's monthly quota, probably back up in Magnolia Beach at Saks. I'd noticed Holly's fingers twisting and twitching like crazy all through the tennis match. She literally gets itchy fingers when she's in manic shopping mode. Also, when she pulled out her iPhone at one point, I noticed a suspiciously fat envelope from Wells Fargo Bank tucked inside her small Celine tote. I was pretty sure Holly had taken out a bunch of cash and was headed to distribute said cash at the shoe salon of Saks.

"She's definitely going shopping," said Bootsie, who'd doubtless noticed the wad of dough herself. "Let's watch the rest of this match, and then you two head back to Magnolia Beach and do a spend-ervention. I've got a couple more matches to watch here, and then I want to hit The Singing Frog."

"Let me guess, that's a bar where your parents got liquored up before they conceived Chip," Joe offered.

"Absolutely not! The Frog is Mummy's favorite boutique in Delray. They get Lilly Pulitzer exclusives. I'm thinking of going Adelia's route, and trying on a couple of Lilly caftans."

"Much as I hate to miss seeing you drown yourself in a flowered caftan, that sounds like a decent plan," Joe agreed. Personally, I loved Adelian's caftans, and thought it might be a good look on Bootsie. I mean, who doesn't love a caftan? They're so '60s-cool. While we watched the tennis match, I pondered whether I could afford to splurge on one myself, and fifteen minutes later, after the hot Chinese tennis player defeated the cute Australian guy, we waved goodbye to Bootsie, who headed south in her preppy sandals at a brisk clip down Atlantic Avenue, while we climbed into the convertible.

Starting up the car, Joe handed me his phone. "See where Holly's phone is pinging on the map?" he said grimly.

I peered in the bright sunlight at the tiny screen. "It looks like she's at the corner of Palm Avenue and Hibiscus Lane," I told him, worry surging through me. I searched for a positive spin to Holly's whereabouts. "Maybe she's returning something she bought last week?" I suggested.

Joe merely raised a contemptuous eyebrow and steered west toward the on-ramp to I-95.

"Do you think she's at Saks? Or maybe Neiman's?" I asked, slumping dejectedly in my seat, hoping I had on enough sunscreen.

"Worse," Joe told me grimly, merging past some 18-wheelers into the northbound lane of the highway. "I know where she is. But I can't even bring myself to say the name of the store. It starts with an H and has handbags named for movie stars and royalty."

Chapter 7

"Holly's mid-meltdown," Joe told me as he roared up the entrance ramp to I-95 and headed back toward Magnolia Beach. "She's having a Howard episode."

I could see true concern in Joe's expression. It's true that Holly is much happier and more stable since she married Howard Jones a few years ago. She doesn't enjoy being alone, and she honestly gets a little manic when Howard isn't around. She seemed to always feel safe and secure with Howard when they first got together. But on and off for the past year, Holly thought he was going to cheat, and when she got the idea in her mind, she couldn't be convinced otherwise. I was positive, however, that Howard wasn't having any flings. He really loved her. And they'd been reunited and doing great since last spring—or so I thought.

"Is it a bartender?" Last year, Holly was convinced that Howard had embarked on a lusty affair with a bartender at the Porterhouse, his favorite Philly steak house. The girl in question was extremely well endowed, and Howard did go to the Porterhouse a lot, but he finally convinced Holly that he only went there for the steak.

"This is worse," Joe told me grimly, Ray-Ban aviators firmly in place, wind whipping back his longish brown hair. "I'll show you on my phone as soon we get to another red light."

We passed through most of town, until we reached a traffic jam as we approached the corner where Vicino and the incipient Gianni Mare stood across from each other.

We both forgot about Holly's marriage woes for a moment, because there was a major scene happening outside Gianni's new place.

The action at the new restaurant resembled the amount of rushing around, chaos, and frenzied construction normally associated with the Super Bowl halftime show. Large white tents had been erected around both the front and side entrance of the restaurant formerly known as The Peacock, blocking the view of the insta-renovations going on within.

As we parked the Caddy, two workers carried out The Peacock's ornately painted sign through the tent flaps and unceremoniously flung it into a huge Dumpster parked on the corner. So much for a piece of Magnolia Beach history, I thought, wondering if I could have e-Bayed the sign to some nostalgic WASP who'd been a devotee of The Peacock's famous crab soufflé, which, Adelia had told us, had once been the town's signature dish.

In front of the Dumpster, a vehicle that resembled a rock band's tour bus and was stamped with an HGTV logo idled noisily. From it emerged cameramen, clipboard-wielding assistants, and finally a beautiful woman in super-tight jeans, stiletto heels, and a low-cut white blouse. Clearly the star of the show, the girl also wore a tool belt and was carrying a fan deck of paint colors.

"Sienna Blunt!" Joe said angrily. "I can't believe Gianni convinced her to do his forty-eight-hour makeover. Plus, it's a travesty that she even has her own show!"

"Maybe it's because she looks great in the tool belt," I suggested. Honestly, the dangling wrenches somehow oozed sex.

"Any girl looks good in a tool belt," said Joe angrily. "That's *Maxim* magazine's go-to look."

"For a pop-up restaurant, this looks pretty elaborate, doesn't it?" I said to Joe, trying to end the Sienna rant. The same workmen who'd dumped the Peacock's venerable placard into the trash emerged from a paneled truck with a replacement sign made of carefully aged French zinc. Hand-hammered into the zinc were elegant block letters reading "Gianni Mare," and a charming, antique-style spotlight was mounted above the large sign. "That sign must have taken weeks to make."

"Chef Gianni isn't the type to pop up," Joe said. "He's more of a plotter and schemer, especially when it comes to taking down Channing and Jessica. Plus, this is a major installation. Pop-ups are supposed to be done quick and on the cheap."

"Would HGTV pay for all of this?" I asked as we watched workmen emerge from the ramp of a truck carrying an enormous, pricey-looking, twelve-arm silver chandelier. They took it in through the tent flaps, followed by additional guys toting matching silver sconces.

"Absolutely not! I priced that chandelier recently for Sophie's house, and it was sixteen thousand dollars. That's close to the whole budget for a TV show makeover," Joe said, looking annoyed. "I mean, even Sophie didn't want to spend that on a light fixture."

"This place is looking very 1997," he added dismissively, as Sienna Blunt directed a group of landscapers carrying lush jasmine bushes in zinc planters inside the white tented entrance. "Brasserie decor is all wrong for Florida."

Personally, I loved the zinc sign, and the planters looked beautiful, but then again, Joe has a habit of dissing any design job he hasn't overseen. He spends most of his weekends, in fact, visiting shops, bistros, showrooms, and hotels around Philly just so he can weigh in on his competitors. A designer show house can enrage him for weeks.

"Let's blow this clusterfuck," he added grumpily as he headed back to the car, stepping aside to make way for a girl carrying a rack of wineglasses.

As I was trying to imagine how hot the beige leather seats that had been baking in subtropical sun would feel through my Gap sundress (twenty-two dollars, end-of-season sale), I heard a familiar friendly voice hailing me from across Ocean Boulevard.

"Doll! Is that you? What are you doing down here?"

TWO BEAUTIFULLY DRESSED men crossed the street. Each wore a crisp white shirt and had a golden tan that spoke of afternoons on the tennis court and lunches by a shimmering pool. They toted neat leather bags from which poked iPad minis. On their leather bags and iPad cases, "Colkett" was stamped in distinctive, tasteful script.

"Kristin Clark and Joe Delafield! We couldn't be happier to see you!" Tim Colkett said, looking genuinely surprised and pleased. The Colketts were Bryn Mawr's preeminent landscape and floral designers, who were known for creating spectacular yards and party settings. They are exceptionally good at what they do, and the two are also extremely nice guys. Holly counts them as good friends.

"Don't you love this town? So overpriced!" added his colleague, Tom Colkett.

"Is Holly here?" asked Tim hopefully. The Colketts had designed many an overpriced party for Holly.

"She sure is," I told him. "I'm staying with her, as a matter of fact. She's over at The Breakers at a workout class right now."

"That's where we're staying," Tom told us. "What a hotel! And I'm guessing you're down here with Sophie," he added to Joe. "She's adorable. We can't wait to get back up north to work on her new house with you."

"Yeah, that'll be great," said Joe, who was clearly as puzzled as I was to see the Colketts. "Are you guys here on a, uh, vacation?" asked Joe.

"I'd call it more of a working trip," Tom told him. "We're helping Gianni with the renovation. Although, since we're staying at The Breakers and not paying a dime, and we'll be starring on the show about this makeover, it's not exactly hardship labor!"

"You made up with Gianni?" I asked, shocked.

The previous spring, during a testy dispute over a bill at Gianni's Bryn Mawr restaurant, the Colketts had been verbally excoriated by Gianni, who'd gone so far as to lob a rock-hard piece of preserved fruit at Tim Colkett. It had taken the unlucky florist weeks to regain his full hearing. The Colketts had been understandably terrified of Gianni and had only agreed to work with him again if they could deal with Jessica, who'd still been the chef's girlfriend at the time.

"We had to make up with Gianni when he offered us this job," Tom said, looking somewhat embarrassed. "I mean, our business in Bryn Mawr is dead in January. No one's even ordering flowers."

"You know our policy," Tim reminded me. "We love any customer, as long as they're rich. And Gianni is currently spending like, well, your friend Holly. He hasn't disputed a single bill. And trust me, finding full-size jacaranda trees for this place hasn't been exactly cheap!"

"I understand," I nodded. "It's hard to pass up work in Florida when there's nothing going on at home." *How is Gianni affording all this?* I wondered as a truck pulled up and the drivers unlocked the rear door, then began trundling out kitchen equipment. "Do you know who his investors are?" I asked the Colketts.

"Er, not really," said Tim. "I mean, we hear rumors, but who really knows!"

"I've gotten some design work down here myself," Joe said, faux modestly. "With the tobacco heiress Adelia Earle. It'll probably end up in *Elle Decor*, which of course isn't as mainstream as HGTV."

"Gianni Mare's theme is one hundred percent blue and white!" explained Tim. "Our concept. That Sienna didn't have a single idea. So we brought in some Chinese export porcelain and helped her match paint colors and come up with a theme for the banquettes and the window treatments. The banquettes are a superb cerulean color piped with bright white and then the curtains are the reverse! All the plates and barware are blue and white, and the ceiling is being hand painted as a trompe l'oeil. The floor, of course, is a blue and white chevron. They're priming the walls as we speak."

"It's gorgeous," nodded Tom. "It's like you've died and woken up in an antique urn. Well, actually I guess you *could* die and end up in an urn, but you know what I mean."

Joe looked devastated. I knew he would immediately shit-can his blue-and-white concept for Adelia Earle's pavilion. He'd never want to do the same theme that the Colketts and Sienna Blunt had dreamed up for Gianni Mare.

"So, will you two be at the opening?" Tim asked me. "I'd invite you myself, but I can't risk being on the wrong end of one of Gianni's moods," he added apologetically. "You know how he gets, and I know you guys are friends with Channing and Jessica."

"We might be there," I told them. "Gianni's always liked Holly. He told her she's definitely invited tomorrow."

"As a matter of fact, we'd better get inside!" Tom said, nudging his colleague urgently. "Because Gianni just pulled up. See ya!"

"PINK," SAID JOE miserably. "I'm going to have to go with pink at Adelia's house. She has way too much green already, and yellow just isn't going to work." He let out a huge sigh.

"I'll call Mrs. Earle right now. She's probably had at least two margaritas since we left. She might not even remember the blue-and-white idea."

"I'm really sorry," I told him. "But pink sounds amazing. Who doesn't love pink! Your pavilion will be a million times cooler than Gianni's place," I added.

"His space sounds like a migraine waiting to happen!" agreed Joe as he dialed Adelia. He perked up. "Pink will be the new color of the season, mark my words. I'm thinking hand painted pink butterflies glazed onto the walls and a trellis-patterned floor. This is going to be way better than that stupid blue theme!"

Chapter 8

As Joe dialed Adelia and cranked up the air-conditioning inside the Caddy, I saw Jessica's thin, tanned face peeking through the fichus hedges on Vicino's patio, a thin plume of smoke rising from where she sat. Her Louboutin strappy sandals were visible beneath the lush green foliage that surrounded the tables in the outdoor dining area.

Not surprisingly, Jessica looked stunned and upset by the level of frenzied construction going on just opposite her own restaurant. And since she and Channing had moved more than a thousand miles to get away from Gianni, I didn't think they'd see his new restaurant as friendly competition. Still, I had to give Jessica credit: a girl with a sprained hand that can balance on five-inch heels isn't going to let her rage-aholic ex-boyfriend scare her off.

In fact, as we idled, a car with "Miami Herald" inscribed on its door parked behind us and a young reporter, followed by a bored-looking photographer with a ponytail and a beer gut, hopped out and approached the boobalicious Sienna. Clearly, Gianni Mare was big news, and the whole instant-makeover angle was only making matters more interesting for local media.

For her part, Jessica gave Joe and me a little wave with her cigarette, but her expression was pure misery as she turned on her heel and disappeared inside Vicino. She obviously hadn't expected Gianni's "pop-up" venture to be an all-out, over-the-top restaurant on steroids.

"Should we stop in and check on Channing and Jessica before we take off?" I asked Joe, who had just surreptitiously gulped down a Xanax. "She looks pretty upset."

"No way," he said. "We'll see those two tonight at dinner. Let's forget about confronting Holly, and hit a couple of antiques stores. I better start buying stuff for Adelia's place before the Colketts steal my pink theme for their next job." He floored the convertible, and we hung a left and headed toward the Intercoastal.

I looked up, admiring the gorgeous phalanx of royal palms that shaded this beautiful road, and the lush banks of pink and red impatiens banked magnificently in a center median. Not one speck of dust or one stray palm frond or wayward coconut marred the perfection of the wide avenue. A woman in a spotless green Jaguar, top up and hair in shellacked perfection, drove past us. Her face was beautiful, but frozen to the point that she might not have actually been alive. But then she hung a right into a bank parking lot.

"Here, check my iPhone tracker," Joe instructed me. "I've got Holly on there, it's the icon at the top right. Just click it, and it'll tell you exactly where she is. And it better not be the Gucci store."

"She's still on Palm Avenue," I told Joe, peering at the screen, where a small circular icon on a map showed Holly's location.

"It's part of a manic episode brought on by Howard being away in Indianapolis," Joe sighed, shaking his head. "That's why she's been working out so much, too." Joe paused at the stoplight before the causeway and looked at me with a concerned expression under his jaunty straw hat.

"She's in the middle of a full-blown Howard meltdown," he said, then gunned the car when the light turned green. "And this time, I don't think she's inventing a problem."

I was truly upset to hear this. And worried for Holly, especially since she seemed so manic. She's naturally skinny and hates exercise, so when Holly starts working out excessively, there's something seriously bothering her. I mean, once in a while, she'll put on a tennis outfit and go to lunch in it, but that's mainly because she looks good in a short white skirt. She doesn't actually pick up a racket or anything.

Everything had seemingly been going well in Holly's marriage over the last six months, or at least I'd thought. She and Joe had even created a "man room" with brown walls, a huge antique desk, and a pool table for Howard at their house in Bryn Mawr, since Howard didn't share her obsession with airy, all-white and pale-gray modern decor. And, understandably, he wanted one small space in their nine thousand square feet of house where he could drink a glass of red wine without fear of leaving a ring on a white marble table. Holly had also received a gorgeous antique ruby ring from Howard as a getting-back-together present, after which they had thrown a non-divorce party at their newly renovated house.

Then Howard had actually taken *time off,* which he never does, and they'd spent August in Tuscany. I mean, how bad could things be?

"Holly had a Google freak-out last week," Joe said, turning left onto the Dixie Highway, which had a charmingly run-down, old-time Florida look to it. There were high-end antiques stores in low-rise shopping centers, and next to the fancy shops, I noticed a few consignment stores. There were also, I noticed, quite a few liquor stores.

"Google Images, actually, was what triggered the Palm Avenue shopping," Joe clarified further. "And the obsession with working out."

"Was there a picture of Howard doing something, you know, illicit?" I asked, worried.

Howard's truly devoted to Holly, or so I'd always thought. He never gets riled up by anything she does or suggests. Take their trip to Italy: When Holly bought out the row of first-class seats behind theirs so that her new leather goods would have their own seats and wouldn't get smooshed on the flight home, did he say anything? Not at all. He just smiled and dutifully toted boxes of Valentino sling backs and Miu Miu leather satchels to seats 3A and 3B. I guess the shoes and bags hadn't wanted to ride in coach.

"Howard's been out in Indiana for almost a month now on that garbage-company takeover," Joe reminded me. "He told Holly he couldn't come down here to Florida last weekend—which he's been doing every Friday since we've been here—because the company he's buying in the Midwest was doing a major charity event that Saturday. It was like Habitat for Humanity.

"Or something," Joe added vaguely, waving his hand dismissively at the notion of Midwesterners banding together to build a house for the needy. It's not worth trying to convince Joe that worthy causes are in fact worthy.

"There was a big indoor barbecue party after the charity thingy for all the volunteers, which was covered by the local paper," Joe explained. "Obviously, Holly isn't going to bang nails or whatever at Habitat for Humanity, but she could have gone to Indiana for the weekend. Instead, she told Howard she couldn't come because she had to help Jessica choose new cocktail napkins for Vicino."

"Picking out napkins probably took about four minutes," I said, concerned. "Maybe she should have gone to Indiana!"

"That won't happen," Joe shook his head. "She wouldn't go anyway, because she doesn't go to barbecues. I mean, where people are eating food like ribs and cheeseburgers. Plus, it's seven degrees right now in Indianapolis, so the barbecue was held in a local college field house, and that sealed the deal. Holly told Howard that she never went to a field house while she was actually enrolled in college, and she isn't about to start now." Joe was still zooming down the Dixie Highway, which was all warehouses and car repair shops at this point. "Plus, Holly claims she only gets on planes that are headed either south or east, like in the direction of the Bahamas," he added.

"Didn't she and Howard go to California two summers ago?" I asked.

"California's different. It's the other states that are an issue," Joe said.

I rolled my eyes at this.

"So what did she see on Google Images?" I asked.

"She saw the daughter of the garbage guy from Indianapolis," said Joe simply. He expertly pulled into a metered parking spot outside a row of antiques stores, turned off the Caddy, and, after scrolling through his phone for a second, handed the iPhone to me. "That's the girl," he said. "At the barbecue."

I had to admit, squinting in the sun at Joe's phone, the girl looked pretty fabulous.

"I was picturing someone different in the garbage heiress role," I said to Joe. We exchanged concerned glances. "This girl looks like she just left Bergdorf's. And she's got, well . . ." With my hands in front of my own sadly underwhelming chest, I made the universal gesture that conveys large boobs.

The photo on Joe's phone was part of the local paper's coverage of the society scene in Indianapolis, and it looked like the indoor barbecue after the Habitat for Humanity event had been a major event. The damning photo was captioned, "Howard Jones, who recently acquired Stewart Waste Management, with Marty, Bubba, and Dawnelle Stewart."

Marty and Bubba looked like your basic good-looking, golf-playing, well-off Midwestern guys in Brooks Brothers dress shirts and khakis. Dawnelle was another matter: She appeared to be in her mid-twenties. She had long and lustrous hair. Her face had adorably large blue eyes, high cheekbones, and a sweet, hopeful expression. She had on what I think was a Dolce & Gabbana bustier dress. And she had a lot of bust to bustier.

"Howard might as well be doing Habitat for Humanity with Kate Upton," agreed Joe. "It's horrible for Holly. All her worst fears confirmed. There are more photos here, too, on this Indianapolis society blog."

"But Dawnelle isn't even standing next to Howard," I noted, attempting to find a positive spin on the situation. "She's over there with her brother, Bubba. She looks a little young for Howard, too."

Joe just stared at me in disbelief. "Young? Did you actually just say, 'She looks a little young for Howard'? Like that's ever stopped anyone," he said finally. "Sometimes you worry me, honestly. I mean, where do you even come up with this stuff? Look, here's another photo of Dawnelle from earlier that day, working at the charity project. She's helping install a sink."

He scrolled to another image where the beautiful heiress, clad in cute jeans and boots for her Habitat volunteering time, was helping Bubba tighten bolts underneath a bathroom vanity (at least, I think that's what they were doing, since I don't know a lot about sinks). Dawnelle looked really good from the side angle, too, given her tight jeans and aforementioned generously apportioned chest. She also upheld the theory that girls look good in tool belts.

Dawnelle appeared to be truly enjoying helping out with the project, too, smiling happily as she worked. "It says on this Indianapolis Style website that Dawnelle personally funded all the bathrooms and kitchens for the project and wrote a check for eighteen thousand dollars," Joe told me grimly.

We looked at each other, and I knew we were both thinking the same thing. Holly's a truly generous person. She'll write a check for any good cause, and frequently does. But there's no way she's ever going to get anywhere near a plumbing project. Hopefully Howard wasn't falling for the do-gooding Dawnelle.

GERDA CALLED HOLLY's phone at six that night, announcing she'd printed a pile of e-mails two inches thick, and that we needed to read them ASAP.

"Where are you, Gerda?" Holly asked her.

"At Barclay's, and I can't get out of house tonight," Gerda said in the manner of a grounded teenager. "Barclay gained seven pounds this week, and we're doing extra workouts tonight. Tomorrow morning, I can sneak out. Barclay has car service taking him to Miami for meeting at nine a.m."

Since it turned out Gerda and Barclay were staying on Seagrape Lane just a few houses down from Adelia, we agreed to meet at Adelia's the next morning at nine-fifteen.

Forty-five minutes later, while I was working on my hair with a flatiron and some de-frizzing spray, Holly came to the guesthouse, trailed by Sophie.

"Ya know what, I'm gettin' tired of Vicino every night," Sophie told us. "Let's stop at Tiki Joe's on the way over to dinner."

I had to laugh as I thought of anyone being tired of Vicino, where each dish was more delicious than the next and waiters were always bringing things like chilled Pellegrino, fresh bottles of pinot noir, and grilled scallops to the table. "Sophie, you co-own the place," I told her. "You can't be tired of it."

"I mean, I love Channing and all," Sophie shrugged. "But I've been there twenty-three nights in a row! Plus, I feel awful that my ex might be the one trying to kill Holly, and I want to take her out for a drink to apologize."

"It's not your fault that Barclay's probably trying to flatten me like a veal paillard," Holly told Sophie. "Anyway, I'm totally up for Tiki Joe's."

"By the way, Kristin, ya need to lose the Old Navy outfits," Sophie told me helpfully, eyeing what I'd thought was a cute sundress. She popped some gum into her mouth, a habit Joe banned when he was present but which Sophie snuck when she could. "Old Navy ain't gonna fly at Tiki Joe's," she informed me, chewing noisily on her Bubblicious.

Holly, who had already gone into the closet, emerged holding a white Milly mini dress with a pretty square neckline and a pair of Prada wedges, both still in the bags they'd been toted home in from the Bal Harbour shopping center. "Listen to Sophie!" Holly told me.

"I feel weird wearing your clothes," I protested to Holly. "I mean, the tags are still on these, and look how expensive they are!"

"*I* feel weird when you wear Old Navy to chic restaurants," Holly told me, turning on her Giuseppe Zanotti heel, Sophie scampering after her like a well-groomed Chihuahua.

"Hurry up. We leave in five minutes for Tiki Joe's."

Tiki Joe's was pretty awesome. It combined the fun, honky-tonk vibe of the Florida Keys with the glossy swankiness of Magnolia

Beach, and it had a '60s, retro vibe. The bar and restaurant were dark and noisy, filled with older men and their younger wives and, in one case, I was pleased to notice, an older woman and her younger guy. Steel drum music was pumping, festive lanterns dangled from the ceiling, and the vibe was totally cool.

Ninety seconds after we sat down, our waiter showed up with two bottles of Laurent-Perrier champagne.

"From the gentleman at the bar," he said, addressing Holly, "for the lady in the black dress."

Men sending Holly drinks was nothing new: This happens pretty much anytime you go anywhere with Holly. As much as she spends on clothing, furniture, artwork, and travel, I don't think she's ever paid for a drink in her whole perfect blond life.

We all peeked to see who the champagne-sender was, though, since he'd been nice enough to buy free bubbly for our whole group. The waiter discreetly indicated a dark-haired guy at the end of the bar closest to the front door.

"Who's *that* hottie?" shrieked Sophie, voicing my own thoughts.

The man was indeed gorgeous. Not in the hunky manner of Channing, or the preppy handsome John Hall type. This guy was more mature, with cheekbones you could hang your dry cleaning from.

Put together Antonio Sabato Jr., any member of the Iglesias singing family, and throw in Robb Stark from *Game of Thrones*, and you get the general idea of the genetically blessed guy with sculpted cheekbones and dark eyes who'd sent the drinks. I tried not to stare as openly as Bootsie was currently doing.

"I'd like to check into a motel with that guy for about four hours," Bootsie announced. "Maybe I got married too young." She seemed like she was about to expand on her thoughts concerning what she'd do once she got into the motel room with the guy, but just then he started walking toward our table.

"Hello," said the Cheekbones politely with an elegant nod of his head to us all. He had your basic American accent but possessed a European vibe in his perfectly tailored sport coat. He also wore some kind of scent that brought to mind new leather, freshly mown grass, cigars, and good red wine. "I'm J. D. Alvarez. Enjoy the champagne."

He gave Holly a polite nod but didn't invite himself to sit at our table—not that we would have minded.

Another head poked around from behind Alvarez. It belonged to a slightly sunburned guy in a golf shirt, khakis, and a belt embroidered with jaunty anchors. His vibe was "Golfed all day, gonna do it again tomorrow!" He was about forty, and attractive, but he looked as though he might be slightly too fond of vodka tonics and porterhouse steaks.

"Scott Simmons," he said, sticking out his hand and shaking all of ours. "Magnolia Beach attorney, businessman, and"—here, he gave a wink of a blue and slightly bloodshot eye—"willing tour guide! You girls should call me anytime!" Simmons realized that he was leaving out Joe while flirting with the rest of the table, so he gave Joe a friendly slap on the back.

"And you, too, buddy. If you need any tee times or have any deals down here you need any legal advice on!" He handed around some business cards and addressed this last to Joe, who barely controlled an eye roll.

"My Honey Bunny doesn't golf—he's a decorator!" Sophie told the Simmons guy.

As Sophie chatted away, the handsome J. D. Alvarez retreated politely back to his bar stool, taking an occasional glance at Holly—who pretended she didn't notice.

I tuned all of this out as I stared down at the business card Scott Simmons had handed over.

It read, "Scott 'Scooter' Simmons, Attorney at Law," and listed an office on Royal Palm Way. This had to be Adelia's neighbor—the guy whose happy hour she liked to liven up with her afternoon target practice. There couldn't be more than one Scooter in Magnolia Beach.

Well, maybe there could be two Scooters—you never know. But I felt sure that this had to be Adelia's neighbor. I could see bells of recognition going off for Bootsie and Joe, too, while they examined Scooter's card. Meanwhile, with Simmons nodding along, Sophie rattled on about how Joe could eat anything he wanted and not gain weight, but he never exercised, let alone swung a golf club.

For her part, Holly had checked out of the conversation. She fixed her lip gloss, glanced at her phone, and gave a couple of quick looks in the direction of the gorgeous J. D. This surprised me a little, because Holly isn't the type to flirt unless it's for a specific reason, like getting a better deal on a car or something like that. She's really devoted to Howard, and she respects their relationship.

After a few minutes, Scooter wandered back to his drink and his bar stool, and Bootsie announced she was starving and it was time to head to Vicino.

Holly was still looking at her phone for a text from Howard—which I hoped would be full of reassurance and erase all vestiges of doubt about the gorgeous Dawnelle Stewart. As we piled into Bootsie's car, though, where I got stuck in the middle backseat, Holly turned her iPhone off, inserted it into her clutch, then closed the tiny purse, but not before I noticed a card inside.

The name on the simple, embossed business card read, "J. D. Alvarez" and was followed only by a cell phone number.

How Alvarez had slipped her the card without any of us noticing, I couldn't tell. My emotions ran toward worry about this handsome guy making a play for my married friend—and a grudging respect for a guy who could sneak his card into a girl's YSL clutch without any one of her four nosy friends noticing.

I felt a quick bolt of worry as I sneaked a quick look at Holly's perfect profile. With Holly in mid-Howard meltdown, one J. D. Alvarez—handsome, cool, who looked like money and smelled like an intoxicating blend of freshly mown grass with a whiff of ridiculously overpriced cologne splashed into the mix—was way too enticing.

I sighed as Bootsie zoomed around the corner toward Vicino. Luckily, Holly doesn't have a business card, because other than being a (mostly) silent partner in Vicino, she doesn't really have a business.

Then things got worse. "Where's your wedding ring?" Sophie said, checking out Holly's bare left hand. "And your engagement band?"

"I'm having them cleaned," said Holly in a carefree tone.

Just then, my phone started ringing with incoming texts.

"It's Martha," I told everyone. "Waffles is having a dog-trum. He's howling at Holly's front door, and angry Bahama Lane neighbors are calling Martha. Can you please drop me off back at Holly's? I'll skip dinner."

The looks that came my way from the front seat called to mind a horror movie I saw recently on Cinemax, in which a single glare melted off the recipient's face. Bootsie didn't even need to tell me that this would never happen with her Labs—I already knew from her expression. Joe started muttering things like "freaking hound" and "who the hell brings their dog to Florida."

Two minutes later, Waffles erupted out of Holly's front door, aiming for me as I climbed out of the car. Then he saw Sophie. He's always had a soft spot for Sophie, who's tiny and easily knocked over, which Waffles does with a certain joie de basset every time he gets the chance.

"Hiya, doggie," Sophie said, reaching out of the open door to pat him on the head. He whined soulfully, turned, and gave me the droopiest, most guilt-inducing Sad Eyes I've ever seen. With Waffles, that's saying a lot, because his patented Sad Eyes look is honestly really sad. My heart sank. I'd dragged him to Florida, which was obviously a lot better than staying in Bryn Mawr, where he'd be freezing and have to stay with my neighbors the Bests. But then I'd left him pretty much all day.

"I can't go to dinner and leave him like this. Look at him!" I said, love welling up inside my slightly sunburned self.

We all gazed at Waffles, who realized he was the topic of our conversation and suddenly perked up.

"You're staying home with *that*?" said Bootsie. "When you could be sitting at Vicino, listening to bossa nova, looking at Channing in a tight T-shirt, drinking Prosecco?"

"And after you spent thirty minutes flat-ironing that mop of hair?" added Joe from the car.

"I know what to do!" shrieked Sophie. "Bring him! I mean, what the hell, I own the friggin' restaurant. Well, Holly and I do, mostly. We can sit on the terrace. The doggie and I can split a petite filet!"

Waffles started wagging and suddenly looked as happy as Adelia Earle when presented with a fresh margarita. He knew he'd won.

Chapter 9

"Is it normal for him to look like that?" asked Sophie, gazing down at Waffles.

As soon as we'd parked at Vicino, the dog had rocketed out of Bootsie's car, going temporarily nuts as he'd headed toward the delicious smell of meats being grilled and pastas being served to diners seated on the outdoor patio.

Before I could catch him, Waffles tangled up his leash in a potted night-blooming jasmine tree and tackled a waiter carrying a twenty-eight-dollar cheese plate, gobbling down the little slices of cheese and fig jam in about four seconds.

Once we were seated on the patio, he finally calmed down as he sat at my feet, panting and drooling happily. Remnants of Brie speckled his ears, and fellow diners looked appalled but soon returned to their conversation.

"I never saw anyone eat cheese that fast!" Sophie said. "Is that why there's so much drool? Doesn't his belly look kinda swollen, too?"

I looked down at Waffles, who lay gazing happily at the buzz of well-dressed people at the tables all around us. The patio at Vicino was subtly lit by lanterns and votive candles, and upbeat Latin music emanated from hidden speakers. The outdoor temperature was perfection now that the sun had set, and it was a balmy seventy-four degrees, with a crescent moon above the palm trees. Waffles sighed happily, rolled onto his side, and fell asleep on my foot.

"He's fine," I told Sophie. "He was probably just hungry." Bootsie rolled her eyes, while Holly, who'd chosen to disregard the entire incident, checked her phone—probably hoping for a text message from Howard. I thought about asking her how Howard was doing but decided against it, in case she was still obsessing about Dawnelle Stewart.

"What's up with Howard?" asked Joe, who's not always known for his tact and timing.

To be honest, Joe can be a little too blunt at times. For instance, he doesn't hold back on telling me when my hair looks terrible, or that the "natural look" I strive for with makeup in fact looks more like I just rolled out of bed.

Joe also isn't shy about saying he doesn't like style that's *too* done, either. He's gone up against Sophie countless times over her proclivity for glittery clothing, shoes, and even furniture, and told her that they would have to break up if she bought a single statue to display at her new house. (Sophie has a love of classical statuary and was hoping to surround her pool with half-nude figures a la the Parthenon.) Then again, Joe's never tactless when he's schmoozing his other decorating clients—he's a model of diplomacy.

"I really haven't talked to Howard," said Holly coolly. "But who's that interesting woman there in the head-to-toe Chanel?"

She indicated a sleek-looking woman in pink two tables away. Bootsie, thanks to her avid reading of gossip columns, had already studied most of the local boldface names and had a full resume for the woman, who not only had a long necklace of Chanel charms but was also currently depositing her phone back into a gorgeous quilted handbag.

"Slavica d'Aranville. She's Magnolia Beach's top realtor. Well, she and her brother combined are the top realtor. They're like the Lannisters in *Game of Thrones*, but without the inbreeding!" said Bootsie. "I read about her in *Town & Country*. Slavica's big thing is creating the ultimate move-in-ready lifestyle. She'll have a full wardrobe from Ralph Lauren and Façonnable installed in closets before clients move in. She pre-hires a chef and housekeeper, and arranges for cheese-and-wine receptions with all the fanciest people in town." Bootsie paused to sip her drink, then added, "The magazine story said Slavica once stayed up all night single-handedly repainting a twenty-by-twenty-foot dining room in Benjamin Moore's Really Red satin-gloss paint before an open house when she noticed a chip in the wall that was invisible to the naked eye. The woman is unstoppable."

Slavica appeared to be in her early fifties. She had a sleek black bob and wore a pink Chanel shift dress. She was exotically beautiful and was seated with a handsome, dark-haired man.

"Is she, uh, Slavic?" asked Joe.

"She's all American," Jessica told us with her usual blasé delivery, as she stopped by our table and joined the conversation. "Used to be named Mandy, but in Florida real estate, it helps to be exotic. Plus, she's obviously stunning, so she gets the best listings. That's her brother with her, Harry d'Aranville. They specialize in the five-million-and-above house and condo market. They've been really good customers since we opened in November, and they pick up takeout a lot, too."

While I pondered the fact that anyone would pay thirty-eight dollars for a takeout pasta, Channing appeared, his Chiclet smile gleaming in the candlelight. He pulled up a chair next to Sophie and greeted her with a kiss on the cheek.

"Channing, I know you've gotta be feeling like crap with all of this going on across the street," Sophie told him. "I mean, that freakin' Gianni's got a lot of nerve doing his restaurant right there. He could have at least picked a location down the block or something!"

Channing's handsome face lost a bit of its hopeful confidence, and he looked across the street, where the hive of activity continued with spotlights trained on guys toting ladders, paint, and furniture in and out of Gianni Mare, followed by cameramen and production types with headsets and clipboards. Luckily, there was no sign of Gianni—which was surprising, since he's a renowned control freak—but there was no denying that Gianni Mare was going to be competition for Vicino, and the HGTV angle was only adding to the buzz surrounding the new restaurant.

Jessica reached out her bony little hand to clasp Channing's.

"Once Gianni Mare is open, Gianni will get bored," she told her boyfriend. "He has the attention span of a hamster. As soon as Gianni gets a few newspaper stories and sees himself on TV, he'll pack up and move on. Plus, Florida is full of celebrity chefs, and Gianni doesn't like that kind of competition."

Channing brightened a bit, while Holly nodded in agreement. She even put down her phone and focused on the conversation.

"Gianni is all about attention!" she said to Channing. "When he catered my almost-divorce party, he had that girlfriend of his,

Olivia, secretly taking pictures the whole time. Then he posted pics on his website and released photos to Bootsie's newspaper. I threatened to never hire him again."

"Yeah, but after that, you had him cater that all-truffle dinner party in September," Joe reminded her.

"That's because you can't host a dinner in Philly and expect people to show up if Gianni doesn't cater it," Holly told him. "I thought the blogging was a little too much, but I'm starting to wonder if maybe I was wrong. Although," Holly paused, and looked at Channing apologetically, "I might have to hire Gianni again for my next party when I get home, especially now that he's going to be on TV. Sorry."

"That's okay," said Channing with his usual good humor. "I'd love to get my own cooking show, so I totally get it."

"Channing, you'd be the next Emeril, but with biceps and a square jaw!" said a charming voice behind us. "Or Alton Brown, but with the body of an Armani model! Or that guy Curtis Stone with . . . well, actually, he's pretty hot as it is. You've got what it takes to be on the Food Network."

"Nothing against Gianni, of course," added another voice hastily. "He's got the muscles and tattoos, which is kind of a cool look, and he's obviously a superb chef. Not to mention that he put us up at The Breakers."

We turned to see Tim and Tom Colkett, handsome and stylish in navy blazers and white shirts open at the collars (showing off deep tans that they seemed to have acquired in just twenty-four hours despite putting in a full day of work at Gianni Mare rather than laying out on the beach). They pulled up chairs at our table and gushed for a few minutes in the direction of Holly, then did some "mwah" air kisses with Sophie, who's also hired them many times, including one time the previous spring for a yard makeover that, Joe told me, cost forty thousand dollars in plants and labor.

"We're starving," said Tim Colkett, waving down our waiter and ordering a bottle of pinot noir, two pizzas, and a grilled branzino, as Tom mimed fainting from hunger. "Not to bite the hand that's paying us, but Gianni's been at the restaurant cooking all day and hasn't offered us so much as a Wheat Thin. Finally, the HGTV guys ordered in some takeout from a hoagie place in West Palm, but we thought we saw you guys out here on the patio, so we snuck over here."

"Actually, we might want to move inside," Tom told him. "I don't think it'll go over so great if Gianni sees us dining here."

"I'd hurry if I were you," Holly told them. "I think he is on his way over."

We all turned to see a tattooed, earring-bedecked man in chef's whites, parachute pants, and Crocs charging across the street, the willowy Olivia behind him.

"Cancel the branzino," whispered Tom Colkett. "We'll get room service." He grabbed Tim's arm, then they vaulted a potted hibiscus and disappeared down the alley behind Vicino.

"WE COME TO spend a little money in your fast-food restaurant," Gianni told Channing and Jessica a moment later. "Olivia and I, we laugh at your orange walls." He pointed inside to the bar. "I keep thinking I get a Big Mac!"

"Whatever you say, Chef," Channing said with his usual equanimity. "I'm sure there's room enough for both of our restaurants, so I'm happy to have you come and dine here anytime."

"I just drink tonight," Gianni told him. "Me, I've been cooking all day so as to have complete perfection tomorrow at my opening party. I would invite you, but I'm sure you have to be here to oversee this . . . little place." He waved dismissively at the bustling patio and lively scene inside the restaurant, while Jessica got up, rolled her eyes, and disappeared into the restaurant.

"Sure, boss," said Channing with a laugh.

I noticed Waffles had woken up and was looking at Gianni, wagging.

"Perfect customer for this place!" Gianni said, taking note of Waffles. "Channing, I see you get dogs as your clientele! This one a big fattie, too." Channing shrugged good-naturedly, while I struggled not to give Gianni a heated reply to this insult aimed toward my beloved mutt. However, the chef had lost interest in the dog and was now focused on Holly, who'd finally put her phone away.

"Holly Jones, I demand that you attend my party tomorrow night!" the chef told her, leaning over to kiss Holly's hand in the manner of Cary Grant circa 1938. "Sophie, you come also," he said. "I know you love to spend the money like crazy, Sophie. I love this about you!"

Olivia, who was clad in a strapless black dress, stood next to him, looking bored, exhausted, and like she could really use a cocktail. I'd never met Olivia, who'd been dating Gianni since the previous summer.

Jessica had mentioned offhandedly that, pre-Gianni, she had once worked at the same downtown Philly restaurant as Olivia, and they'd been on good terms but hadn't really been friends. Apparently, around the same time Jessica had kicked off her hot-and-heavy affair with Channing, Olivia had started hanging out at the bar of Gianni's Bryn Mawr trattoria. From what Jessica had heard, as soon as she and Channing had taken off for

Florida, Gianni had offered Olivia a job as part-time manager of his Ristorante Gianni and had soon convinced her to date him.

I noticed Olivia and Jessica acknowledge each other with a nod, but it was hardly a warm greeting—understandable, given the awkward circumstances. Olivia had replaced Jessica both professionally and personally.

As per usual with Gianni's girlfriends, Olivia was fifteen years younger and very attractive, and she seemed to be rapidly losing patience with his tantrums and public outbursts. At the moment, she was both texting and hissing a drink order to a passing waiter while Gianni regaled Holly and Sophie with the details of the opening party he'd planned for the following night, including a shipment of something called gamberetti, which he was having shipped in from Italy.

"The gamberetti is the juiciest, most delicious, most incredible shrimp in the world!" Gianni proclaimed.

I perked up a bit at this, since I have an embarrassing but unbridled obsession with shrimp. Shrimp from the Mediterranean? This honestly sounded pretty awesome. I'd wanted to skip Gianni's party, if indeed I could even wangle an invitation, but after all the Progresso soup and peanut butter I'd been eating at home this winter, the prospect of gamberetti was intriguing.

"Olivia, she have to haul ass down to Miami International on Sunday to pick up six crates of shrimp!" Gianni told us, giving Olivia a condescending pat on the tush. "She do the schlepping for Gianni!" The chef gave his girlfriend a little squeeze while she sipped at her vodka with what I considered to be remarkable self-control.

I felt for Olivia. It couldn't feel good to run Gianni's errands. Plus, I'd forgotten his habit of referring to himself in the third person. That had to be painful to listen to on a regular basis, too.

Gianni had (thankfully) turned to head inside to the bar, taking Olivia's elbow to steer her in that direction, when all of a sudden, a commotion broke out at the table of Slavica and Harry d'Aranville. The elegant Slavica had turned green under her deftly applied makeup, and she was trying to rise, balancing unsteadily on her beige quilted pumps. Harry, who looked a little woozy himself, had one of Slavica's elbows, while a nervous-looking waiter supported her gently.

"Bathroom!" Slavica moaned.

They rushed her indoors toward the restroom, Channing looking alarmed as he followed Slavica, while the happy buzz on the patio came to a crashing silence.

Where most people would keep out of the way of such a debacle, politeness demanding that someone who appeared as ill as Slavica be given some space and privacy, Bootsie isn't most people. She was out of her seat and at a dead run, her tall, flowered back disappearing inside the restaurant within seconds of Slavica's restroom run.

A few minutes later, Bootsie returned, the excitement of fresh news written all over her face.

"This isn't good," she told us. "Slavica's puking in the ladies' room. Jessica's in there with her, while the brother is hovering outside. He said it had to be the clams. And Channing is freaking out, because bad shellfish can ruin a restaurant in this town, especially when it was consumed by the top realtor in Palm Beach County."

Chef Gianni and Olivia appeared on the patio behind Bootsie, pausing for a moment at our table.

"Too bad for Channing. He serve this lady the bad Florida littlenecks," said Gianni happily. "And I'm sorry for you, Sophie, I hear you got a lotta money sunk in this Ronald McDonald restaurant."

"Everything will be okay!" Sophie squeaked. "Slavica's probably got a stomach virus."

"No, is from old clams," Gianni said positively. "I seen this before. The projectile vomiting is always from the bad fish."

"Look," Sophie said, as we passed the table Slavica had vacated in such a hurry. "That's so weird!"

The waiters had immediately removed all traces of Slavica and her brother's meals, but on the otherwise bare table sat a package of Imodium.

"That's good stuff!" Sophie told us. "Barclay lives on it, since he's got major Irritable Bowel Syndrome. And who wouldn't, the way he eats!"

Joe and I exchanged glances. The Imodium was clearly a nasty little joke and confirmed what Gianni was saying. *Someone knew Slavica was going to get sick.* And Gianni was in prime position to have deposited it on the table.

Gianni rudely grabbed Olivia's arm and headed toward the street.

"Looks like I open my new place just in time," he called over his shoulder. "This place gonna be out of business in a week!"

Chapter 10

THINGS SPIRALED DOWNWARD quickly that night after Slavica lost her clams in the ladies' room at Vicino.

The town's top realtor emerged from the chic white restroom after twenty-two minutes of solid (well, uninterrupted) barfing, supported by Bootsie, who wasn't about to miss such a gossip-worthy event no matter how messy, and Jessica, to whom Slavica muttered dire threats.

While diners and Vicino's bar crowd watched, agape at the sight of the Chanel-clad Slavica stumbling toward the front doors, the realtor's brother implored her to let him drive her to the ER, but Slavica merely whispered that she needed to get home—to her own bathroom—ASAP.

Channing, pale beneath his tan, gallantly assisted Bootsie and Jessica in helping Slavica down Vicino's front steps while Harry brought the car around. But even Channing's charm and genuinely kind nature failed to smooth over the society broker's rage and embarrassment over having a puke-a-thon in a public setting.

"This is the last you'll see of me at your restaurant," Slavica hissed to Jessica and Channing as Harry assisted her into the backseat of his Porsche Cayenne. "But not the last you've heard of me."

HOLLY GOT A call from Channing at 8:45 the next morning, asking her to stop over at Vicino, where he thought he'd made some discoveries that explained the Slavica situation. She promised him we'd be over ASAP but that we had a previous appointment with a computer hacker friend.

"GERDA!" SHRIEKED SOPHIE as the Pilates pro walked into Adelia's living room thirty minutes later. She popped up from her seat to give Gerda a huge hug, while Gerda gave her an awkward shoulder pat. I could tell that Gerda was touched, though, since she looked simultaneously pleased and uncomfortable with Sophie's display of affection.

I couldn't really understand Sophie's devotion to Gerda, who's not exactly warm and fuzzy, and also has told me repeatedly that Waffles is, well, portly. I never asked her for this input, either. (Her exact words were "He is fat load.") But then again, Gerda and Sophie have been through a lot together, and Gerda lived with Sophie when she and Barclay first split up. I guess they'd formed their own weird bond.

"Mrs. Earle, may I present our, uh, acquaintance, Gerda," Joe told Mrs. Earle. "Gerda . . . what's your last name again, Gerda?"

"I don't use a last name," Gerda told him.

"Anyway, Gerda works for Mr. Shields, and she has some information we need about that new restaurant I was telling you about, Gianni Mare. At least, we think she does," Joe said.

"Wonderful! I love gossip, especially if I can get it right in my own living room. Sit down and have a margarita, dear," Adelia told Gerda, gesturing to a green and white chintz armchair.

Gerda gingerly took a seat, taking in the charming surroundings and the gorgeous pool just outside the French doors, as well as the little china bowl of Stokes cigarettes. She'd arrived in her usual track suit with the jacket off in deference to the warm weather and a Lycra workout top underneath. Gerda is usually stridently anti-alcohol, anti-smoking, and anti-junk food— basically, she's against anything fun— and I feared she would blast Adelia about the evils of drinking, especially at this hour of the morning, but she didn't. Gerda was in an oddly pleasant mood. Something close to a smile actually seemed to be fighting for space on her face. Well, not a smile, but she didn't seem quite as pissy as usual.

"I don't drink," she told Adelia. "But thanks."

"You don't know what you're missing, dear!" hooted Adelia. "Have some lemonade then. Ozzy will bring it." Her assistant disappeared toward the kitchen, while Gerda nodded approvingly toward the pool.

"This is nice place," Gerda said. "Lot of nature and plants."

"Thank you," Adelia said. "I understand you're from Austria? Beautiful country. I had my second face-lift done there."

"From the Alps," nodded Gerda. "Lot of top plastic surgeons near my hometown. In the clinics. Also, the spas where one gets the colon cleaned out with the hose. Very healthy."

"I've done it all, darling!" Adelia hooted. "Left me as empty as this tequila bottle," she added, indicating a drained flacon of Patrón Silver, "and limp as a stale Triscuit."

"Gerda was telling us about some e-mails she happened to see on Barclay's computer," I said, hoping to avoid the finer details of colonic procedures. "Were you able to bring them, Gerda? Thank you, by the way."

"I have," Gerda confirmed, opening her black nylon knapsack and pulling out a slim sheaf of papers. Joe, Holly, and I all sat on the sofa and passed them back and forth, scanning them quickly for mentions of Channing, Jessica, Vicino, or Sophie's investment therein. Meanwhile, Gerda and Sophie caught up a little.

"Are you drinking the kale smoothies?" Gerda was asking Sophie disapprovingly. "I can see in your skin, you been eating a lot of meat, and not exercising."

"I did a couple of classes with Holly at The Breakers," Sophie told her nervously. "Maybe I haven't been working out quite as much as I used to."

"News flash! Barclay has sunk a ton of cash into Gianni Mare," Holly announced excitedly, brandishing one of the e-mails. "This e-mail copies Gianni and Barclay's lawyer about a transfer made into Gianni's account. He's into that place for over four hundred thousand dollars."

"I knew that place was too expensive for HGTV!" screamed Joe. "When I auditioned for my own show, they told me no project would go over fifty grand. Can you believe they said they thought I'd have trouble sticking to a budget?"

"You do have trouble sticking to a budget, Honey Bunny," Sophie told him. Luckily, Adelia, whose budget Joe was currently exceeding, seemed to miss Sophie's comment. "But that's okay, I do, too!"

"HGTV picked up the first fifty thousand for the renovation of Gianni Mare," nodded Holly, continuing to scan the papers in front of us. "After that, Barclay financed the rest of the restaurant with a couple of other minor investors." She paused for a moment to read.

"Barclay e-mailed Gianni back in December to make sure that Gianni Mare 'puts Vicino out of business within a month so that bitch Sophie loses every dime she put into it.' And I quote."

"What an asshole!" shrieked Sophie. "Oh, sorry, Mrs. Earle," she added. "I'm from Jersey. Sometimes my language gets kinda dicey."

"Please, dear, I'm from Virginia. I can curse the hair off a dog," Adelia said, waving a languid hand as she sipped her drink.

"And it's not just me he's screwing," Sophie said. "Channing and Jessica can't afford to lose Vicino."

"By the way," Adelia said, "I don't like what's happening to your friends at Vicino. Slavica already called me to tell me about getting sick, along with everyone else she knows. So tell this Channing person that I'm going to move my annual Reptile Preservation Foundation to his restaurant. It's next week! I'll have Ozzy tell all the ladies that it's going to be at Vicino."

"That's real sweet of you, Mrs. E.," said Sophie. "Cause Channing and Jessica are poor, like Kristin and my Honey Bunny here. I mean, for me, the two hundred grand ain't a big deal. Not to brag or anything," she added. "And wait a minute. Won't Barclay want to be at the opening of Gianni Mare tonight?"

Gerda shook her head firmly. "Barclay talk to me a lot when he's drunk," she told us. "Which is pretty often.

"He said his lawyers tell him not to go to Gianni's opening. He's trying to keep quiet about investing in this restaurant. Lawyers told him it open up a big can of worms if you"—she indicated Sophie—"try to get half of that place."

"Well, I'm going to. And he better not go after my stake in Vicino!" Sophie fumed.

Gerda shook her head. "Mr. Shields heard last night about

someone getting sick at that place. He was drunk and tells me Vicino going to be out of business soon," she said grimly. "Bad clams, plus he said he heard through grapevine about someone getting almost run over in alley behind it. He doesn't care about getting half of it. He says it will be half of nothing."

Bootsie, Holly, Joe, and I exchanged glances.

"How does Barclay know that Vicino's going to be out of business?" Holly asked. "Is *Barclay* the one who's behind all the problems?"

"I CAN'T FIND any e-mails in which Barclay mentions bad clams or the Death Chevy," Joe told us, taking a look for himself through the stack of printouts.

"But it looks like Barclay's cc'd someone else on some of these e-mails about Gianni Mare," Joe told us. "He's e-mailed an S. Simmons a bunch of times about whether Vicino violates any Magnolia Beach zoning laws, which he's hoping it does. And he's got Simmons working on setting up some surprise health code inspections."

"Scooter Simmons, most likely," snorted Adelia, a bit tipsily. Her snort was somehow refined, but extremely derisive. "My next-door neighbor. Has a part-time position advising the town zoning board. He'd steal cookies from a Girl Scout."

"We met him last night at Tiki Joe's," Bootsie told Adelia. "Scooter! What a dumb nickname!" Joe rolled his eyes at this, since Bootsie never seems to realize that the name Bootsie, is, well, somewhat debatable in itself.

"Well, Scooter e-mailed back that he'd look into it, but that as far as he knew, Vicino's up to code, but he'd definitely set up something," Holly told us, still reading. "But here's something weird. This e-mail's from last week, and Scooter wrote that when

Barclay got into town, they'd sit down and take care of business. Listen to this, he even listed an agenda for their meeting: Point 1. Hotties. Point 2: Condos."

"Hotties?" Sophie repeated, jumping up and grabbing the page from Holly. "What the heck does that mean?"

Gerda looked uncomfortable and stage-whispered to Sophie, "I think I know. But I don't want to say in front of this lady." She made a not-so-subtle gesture in the direction of Mrs. Earle.

"Don't hold back on my account," Adelia told her. "If there's dirt for diggin', hand me a shovel!"

"The hotties are, well, paid ladies," said Gerda, looking embarrassed. "They come over yesterday while I was at tennis match. I see two of them leaving when I come back. They don't spend the afternoon with Barclay for free, trust me on this one."

"Hookers!" Sophie shrieked, throwing down the page she'd grabbed from Holly. "Again with the hookers! I gotta call my lawyer." She snatched up her phone and was heading out toward the pool when Joe stopped her.

"Sophie, the e-mail also mentions condos," he said, reading over the page she'd tossed aside. "Is Barclay buying a condo down here? You might want to mention that to your lawyer."

"You bet," she said. "If Barclay's getting a condo down here, I'll own half of it by the time my attorney's done with him."

WITH GERDA, YOU never knew what was going to happen next, and once again, she surprised us all by striking up an unlikely bond with the tipsy Mrs. Earle. While Sophie made the call to her lawyers, Gerda and Mrs. Earle wandered over to admire Adelia's display of vintage framed magazine stills and Stokes cigarette ads. Gerda seemed intrigued, though I'd have thought that learning that tobacco money was the source of all the splendor of Adelia's home would have set Gerda's health-nut radar off. Instead, Gerda looked impressed.

"This style, I like," Gerda told Mrs. Earle approvingly, looking at her debutante photos. "Classic. Not like the flashy clothes people wear today."

She nodded in the direction of Sophie, who was storming back into the living room in a yellow silk Versace sundress and teetery gold sandals. "This is what I mean. Too flashy."

"Henry said he'd check around and call me back in a few minutes," Sophie told us, ignoring Gerda. "He thinks there's no way Barclay would buy a condo right now, though, since it would technically be community property until we sign off on the divorce."

"That's Divorce Law 101," Holly said, looking up from the sofa, where she was still scanning the stack of printed e-mails. "When Howard and I got our almost-divorce, you wouldn't believe the stink my lawyers made over me buying a house. I'm sure Barclay knows that though.

"Wait a minute!" Holly added. "Right here, at the end of the e-mail trail, there's another mention of condos," she said, holding the last page aloft. "Barclay's going to *build* condos, not buy one. Scooter wrote to Barclay that he has a meeting planned for them today with a guy named J. D. Alvarez, and that the three of them are just about ready to break ground on the condos."

Holly looked up, eyes wide with surprise. We all remembered J. D. Alvarez from the tiki place, since, as mentioned, he'd looked and smelled extremely good.

"We met Mr. Alvarez at Tiki Joe's last night, too," Joe informed Adelia and Gerda. "He sent us champagne. Well, he mostly sent it to Holly, but there was a lot of it."

"This guy was hot!" Sophie told Gerda and Adelia. "If I wasn't dating Joe, Mr. Alvarez would be at the top of my to-do list."

"I wish I knew this town better. I'm not sure what Scooter's talking about," mused Holly. "He says here that once they get a few details done with, they can get the schoolhouse torn down and start construction."

"I know exactly what Scooter's talking about," said Mrs. Earle, her face flushed pink with anger. "That little rat is making a run at putting up condos on the site of the old Magnolia Beach Schoolhouse."

Adelia told us that Scooter's family had long owned real estate in South Florida, most of which had been sold and developed, making the Simmons clan a very wealthy one. One of the most sought-after pieces of land they'd held onto for years was down past Palm Avenue: approximately seven acres of oceanfront land around a tumbledown former schoolhouse. It was worth millions, being the only undeveloped site of its kind on the island.

Scooter, his stepmother, Susie, and Scooter's younger half-brother, Bingo were the main holders of Simmons Properties these days, but Susie and Bingo weren't as ambitious as Scooter. Bingo, in fact, was an avid environmentalist, and while he'd once been a bit of a party animal, these days he spent his time saving things like manatees and rare seagulls. While Scooter was an avid consumer of bacon and Scotch, Bingo stuck to a vegan diet and limited himself to one margarita per day.

"He does seem to smoke a lot, though," Adelia said vaguely. "Very fragrant, too, and he rolls his own cigarettes!" At this Ozzy gave a polite smile.

"Scooter's next door to my left, and Bingo lives just on the other side, to my right," Adelia explained. "Take a peek through the hedge in the backyard. Bingo's got a charming cottage, but he spends most of his time in the backyard. He lives in a—what do you call it, Ozzy?"

"A yurt," Ozzy told us.

"I'll send Ozzy over there to get Bingo. He doesn't believe in phones," Adelia told us. While Adelia dialed Susie Simmons, who lived on the next street, we all went out to peer through the tall hedge to the right of Adelia's pool. Joe pulled aside some of the dense shrubbery, revealing a pretty yard, slightly overgrown with citrus and avocado trees. The yurt was there, too: Along the lines of a teepee, it was a sizable structure in cylindrical form with some lovely lemon trees flanking it. Given the beautiful nighttime temperatures in Magnolia Beach, I could imagine it being a pleasant place to spend the night.

"I usually hate camping, but that looks pretty nice," Joe shrugged. "The grapefruit trees are pretty, too."

Adelia reported that she'd reached Susie Simmons's dog-sitter, who was minding Susie's dachshund while its owner was on a Turner Classic Movies cruise to St. Lucia. The dog lady said she would try to reach her employer on board the ship—which might take a day or two, she explained, because Susie rarely used her cell phone. In fact, the flip phone was sitting right here in Susie's kitchen.

Five minutes later, a man arrived at the door to Adelia's living room, giving a little knock on the door frame as he walked in behind Ozzy.

"Bingo!" said Adelia. "Your brother's up to no good again. Have a margarita and sit down, dear."

"You know I don't drink before five," said Bingo with a friendly smile. "But thanks."

As Bingo shook all our hands and we exchanged greetings, I noticed he resembled his half brother but was taller, leaner, and had a brown ponytail, which gave him an appealing 1970s vibe. He wore a white cotton shirt, faded jeans, and flip-flops, and he emitted a vaguely smoky aroma, which might have been the scent of patchouli . . . or possibly something stronger.

"So what's this all about, Adelia?" Bingo said, seating himself next to Bootsie on a chintz love seat.

Gerda handed over the pertinent document, which Bingo scanned quickly, shaking his head. Then Sophie sketched out a quick description of her ex Barclay, and his apparent budding partnership with Bingo's half-brother.

"Scooter promised me and Mom that he'd never try to develop that land!" Bingo said, running a hand over his tanned forehead and ponytail, looking upset. "He knows there's a jacaranda on the property that's over two hundred years old, plus Bahamian swallowtails nest there, and they're almost extinct." He scanned the e-mails again.

"Let me go talk to him," Bingo said. "Maybe Scooter's getting scammed by this guy Barclay."

"I doubt it," snorted Adelia. "Your mother always told me Scooter was a little sneak."

BINGO CAME BACK moments later, reporting that Scooter's housekeeper had told him that Scooter was down in Miami for the day (probably with Barclay, I thought), but was due back for the opening of Gianni Mare at 7:00 p.m.

We all agreed to meet Bingo at the big opening party, except Adelia, who said she never missed *The Voice* elimination round episodes. With that, Bingo left, while Joe and Sophie made a quick detour to the Versace boutique in Palm Beach, which Sophie had convinced to open early on a Sunday for her. The dress that Lady Gaga was wearing in her current issue of *Marie Claire* had finally gotten FedExed in.

Bootsie, Holly and I headed over to Vicino to see what Channing had called about. When Bootsie pulled up outside the restaurant ten minutes later, we could see that Gianni Mare was a hive of frantic pre-party activity. Workers were carrying in massive potted trees and armloads of flowers, and painters were applying a glossy white finish on the French doors out to the patio. Next to a small outdoor bar, musicians were assembling sound equipment, and cases of wine and champagne were wheeling past us as we parked.

This was all well and good. But after Gianni's evident happiness at the Slavica episode—not to mention his insulting Waffles—I'd privately resolved the night before that I wouldn't go to his opening party, even though he'd invited all of Magnolia Beach and much of the state of Florida.

Even Holly and Bootsie, who don't usually miss a party, had made some bold statements that we shouldn't support Gianni's new place. However, I could tell the three of us were having the same thoughts as we took in the party preparations: *Gianni being somewhat of an expert in throwing seriously awesome parties, his opening promised to be pretty fun.* I mean, there would be a live band, all those flowers, the champagne, and those shrimp being flown in from Italy. . . .

Just then, a bakery truck arrived and opened its doors, unleashing the sumptuous scent of just-baked baguettes and Italian loaves. A guy began toting brown paper bundles of the gorgeous bread right past us into Gianni's front doors, which had a similar effect to waving bacon under Waffles's nose.

Bootsie made "mmm" noises, and even Holly, who doesn't eat bread, took a delicate sniff and took on a hungry look. Right behind him, a girl carrying boxes labeled *Louis the Cheese Purveyor* was toting in oversized wheels of Parmesan and Asiago. More cases of wine rolled by after the cheese girl.

The three of us exchanged glances, and Bootsie said what had to be said.

"Screw it, we're going to Gianni's tonight!" she exploded. "Sorry, Holly, I know you and Sophie have money in Vicino, but there's no way I'm missing this party."

"That's okay," Holly said, shrugging her shoulders, which were encased in a little sleeveless Lacoste dress. "I'm going tonight, too. I'll tell Channing and Jessica that I'm there to make sure we're on top of Gianni's plots and schemes to take down Vicino. But obviously, I can't be in Magnolia Beach and *not* be at Gianni's opening. I'd have to leave town and never come back."

"I'll tell Channing that I have to be at the party to write a story for the *Gazette,*" Bootsie said. "Which is true! I'm getting the *Gazette* to pay for all the gas I used getting down here, and I'm not taking vacation days, so I need to turn in something about Gianni's bash.

"And I need some Asiago cheese, stat!" Bootsie added, whipping out her mobile. "Martha said she was going to the supermarket. Maybe she can grab some Asiago for tomorrow's omelets—do you think she'd mind if I sent her a quick text?"

I stayed silent, thinking if I was Martha I *would* mind getting texts about cheese. Also, I was still mad about what Gianni had said about Waffles—he'd called my dog a fattie. *I shouldn't go tonight.*

Just because Gianni Mare looked like it was going to open with an all-out, five-star, champagne-fueled bash—with special gamberetti being flown in from Italy, and heavenly smelling bread, not to mention a band and deejay—didn't mean I needed to ride Holly and Bootsie's coattails into the party. I mean, I could exhibit some backbone and stay home with Waffles and watch *Friends* reruns. Plus, I was honestly pretty tired and could use an early night. And there was that fluffy white terry robe in the guesthouse, which I hadn't spent nearly enough time in.

Bootsie gave me an appraising look. "Don't think you're going to skip this party," she told me. "First of all, I know for a fact you can't stop thinking about those giant shrimp Gianni's getting. And another thing—I didn't drive you and that mutt fourteen hundred miles so you can sit home in a bathrobe."

Phew, I thought. I really didn't want to miss this shindig.

"LISTEN, ANY RESTAURANT can mistakenly serve a piece of meat or fish that's got potentially dangerous bacteria in it. But I can't stress this enough—we double-, triple-check everything that comes in and out of this kitchen," Channing told us a few minutes later. He seemed to want to unburden himself about how upset he was about Slavica getting sick and also explain himself to Holly, his biggest investor.

I knew Holly trusted Channing. Still, he clearly felt terrible about the incident, and talking about it seemed to be helping him process what had happened.

"We only buy from the absolute pickiest, most selective and meticulous purveyors in Palm Beach County," Channing continued. "Most of the fish we serve comes from within twenty, thirty miles from where we're standing right now."

Bootsie, Holly, and I were perched on stools in Vicino's kitchen, which luckily had one small window that faced the alley and had no view of the buzz of activity at Gianni Mare. Channing was running his hands through his wavy brown hair as he explained to us why he was so puzzled about what had happened to Slavica the night before. While he talked, his sous-chef Rob, an old friend of Channing's from culinary school, was Lysoling the stainless steel counters, though they were already gleaming. Both chefs had been up most of the night, methodically inspecting every single item of food in the walk-in fridge and freezer. Bleary-eyed, they'd torn apart the kitchen to try to figure out how Slavica could have possibly gotten so ill.

"We buy from only two seafood vendors: Locally, we deal with the Martinez Brothers, who are incredibly good. They have exclusive deals with a few local fishing boats, and they're absolutely nuts about safe storage practices and transporting fish. As soon as it's off the boats and on ice, it's literally on its way here. And then there's Maine Coastal Catch, a company that overnights some of our shellfish, plus trout and bass caught up north. Their lobster and cold-water fish are seriously pristine," Channing told us, handing around mugs of coffee he'd just brewed.

"But we rarely sell fish that isn't caught locally—to be honest, I'd like to insist on going one hundred percent local and sustainable, but customers want lobster," the hot chef continued. "But all the clams we sell are all harvested in Florida. Plus, clam farming is a totally clean industry—no chemicals or antibiotics, since clams can't tolerate them. There's great shellfish down here—the littlenecks from the Keys are delicious, and then there's the Florida Spike, the Moccasinshell, the Chipola Slabshell. All fantastic!"

Channing, though clearly sleep-deprived and upset, looked briefly enthused about the local seafood harvest. He opened a stainless steel door and stepped briefly inside the walk-in refrigerator to pull a rectangular white plastic container slightly larger than a shoebox from a shelf in the back. He lifted the lid so we could see the shellfish it contained.

"I'm pretty sure these are how Slavica got sick," Channing said. "Any clam that's alive should be totally safe to eat.

"See these? Notice anything?"

The small pile of tiny clams nestled on a bed of seaweed looked benign enough.

The three of us all shook our heads, admitting we didn't see a problem—but then again, Holly doesn't eat, Bootsie can't cook, and I wouldn't know a mollusk unless it came in a can of Progresso Clam Chowder. Given Slavica's reaction last night, we all kept our distance, as if one of the small bivalves might leap out of the Tupperware and somehow attack us, horror-movie style.

"They're bad clams—dead clams. And they're not from Martinez Brothers—this isn't the Martinez packaging. Usually Rob and I log in all the deliveries, and we would never have accepted these, but when dinner prep is on, it's crazy-busy in here. One of the staff might have signed for the clams without checking with me first.

"We serve forty-two-dollar seafood risotto and fifty-dollar steaks—we can't afford to be anything less than perfect." Channing explained that he'd sent the staff home at eleven after the dinner service so that he and Jessica could inspect the kitchen, finally realizing that someone must have delivered the rogue clams when he was distracted. "We can never, ever serve another bad clam—if that's what it was—again. Especially because Slavica's the most connected woman in all of South Florida."

"She's been on the phone and Yelp all night," Jessica said sourly, coming in from the dining room, holding up an iPad with the foodie website open. "She described her experience here. In detail."

"There was one other giant clue that the clams were the culprit," added Rob. He held up a colorful little box. "This was left right behind the box of dead shellfish—a bottle of Pepto-Bismol. I guess whoever delivered the bad clams decided to make one hundred percent sure we got the message."

"Is it hot in here, or is it just that I'm looking at Channing?" Bootsie leaned over to whisper to me and Holly. She's always close to an overheated, full drool when she sees the hunky chef, but actually, the room temperature was noticeably on the rise. She grabbed the plastic top of a food bin and started fanning herself. "I mean, I know we're in the kitchen, but the stove isn't even on."

It was getting kind of sweltering. Jessica overheard our whispered conversation and, obviously, took note of Bootsie's somewhat dramatic self-fanning.

"I'll go turn up the A.C.," Jessica said, disappearing into the dining room.

"I say we completely start over today in the kitchen—clean slate," suggested Rob. "Let's toss everything in the fridge. Most of the suppliers aren't open today, but I can call in a few favors and also hit some of the upscale markets. Then tomorrow, Monday, we'll be able to completely restock."

"Let's do it," Channing agreed. He gave us a rueful version of his usual charming grin. "I'm thinking between Slavica on Yelp and Gianni's opening, we're not going to be all that busy tonight. We won't need to buy all that much."

"The air-conditioning's broken!" Jessica said, bursting through the doors from the dining room, a note of panic in her voice. "I turned it on and off three times, but it's not starting up." She temporarily buried her face in her hands in a very un-Jessica-like display of emotion.

We all understood the reason Jessica was overwrought. Bad fish was bad news, but no air-conditioning was the kiss of death in South Florida.

CHANNING AND ROB checked the thermostats, then went outside to look at the cooling unit near the trash bins. They came back three minutes later, their faces grim.

"Someone vandalized the unit," Rob told us. "Smashed in the coils and cut the line."

"I know you didn't want bad PR for the restaurant, but I really think you need to report all of this—including the fact that you guys almost got run over in the alley," I told Channing and Holly. "And the bad fish delivery—if that's what it was—sounds like something that the police should know about, too."

WHILE THEY WAITED for the police to come and Holly reassured Channing that she and Sophie could both use the tax write-off of a losing restaurant, I discreetly ogled Channing. I couldn't help noticing that even when he was depressed, the guy looked absolutely gorgeous, like the male models in Gucci ads who are pouting so much that you wonder, If you're in a Gucci ad, how bad can your life really be? I refocused, putting away thoughts of cologne ads and trying not to stare at Channing's muscular arms and chiseled cheekbones.

Actually, now that I looked a little closer at the gorgeous chef, I realized that stress had taken the tiniest, most infinitesimal toll on the movie-star-ish Channing. He looked slightly thinner and perhaps a shade paler than a couple of days before. Inwardly, I gasped, aghast at this crime against nature's eye candy. I determined not to say anything, but the thought seized me: Channing couldn't lose his looks! Sure, Vicino's food was absolutely delicious (at least to my unrefined palate), but the stunning pair of Jessica and Channing were at least half of the restaurant's attraction.

Something was different about Jessica, too, I realized. Her long blond hair was as glossy as ever, and she'd always been bone-thin, so that hadn't changed. Her outfit was casual, but obviously as expensive and chic as ever. I'd have to think this over and sneakily assess Jessica when she reemerged from the office. There was just something a little bit off. Normally, I don't notice, or look for, flaws in my friends. With these two, though, perfection had always been the baseline. The fact was that the pair that Bootsie and I sometimes (after a few cocktails) referred to as "Janning" or "Chessica" were so gorgeous that the slightest variation in their appearance was noticeable.

Sophie wasn't quite as subtle in her assessment, though, when she arrived.

"Channing, ya look like crap!" Sophie said thirty minutes later, having completed her Versace run.

The police had left after looking around, making some notes, and advising the handsome chef to have a talk with all employees about new policies for deliveries and safety procedures. They'd also send a detective out to do some additional investigation, they told us. Channing was out front, informing the bartenders and waitstaff there'd be a mandatory staff meeting at 11:00 a.m. Sophie had taken one look at the chef and began to loudly voice exactly what I'd noticed earlier.

"First of all, you look like you've been skipping workouts, and maybe not eating enough protein," Sophie told the stressed-out Channing.

She plopped down on a bar stool and examined Channing with the critical eye of a housewife eyeing a bone-in rib roast at the meat counter.

"You gotta get a little sun," Sophie told him. "This is Florida, hon. Or go for a spray tan. You don't want to be as pale as this one"—here, she indicated me—"which obviously doesn't look good, and start eating more! Make yourself some grilled chicken and sautéed kale, pronto!" The years with Gerda lecturing her about eating healthy must have rubbed off on Sophie. She sounded ready to join the *Today Show* as a fitness correspondent/nutrition expert.

She reached up and fondled one of Channing's still bulging, but slightly less impressive, biceps. "Don't forget, these ladies who come in here want to see a cute, hot, tanned chef! These, and, well, your tush and your abs, and your whole package—show what your momma gave you, Chan! Shake your moneymaker!"

Channing and Bootsie both cracked up at this, and even though I'd just been insulted, I burst into laughter, too. Even Holly, who's not one for hilarity most of the time, especially when she's mid-Howard-meltdown, smiled a little.

"It's a restaurant, Sophie," Bootsie told her. "Not *Magic Mike*."

"When you look like this one," Sophie indicated Channing here with a tiny hand adorned with three giant cocktail rings, "everything is *Magic Mike*. Ya think I'm investing here cause he cooks so great? Sorry, Chan, I mean you do cook great, but I put my money in this place because with your skill and your looks, you're the whole package." She giggled. "There's that word again—I can't stop mentioning your package!"

"We should uh, leave and let Channing get back to work," I told Sophie, embarrassed.

"That's okay," Channing said, still laughing. "I know what you mean, Sophie."

"Good, cause I'm staying for the staff meeting," Sophie informed him. Just then, Jessica appeared, a tiny frown creasing her pretty face.

"I'm calling security firms, but we can't get cameras installed until the end of the week at the earliest," she told us. "I called seven places, including four companies in Miami. Apparently, crime is so nuts in Miami that there's like, round-the-clock installations going on down there."

"Let me make a few calls, too," Holly said, plucking her iPhone out of her Lanvin bag. "My parents come to Magnolia Beach a lot. Maybe they know someone."

Meanwhile Sophie was staring at Jessica, seemingly unconcerned about the security measures being discussed by Channing's girlfriend/business partner.

"Am I the only one who's got working eyeballs around here?" Sophie demanded. "What the heck is happening with Jessica wearing flats. Ya look horrible in flats! Jessica, where are your Louboutins?"

That was what I'd noticed earlier, I realized, when I'd thought Jessica looked different. Vicino's manager was wearing a little pair of ballet flats rather than her ever-present teetering four-inch heels. She and Channing were truly off their game.

JUST THEN, A tall, broad-shouldered guy in a blazer and khakis showed up, explaining that he was a detective from the Magnolia Beach Police Department. Sophie took one look at him, shrieked, and ran over to give him a huge hug and kiss.

"Zack Safina!" shrieked Sophie. "What are you doing in Florida?"

"Sophie!" said the guy, hugging her back.

"This guy and I—we dated for most of high school," Sophie told us, giving Zack a wink that seemed to convey some hot-and-heavy memories from their youthful romance. "He was the biggest football star and played lead guitar in a band! I mean, he was the coolest guy and the prom king!"

Zack Safina modestly waved away Sophie's compliments, though he looked pleased. "You were the beautiful cheerleader, Sophie," he pointed out. "And you were always such a sweetheart. Still are!"

"So, are you married?" Sophie asked. "How's your brother doing, the one who dated my cousin Angela?"

While Zack told Sophie that no, he wasn't married but had almost gotten engaged a couple of years ago until the girl had moved to Fort Myers and left him for an attorney, I noticed Joe listening miserably, looking like he'd like to go drown himself in the ocean.

Since I've often felt the same anytime I catch sight of Lilly Merriwether, the gorgeous ex-wife of my veterinarian boyfriend, I felt awful for Joe. Zach Safina was pretty good-looking, resembling a hot TV detective. Plus, the guy seemed nice.

After detailing her long and contentious split from her ex, Sophie suddenly remembered that she had a boyfriend, and that he was standing right next to her.

"This is my Honey Bunny, Joe," she said to the detective, who shook Joe's hand with his own brawny grip.

"Great to meet you!" Detective Safina told Joe. "You're one lucky guy!"

"Thanks," Joe said. "Well, I better get going. Work to do."

"Yeah?" said Zack Safina. "What line of work are you in?"

"I renovate houses," Joe replied. This was true, even if Joe isn't usually jackhammering up old tile or anything like that. I had to agree that this was a better way to present his line of work to Sophie's hot-detective ex-boyfriend.

"He also knows a ton about paint colors!" Sophie told Zack proudly, but Holly, also sensing that Sophie might be about to go on a long description of how Joe could get really picky about fabrics, interrupted her.

"You know, Detective Safina," Holly said, giving him her full almond-shaped, blue-eyed gaze, and coming over to put a thin, tanned hand on his forearm, "I'd love to show you where I almost got run over the other day. First, this red car came whipping around the corner . . ." With that, she steered him toward the kitchen and the back door, the detective looking predictably pleased at having a willowy blond girl hanging on his arm.

Safina followed Holly out to the alley, while Joe turned and made for the front door, looking pissy and muttering that he was heading to Adelia's.

At Sophie's insistence, we stayed for the staff meeting. Calmly and professionally, Channing explained that while Vicino was fine, and business was good, there were new procedures to be followed. A list of approved vendors was posted by the back door. Only the vendors on the list were to be allowed inside with deliveries. And either Channing himself, Rob, or Jessica would be on-site all day to accept, check, and log in every lettuce leaf, grain of rice, sprig of rosemary, and most definitely any fish or meat that came through the doors.

The staff was exchanging worried glances. They knew that with a few more bad clam incidents, Vicino would be circling the drain.

Meanwhile, Jessica was answering the phones, and reservations were being canceled at the rate of two or three every ten minutes. "Slavica's still working overtime on this," she whispered to us as we left. "I just went on Yelp, and she even detailed the gory details of her twenty-two grisly minutes inside our restroom. She described every clam as it came back up, down to the color and texture as it flew from her mouth into the toilet!"

Holly raised her hand to her mouth as if to stave off an episode of nausea herself, and I felt my own stomach do a flip-flop.

"It was mostly yellow and green," Bootsie told us helpfully. "I could see most of what she was puking up, and obviously the texture was really slimy."

"I'm calling Yelp now," Jessica said, "to get Slavica's review pulled down. I don't like to lie, but this could kill Vicino, so I'm going to tell them a disgruntled employee wrote it." She punched at her phone, then looked up as we headed out the front door.

"Gianni has to be behind all of this," Jessica whispered desperately. "He never lets go of a grudge."

"Ya know, the air-conditioning and the bad clams could also be Barclay," Sophie said ten minutes later at Adelia's house, where Sophie had insisted we go check on Joe, who, she'd noticed, "seemed a little mad."

She looked over at Joe. "What do you think, Honey Bunny? You think Barclay would try to put Vicino out of business?"

"Don't talk to me," Joe told Sophie.

This was not the Joe Delafield who conducted business over crab salads with ladies in St. John Knit suits and took his clients on fun field trips to Sotheby's auctions. Gone were the crisp white Thomas Pink shirt and tropical-weight J. Crew blazer, complete with yellow silk pocket square I'd seen him charming Adelia in for the past couple of days.

Joe had changed into torn khakis and a white Hanes T-shirt, and was lying on his back in Adelia's pool house, chisel in hand. Up on a ladder near Joe was Frank, a painter who wore jeans and a Budweiser T-shirt and was taking down loose crown molding around the ceiling.

"I'm not in a good mood," Joe announced. "Frank here needs help ripping out the rotten woodwork, and his assistant Gus is on a fishing trip in Islamorada, which he *claims* he couldn't postpone. Even though I offered Gus ninety bucks an hour."

"It's Gus's fifteenth wedding anniversary," Frank told us from his prone position as he easily pried free a flimsy section of floorboard. "He's had the reservations on the boat for five months, and he prepaid for the hotel. His wife threatened to divorce him if he canceled."

"Like that's a good excuse!" Joe hooted, wiping sweat from his brow with a dirty rag. "And just because it's Sunday, all the other guys Frank usually works with can't help out today. So here I am."

Evidently, meeting Zack Safina had galvanized Joe into doing some physical labor, which was surprising, but not a total shock.

I've seen Joe at work many times, and he's not afraid to get his hands dirty. Well, he's a little afraid. But I've seen him grab a paintbrush many times, and even adjust things like the temperature on hot water heaters and finish up the wiring in flat-screen TVs.

So while Joe's accumulated some contracting skills over the years, prying up floorboards and rotten wainscoting didn't seem to be one of them. Frank had a technique that involved using a crowbar as a lever that seemed quite effective on the molding, while Joe was working on some flimsy wainscoting along the little structure's interior walls with little success.

"You need to get the chisel underneath the wainscoting more

securely," Bootsie told Joe. Bootsie's actually pretty handy, thanks to growing up with two brothers, plus she's just interested in that kind of thing.

"Put some muscle into it, Honey Bunny!" Sophie said encouragingly.

"Fuck off, sweetie!" Joe told Sophie.

Holly rolled her eyes and walked back toward the house, eyes glued to her phone, while Sophie muttered things like "Yeesh," and "Ya don't have to get that mad," and followed Holly.

Bootsie watched Joe for a full minute, then rolled up her Lilly Pulitzer pants and elbowed Joe out of the way while grabbing his tools. "Let me do this," she told him. "Go work on the fabrics. Please, I can't bear to watch."

"Great!" said Joe, looking relieved and jumping up.

"Nice," said Frank, giving Bootsie an admiring glance as a section of wainscoting peeled away as easily as wrapping paper from a gift on Christmas morning. I was honestly kind of impressed myself.

Joe headed for a green-umbrella-covered table and pulled some paint chips out of his tote bag, clearly thrilled to be done with manual labor. "Do you think Decorator's White will work for the interior and the window seats? Glossy or matte?" he asked me. "And should we try to get Ozzy to make us some lunch?"

Chapter 11

"WE DON'T HAVE time for lunch," said Bootsie, who'd finished her wainscoting task in about three seconds. "I'm feeling my inner detective kicking in, big-time."

"Ya know, it could be that Barclay hired somebody to drive that killer Chevy and screw up the air-conditioning at the restaurant," Sophie said, plunking herself down next to Joe.

"But I don't know—messing up the A.C., running people over in an alley—it kinda seems like stuff Gianni would do, don't ya think?" Sophie added. "It's all focused on Vicino. Barclay usually thinks bigger than that when he's trying to ruin someone's life."

"You're right," said Bootsie, a light coming on in her eyes—which concerned me, since this gleam often signifies a risky plan being hatched. "Gianni likes to do small-scale mean stuff. Not that running someone over is small scale, but you know what I mean. Sophie, I think you're onto something with this Gianni idea." She drummed her fingers on the table, then jumped up and, to my dismay, seized hold of my shoulder with a tennis-honed iron grip.

"We'll call Holly and head to The Breakers. I have a plan!

Gianni's overly confident," Bootsie said, her face taking on the faraway, slightly insane focused look she gets when she's about to go Full Snoop. "Which is a good thing. He'll make a mistake soon." She dialed Holly. "You're at The Breakers? And you said you're best friends with the concierge there, right? Perfect!"

Dread rose within me as Bootsie two-wheeled out of Seagrape Lane and headed for the luxury hotel. It was only 12:45 on this gorgeous, sunny day, but I felt like I'd been awake for about three hundred hours. I sighed, thinking I'd give anything to join Waffles at the guesthouse, where Martha had texted me he was peacefully napping, and to jump in that fabulous pool. However, I had to concede that in a weird way, Bootsie turning the focus to Gianni made some sense. He had the biggest motive against Vicino, whether or not he was getting a piece of the condo deal Barclay and Scooter were working on.

"Are you going to follow Gianni today?" I asked her. "He's probably over at his restaurant, not at The Breakers. Maybe we should head over to Gianni Mare instead."

"My plan is way better than following him!" Bootsie told me as we barreled down an absolutely beautiful lengthy drive flanked by ornate plantings and tall palms toward the massive 1920s structure, the ocean glistening behind the hotel.

"STEFAN, I HAVE a tiny favor to ask you," Holly said to the concierge at The Breakers seven minutes later. We'd dropped Bootsie's keys with a parking attendant, and I followed her into a massive and gorgeous lobby with a triple-height ceiling, columns, tall French windows, and oversize chandeliers, where Holly was waiting for us.

"Have you met Stefan?" Holly asked us. "He's the single best connected person in all of Palm Beach. Stefan basically *is* Palm Beach."

Stefan appeared pleased at Holly's assessment, and lived up to his reputation as concierge par excellence. While listening attentively to Holly, he simultaneously gave a significant glance to a bellboy who wasn't running out quickly enough to help a flustered-looking family with three toddlers bring in their bags and strollers. At the same time, Stefan merely looked at a tiny bit of paper that had somehow fallen onto the lobby floor near the check-in desk, and two maintenance workers dashed over to remove the offending scrap. Then a man dressed in chef's garb appeared with an invoice, which Stefan initialed while genially shaking hands with an older couple who'd just valeted their car and were heading poolside for a late lunch.

I was impressed. Stefan's navy blazer and striped tie were absolutely flawless. It seemed destined that Stefan would end up running this hotel, and doubtless owning a piece of it, too. The guy had success written all over him. However, he probably hadn't been bargaining for dealing with someone like Bootsie when he'd woken up on this breezy, flawless Florida day.

"Anything," Stefan told her, smiling down at Holly, who'd led the four of us over to a table in the elegant Tapestry Bar just off the lobby.

"We need a maid's uniform, size six, and a key to Chef Gianni Brunello's suite," Holly told him.

Stefan didn't look happy to hear this request. "Anything but that," he said.

Bootsie and Holly had sketched out a two-pronged plan in a quick, whispered conversation in the lobby. While the scheme was fluid and not all that coherent, the gist seemed to be that Bootsie would break into Gianni's suite disguised as a housekeeper and ransack it.

"I'll be in and out in five minutes," Bootsie informed Stefan as she downed a quick Bloody Mary. "I'm an investigative reporter— I'm really quick, and I never get caught."

I knew this last to be untrue, but I kept silent. Bootsie does get caught snooping fairly often.

"Come on, Stefan," said Holly with the full force of her almond-shaped blue eyes and dazzling white smile. I also noticed her discreetly handing him a nice stack of bills under the table. "Just one little key card. You know you hate Gianni and Olivia."

Stefan's face betrayed that this was in fact true. He was wavering.

"You told me yourself they aren't nice to the staff here," Holly reminded him. "And they barely tip. We're doing you a favor! Gianni might have tried to kill me, and you don't want guests like that lurking around your hotel."

Stefan caved, but he looked really nervous. "Please, I need this to be very quick," he told Bootsie as Holly discreetly handed him another bill. "And what if Gianni comes back from the restaurant and finds you in his suite? He knows you from Pennsylvania, right?"

"He won't notice it's me," Bootsie said confidently. "Gianni isn't the type of guy to focus on a maid. I'll be like wallpaper."

I wasn't so sure. I mean, Gianni's been in Bootsie's company quite a few times, both at home and down here in Florida, so there was every chance he might recognize her. I didn't voice this, of course, since Stefan was already heading toward the employees' area deep in the recesses of the hotel to procure the maid outfit.

On the plus side, I thought, Bootsie's very attractive, but her preppy, sporty brand of cuteness isn't Gianni's type, and he never really pays attention to Bootsie (or me). He tends to date skinny actress types in seven-hundred-and-fifty-dollar strappy sandals, like Jessica and Olivia, and drool over girls like Holly, who pay him to throw elaborate parties.

"Don't Olivia and Gianni share the suite?" I asked Holly, thinking that I'd probably rather Bootsie face down Gianni than have Olivia discover us mid-ransack. Olivia seemed fairly miserable, and I pegged her as a girl whose temper might be a little scary.

"Stefan said Olivia has her own room," Holly said. "Gianni stays up really late and watches TV all night, so Olivia came down the first night to the front desk and made a big scene about needing the adjoining room next to Gianni's suite. Plus, she said she needs the closet space."

Stefan returned and reluctantly handed Bootsie a bag marked "The Boutique at The Breakers." "Everything you need is here," he said. His cool, calm mien had morphed into the look of a man who knows he's taken the wrong track but realizes the train's already left the station.

"Please return the uniform and key ASAP," he whispered.

"Oh, of course!" Bootsie said airily to his departing blue-blazered back. "Within minutes! Now, Kristin, you come with me to the suite."

"Bye," said Holly, gathering up her phone and sunglasses and hopping down from her bar stool.

"What!" I said desperately. "How did I get involved in this? And you're not coming with us?" I aimed this last at Holly, who'd picked up her bag and was heading out of the bar.

"I've got to get my hair blown out for tonight. Plus, Gianni knows me!" Holly said. "If you two get caught, he probably won't know who you are. He only pays attention to really rich people or, well, girls who don't go around in Old Navy!"

Four minutes later, after Bootsie discreetly knocked on the door to Gianni's suite and received no answer, she inserted the key, and the door clicked open. Against every instinct, I went inside with her. Bootsie was in full maid regalia, while I was in a seventeen-dollar tank dress. Bootsie had told me that if we got caught, she'd say she was training me and I hadn't been issued a uniform yet.

Once again, I'd been left holding the bag as Bootsie's unwilling accomplice. I could have bolted from The Breakers and walked home, but I was honestly scared to leave Bootsie to her own devices. This felt like one of the dumber things I've done at Bootsie's insistence, and there have been quite a few already in the two decades since we met as seventh-graders. I sighed, then got distracted by the view once inside the suite.

"This suite is pretty awesome!" I said, forgetting to whisper. There was a huge living room with an overstuffed sofa and cushy armchairs in soothing shades that evoked the hues of sand and ocean. The walls were papered in a pretty trellis pattern, and the entire front wall of the suite opened via sliding doors onto a wide terrace with captivating ocean views. At left, the bedroom was anchored by a king-size bed with a stylish British Colonial headboard and the crispest of linens, and it had another huge balcony. There was a massive marble bathroom, roomy closets, and even an extra powder room in the living area.

I felt an irrational spark of jealousy about this fancy suite. I had my own guesthouse, so I wasn't sure why I felt envy at Gianni's cushy setup. Holly's Bahama Lane place was fantastic, obviously, and Martha was giving Waffles one of the best weeks of his doggie life.

If I was completely honest, the main attraction of the fancy suite, in addition to the fab bedding and ocean views, was that I wouldn't have Bootsie and Sophie barging in a couple of times a day.

"The maids haven't been in to clean yet!" Bootsie said triumphantly. She grabbed a small, half-filled plastic trash bag out of Gianni's bathroom and stuffed it into her L.L.Bean tote, then began rooting around on the little desk in the living room, loudly inventorying its contents.

"Matches, Tic Tacs, the card from a tattoo parlor in Miami, Italian candy"—here, she popped a few candies into her mouth—"this is all useless."

She opened the desk drawer and grabbed a handful of loose papers and receipts. "Jackpot!" she said, and stuffed them into her apron pocket. I felt really uncomfortable now, but there was no way to slow Bootsie down. She made a quick run to the bedroom closet, where she told me she'd never seen so many pairs of Crocs, and did Gianni really need three leather jackets in this heat?

I opened the front door of the suite and peeked out into the hallway—empty. Still, what if Gianni came back to take a nap or change clothes before his dinner service started?

"Let's go!" I hissed over my shoulder to Bootsie. "You've stolen the trash and receipts, so we're good now."

"I need to take a quick peek around Olivia's room," Bootsie said, popping up next to me, carrying her tote. She'd also pilfered the box of Italian candy and the Tic Tacs, I noticed. She hung a left and opened the connecting door into Olivia's quarters without even knocking to see if Gianni's girlfriend was home.

Defeated, I closed the door into the hallway and followed her, hanging back and whispering things like "Hurry!" and "Gianni will have us arrested!" while Bootsie flung open the doors to Olivia's hotel-room closet. I also noticed that Olivia's room, while certainly beautiful and roomy, was about a third the size of Gianni's own roomy digs.

"This is almost in the Holly category of closet awesomeness!" Bootsie said with some admiration.

From my scared perch by the connecting door, I couldn't see the closet, so I ran over for a quick peek. It was a pretty fantastic closet: It was full, but not overly crowded, and organized by color. It also had a serious shoe rack that Olivia must have brought with her. Or maybe The Breakers supplied things like shoe racks.

"Okay, I'm ready," said Bootsie, who was rooting through Olivia's makeup stash in the bathroom. "I don't think Olivia's got anything relevant in here—I mean, Gianni treats her like dirt and has her running errands all the time. If he's messing with Vicino, Olivia probably doesn't even know about it."

Relief flooded me as we closed the door behind us and began a quick trot down the long corridor toward the elevator. Halfway there, a door opened and a guy in a bathrobe poked his head out.

"Miss?" he said.

Bootsie completely ignored him. "Um, you from Housekeeping there?" he said more loudly.

"Yeah?" Bootsie said over her shoulder in a rude and very un-Breakers-staff-like way.

"Could I please get more towels? And a bucket of ice and some fresh water glasses?" he asked politely, rustling around in the pocket of his robe to pull out some cash.

"Sure!" Bootsie said. "I'll take care of that right away." She pocketed the ten bucks he handed over. Pretty generous, I thought.

"Thanks!" said the guy, going back into his room and shutting the door.

At the elevator, the down button pinged softly, and we got into the empty car.

"Let me guess—you're not going to get him the towels and the ice," I said to Bootsie.

I was actually beyond embarrassed at this point. I also would have given anything to be home in Bryn Mawr. Any place on earth that Bootsie wasn't would be okay, come to think of it.

"Absolutely not," she said. "This money's going to buy us two cappuccinos to take back to Holly's. Then we can go through Gianni's trash and receipts."

BOOTSIE DE-UNIFORMED IN the ladies' room off the lobby. When she reemerged, I noticed she had neatly folded the uniform and put it in her giant tote.

So, she was stealing the housekeeping outfit.

"You told Stefan you were giving that uniform back!" I reminded her.

"I'm borrowing it just for another day or two," she informed me. "Part two of my plan comes later."

I gave up and followed her to the little coffee bar at the hotel, where we ordered our cappuccinos. As we were leaving, I saw Gianni swing in through the lobby doors, doing a few greetings and air kisses along the way. Thankfully, we then took off for Holly's.

Since Martha is a by-the-rules kind of person, and definitely isn't someone who goes through other people's garbage, we decided to go through Gianni's stuff in the guesthouse. Waffles got up from watching *The Chew*, looking interested.

There were receipts from Tiki Joe's and from The Breakers gift shop, and car service bills from the airport, all of which seemed pretty straightforward.

"The car service receipt shows that Gianni did get here on Friday," Bootsie said dejectedly. "So he probably didn't try to run Holly over, unless he snuck down to Florida earlier in the week." She rummaged through a few more slips of paper, came up with a few girls' numbers (which Olivia probably wouldn't be too happy about), then held up a full-page printout.

"Finally!" Bootsie shouted. "An invoice from Maine Coastal Catch." We studied the paperwork, which showed a shipment of ten dozen Ipswich clams and four dozen live lobsters to Gianni Mare and was dated yesterday. "The day of the killer clams!" Bootsie said.

"But these were delivered to Gianni's restaurant, and Channing says this is a really reputable supplier," I reminded her. It didn't seem like much to me, but Bootsie said she'd head over to the seafood supplier tomorrow, and I halfheartedly agreed it was worth checking out further. In the meantime, I needed to convene with my blow-dryer and a bunch of hair potions. There was no way I could show up at Gianni's opening with Florida frizz.

Chapter 12

A LINE OF valet parkers, Town Cars, and the HGTV bus still idling outside the restaurant greeted us at Gianni Mare's, which had a seriously festive air on its opening night. Beautifully dressed older couples were arriving, the HGTV cameraman was filming, and the ponytailed photographer from the *Miami Herald* was snapping away. A few glamorous-looking models who'd been hired for the event greeted guests at the door under the hammered silver "Gianni Mare" sign.

On the patio, Sienna Blunt, looking extra sexy in a low-cut white top and skirt and holding a wrench, was being filmed by another camera operator as she pretended to tighten the hinges of the French doors that led from the dining room. All of the Colketts' hard work had resulted in a chic, lushly landscaped front patio space, lit by silver lanterns and banked with massive jasmine and hibiscus trees set in blue and white Chinese-export planters.

The outdoor patio, where a jazz trio was sawing away on instruments and a vocalist was cooing "The Girl from Ipanema," had blue inlaid mosaic tables and beautiful blue toile banquettes.

It was somehow both classic and modern, and totally gorgeous. I saw Joe's eye twitch, a sure sign he was entering a jealous funk.

"We get it," he said dismissively. "Blue and white. Classic Florida with a twist. I mean, for me, this is Decorating 101."

I wasn't sure if it had been Sienna Blunt or the Colketts who'd taken the theme and run with it, but when we stepped inside the restaurant, I felt my jaw drop slightly: Decorating 101, this was not.

Lit by votive candles and already abuzz with a happy crowd, the restaurant space somehow combined sophistication and coziness: The floors had been painted a snazzy blue and white chevron pattern, giving a modern flair, and were bordered with inlaid blue-and-white porcelain tiles. On every available surface, colorful ginger jars of various heights were bursting with about eight thousand bright-blue hydrangea blossoms (which must have cost a fortune to fly in), and a buffet held huge platters of oysters, olives, and Italian cheeses. The walls had been painted a gleaming deep cerulean that glowed under the massive silver chandelier, and an antique mahogany bar ran along the right wall of the restaurant, around which guests were gathered three-deep. The banquettes that lined the interior of the restaurant were the same shade of stunning blue as the walls, and as expected, every dish in the place was classic white and blue.

"They've got a full restaurant service of Ralph Lauren's Mandarin Blue china!" Joe marveled. "I've used it for clients, but only in their homes. It's way too expensive for a restaurant. Every time a plate breaks, Gianni's going to be out twenty bucks." This seemed to cheer Joe up. "Drinks?" he asked.

"Hey!" said Tim Colkett, zooming over to greet us. His tan was even deeper than it had been the day before, and he looked tired, excited, and nervous. "How do you like the design? Because, and this isn't to throw Sienna Blunt under the bus, we did one hundred percent of the job."

"It's fantastic," Holly told him, ignoring Joe's pissy expression. "Seriously, Tim, this is like waking up in I Dream of Jeannie's bottle, if she'd been into Chinese-export china, that is. It's so beautiful."

"I gotta admit," Sophie told him, "ya outdid yourself!" She gave Tom a hug. "And trust me, as much as I like you guys, I wasn't rooting for you. I'm on Channing's side in this restaurant war."

"Listen, doll, I'm sure there's room for two great bistros in this town," Tom told her. "I mean, look how many customers are here, and the party officially started thirty seconds ago." Magnolia Beach residents were indeed streaming through the door in droves, grabbing glasses of wine from waiters and loading their plates at the buffet.

"Where's Tim?" asked Bootsie in her typical blunt fashion, scanning the room and pulling out her reporter's notebook. "And where's the chef?"

"Tim's changing. He got behind schedule today helping Olivia pick up the gamberetti and the wild boar fresh off the plane from Italy," Tom told us nervously. "There was a tiny issue with bringing in meat that was basically unregulated wildlife, but Tim drove down to Miami, and they got it straightened out." He leaned over and whispered, "The paperwork wasn't a hundred percent finalized back in Rome. But Gianni sent down five hundred in cash, and once that got handed out to the right people, there was no problem. Some airport guys even helped them load it into the truck."

"Ms. Jones," a deep voice addressed us, and we all turned to recognize J.D. Alvarez, the dark-haired forty-something guy who'd sent Holly champagne the night before at Tiki Joe's.

"May I get you another drink?" he asked, directing the question to Holly but including us with a polite nod that encompassed our whole group.

"Sure! I'll have a margarita," said Sophie. "But this one's married, just so's you know." She pointed at Holly, who kept her cool but looked like she'd like to give Sophie the same skin-it-and-roast-it treatment that the wild boar was currently undergoing in Gianni's kitchen. J. D.'s eyebrows shot up at Sophie's announcement, but he didn't seem unduly upset by Holly's marital status.

"Where ya from, J. D.?" queried Sophie.

"I spend most of my time in Miami," J. D. said. "Then part of the year I'm in New York, and I have some business in South America and in London."

I could see Holly's eyes light up with interest. J. D.'s life did sound pretty glamorous. Howard's garbage empire expanding to Indianapolis couldn't really compete with the places J. D. had just mentioned.

"Hey, man, I know you!" said Tom Colkett. "You're a friend of Gianni's, right? I've seen you around the restaurant a few times this weekend."

"I made a small investment in this restaurant," J. D. said politely. "Of course, Chef Gianni's the one who's really putting in all the hard work."

J.D. flagged down a waiter, who refilled all our glasses. Then he excused himself, saying, "I apologize, I need to make a quick phone call outside. I hope we can talk more afterward." Obviously he meant Holly, but I had to admire his good manners.

As he walked out the front door, I noticed that not a single wrinkle marred the back of his perfectly tailored gray sport coat. I don't know how some people can maintain that level of perfection.

I mean, Holly does, but she has Martha, and special dry cleaners who charge forty dollars to steam a single silk blouse.

"Well, I'll go see what's up with the food. The boar's roasting on a spit and Chef Gianni is grilling the heck out of the gamberetti. I think Gianni will be out here mingling any second, though."

Tom Colkett wandered away and Bingo Simmons walked in, still in his jeans and sandals outfit, and gave us a wave. As he approached us, Scooter entered the restaurant, too. His eyes lit up when he saw Holly and Sophie in the crowd, but when he caught sight of Bingo, his expression turned to anger and he headed right for the ponytailed environmentalist. The two were soon arguing in a corner—after Scooter hit the bar and grabbed them each a drink.

At that moment, I heard Crocs scrambling on expensive fabric as the jazz band's instruments suddenly crashed to a halt. All eyes turned to the bald, muscular figure that had climbed atop a blue banquette.

"Welcome to the greatest restaurant Florida has ever seen!" shouted Chef Gianni.

I COULDN'T BELIEVE it. The room actually broke out in applause, and discreet cheers arose from the crowd. Chef Gianni—undeniably a talented cook with a knack for generating publicity—had convinced the residents of this beautiful town that he was the chef of the moment. Apparently, though Magnolia Beach had appeared to be a very festive place before Gianni had gotten here, the town couldn't survive one more minute without his handmade pasta and spectacular frutti di mare.

Olivia, looking annoyed but very stylish in a strapless column dress and towering heels, handed Gianni the jazz singer's wireless microphone as Tim Colkett appeared in the dining room after her. Gianni, for his part, looked primed to make a speech in his parachute pants, his chef's white jacket sleeves turned back to show his muscles and tattoos, and his gold earrings glinting.

"I want everyone to come back every night this week, Gianni wants to meet every one of you and become your friend," said the chef. "We like to thank the HGTV and the sexy Sienna Blunt!" Sienna waved from her spot next to Gianni, while cameras filmed the speech and her reaction to it.

"And I want to thank the real money my investors put into this place, because HGTV, you kinda cheapos!" Gianni shouted. "Just kidding!"

He didn't look like he was kidding, I thought to myself, as some of the production staff standing near Sienna pursed their lips, looking pissed off at this assessment of them as cheapskates. I noticed the Colketts looking upset, too, since Gianni didn't thank them.

Meanwhile, Scooter and Bingo were getting into it in the corner, their angry exchange competing with Gianni's speech.

"That's the one piece of land we agreed you'd never jack up with condos!" Bingo said, his voice rising above the buzz of the crowd.

"You've had too much to drink," Scooter told him as heads swiveled curiously.

"Dude, I have not," Bingo said. But he sounded a bit wobbly, and he was gripping the back of a chair. "I've just had this. My one daily mojito."

"Hey, shut up over there," Gianni told them from his perch on the banquette. "That guy Scooter has money invested in this place, otherwise I throw them out!" he added to the crowd. "Hey, Scooter, you pissing me off. Go outside!"

Scooter complied, taking Bingo's arm and dragging him out to the patio, while Gianni made a rude hand gesture in their direction, then returned to his monologue.

"Anyway, we got a special treat today, the gamberetti flown over from Italian Riviera this morning, and the fresh-killed wild boar from Toscana. The boar, big delicacy in Italy, it's called a *cinghiale.* We roast the crap out of this motherfucker today, after my girlfriend Olivia give a few bribes at Miami Airport."

Olivia looked irked as her illegal activities were broadcast to the crowd, but no one seemed to mind, and the crowd murmured admiringly.

Gianni, thankfully, wound up the speech. "*Mangiamo*!" he screamed with a little jump from the banquette down to the chevron floor. "Bring in the *cinghiale*!"

Two waiters, uniformed in khakis, navy polos, and white aprons, burst into the dining room from the kitchen, bearing aloft a huge white platter with a hefty roasted boar atop a bed of fresh rosemary.

More cheers broke out as the aroma of garlic, mingled with a gamey, pork-y, and undeniably deliciously meaty fragrance, wafted our way. The crowd moved in a wave toward the buffet, where Gianni began carving up the unlucky beast and serving it on tiny cocktail plates.

"That smells awesome!" said Bootsie, making a move toward the *cinghiale*.

"It sure does," shrieked Sophie, the former vegan.

"What is it with Chef Gianni and pigs?" said Holly, glancing around for another waiter with trays of champagne. "*Is* boar part of the pig family?"

"Who knows?" Joe said. His eyes took on a faraway look that

I recalled from our days in high school in history class. Joe had been quite a good student, and he possessed a thirst for knowledge that had led him to spend much of his time in the library in those pre-Google days. "I might just research that," he said, pulling out his phone and typing in the word "boar."

Just then J. D. Alvarez came back and began talking to Holly, while I looked hopefully toward the kitchen, wondering when the gamberetti would appear. The boar did smell amazing, but I wasn't sure about eating a creature that had been gamboling through the woods of Tuscany and then, in the next second, was dead on the back of a truck and headed for the Rome airport, fated to become cocktail fare in Florida.

Just then, though, I saw movement on the patio—not polite, party mingling, but what looked like a scuffle.

"I think Scooter's fighting with Bingo!" I told Joe and Sophie, catching a glimpse of Bootsie elbowing her way toward the front of the wild-boar line as I wound through the crowd toward the patio doors.

The three of us arrived just as Bingo went down hard on the patio's brick floor. I couldn't see if he'd been punched by Scooter or had merely fallen, but Bingo lay there, face up and moaning. A couple of chairs were overturned around him, and his mojito glass was shattered all around him.

"Poor Bingo!" shrieked Sophie. "Do you need a doctor?"

"He's fine," Scooter told us dismissively. "He just needs to sleep it off. Too much to drink, and he smokes too much ganja. You, kid"—here, he snapped his fingers rudely at a busboy who'd come out to check on the situation—"help me get my brother out to my car."

Gianni peeked around the door, but he didn't seem too worried about a guest having fallen flat on the bricks.

"Scooter, your hippie brother have too good of time!" he said. "Get this drunkie out of here. I don't run tacky place!"

"I don't feel right about Scooter taking his brother home," I whispered to Joe and Sophie—and Bootsie, who'd appeared next to us, forking in a plateful of *cinghiale*. "Scooter's so sneaky. Maybe we should offer to drive Bingo."

"We'll follow them to make sure he's okay," Bootsie said, putting down her empty plate and making for the street on the heels of Scooter, who had an arm around his brother and was half-dragging, half-supporting him as they headed for Scooter's BMW.

As I stepped off the patio, I felt a strong hand close over my wrist, and the faint scent of Irish Spring soap wafted toward me. I looked down to see a tanned hand, white shirt cuff, and navy-blazer sleeve. I felt a shiver pass down my neck, then looked up into the dark-brown, black-lashed eyes of Mike Woodford.

What was Mike doing in Magnolia Beach?

SHOCK, SURPRISE, AND a pleasant tingly feeling shot down my spine, but since Bootsie was already behind the wheel of her Range Rover, I told Mike we had a quick errand to run, and that I'd be right back.

But Scooter didn't take the right turn that would lead back to his and Bingo's houses. Rather, he turned left and headed over the bridge toward the West Palm Beach business district. Three minutes later, he took the exit ramp for the airport. Bootsie, who Scooter didn't seem to have noticed on his tail, steered her car a dozen spaces away from him under the well-lit outdoor long-term parking and turned off her lights. It was 8:30 p.m., and Bingo was walking better now but still looked groggy. Scooter grabbed his briefcase out of his backseat, and he and Bingo took off for the airport entrance.

"I'll be right back!" Bootsie said. "You three stay here."

Five minutes later, Bootsie returned, looking dejected. "Scooter went to the American counter and bought two tickets, but I couldn't hear where he was heading," she reported. "Then they went down to security, and that was it. They're gone."

"Did Scooter just kidnap Bingo?" I wondered.

"Bingo went willingly enough," Bootsie said. "He seemed a little out of it, but he wasn't putting up a struggle."

"If we were back in Jersey, I'd say Scooter slipped him a mickey," Sophie said, assessing the situation. "Coupla Klonopins is what Barclay used to use."

We nodded, because Sophie honestly knows more about this kind of thing than Joe, Bootsie, and I do. In this case, given that Bingo wasn't drunk and hadn't seemed high when he'd arrived at Gianni Mare, she was probably right. Scooter could have drugged his brother and was currently getting him out of the way—hopefully not permanently.

We exchanged worried glances. "Er—should we call the police?" Joe asked.

"I'll call Zack Safina!" Sophie chirped. "He gave me his number today."

"Wonderful," said Joe.

"I need to go back to Gianni's," I told them.

"I saw that guy Mike Woodford there!" Sophie told me while dialing. "You two going to get some lovin' tonight? You got that whole guesthouse just sitting there with a king-size bed."

"No!" I told her, and launched into a speech about being one hundred percent committed to John Hall, when Sophie waved me into silence and started to talk into her phone to Zack Safina about Bingo and Scooter.

"Nothing Zack can do unless someone reports Bingo missing," Sophie told us when she ended the call. "We'll have to wait it out a little."

As I CLIMBED out of Bootsie's backseat when we got back to Gianni's, I noticed two texts had come into my phone.

John Hall was checking in to say hi, while Holly said she was going to Tiki Joe's with J. D. Alvarez. While I frowned at this news, a third text arrived: Mike Woodford messaged me that he was at the bar at Vicino.

As I walked to Vicino, across the street from the din and clamor at Gianni's opening, I noticed what an absolutely beautiful night it was. A little breeze ruffled the bougainvillea that climbed on Vicino's exterior walls, and tree frogs chirped from a park just down the street. The hubbub from Gianni gave the whole street a festive vibe, as did the Latin music the band was gamely pumping out.

Truth be told, this was a pretty romantic place to be, especially in mid-January.

But Vicino was a dismal sight with only two tables occupied. One banquette held a group of older ladies in sneakers who I guessed were out-of-towners sent to Vicino by a hotel concierge—this I knew because in four days, I hadn't seen a single resident of Magnolia Beach in sneakers, and when I'd put on running shoes to walk Waffles, Holly had been upset and ordered me to immediately remove them. The other table was occupied by a pair of teenagers on a date, who were drinking Sprite and sharing a wood-fired pizza.

This was not a money making night. To make matters worse, the windows were open, thanks to the broken air conditioner, allowing music and a happy, *Dolce Vita*-style buzz from across the street to waft in. Vicino's skeleton crew of staff—due to the lack of customers, Channing had sent home most of the waiters and cooks—looked depressed. I couldn't believe this was the same spot where, barely twenty-four hours ago, couples had been clustered near the bar, waiting for tables. Thanks to Slavica's anti-Vicino campaign, Magnolia Beach insiders were done with Vicino.

I gave Mike a quick update on how great Vicino had been doing—until last night—before Channing emerged from the kitchen and greeted Mike warmly with a back-slapping man-hug. They'd worked together a few years back at Sanderson, the farm and estate owned by Mike's aunt Honey.

It was a little warm inside, given the broken air-conditioning, but not terrible. But the vibe was still unnervingly grim. I caught a glimpse of Jessica sitting on a stool in the kitchen, looking inconsolable and scrolling through something on an iPad—hopefully Yelp had taken down the Slavica posts.

"Sorry about the air-conditioning," Channing said, flashing perfect white teeth in a brief version of his usual buoyant smile. "We're hoping to get someone out to fix it first thing tomorrow."

"Don't worry, man," Mike said to Channing, pulling out a couple of stools so we could sit at the bar. "It's a beautiful night. Perfect temperature. And my aunt Honey's cottage, where I'm staying, doesn't even have air-conditioning. We just open all the windows and let in the breeze.

"Hey, can we order a couple of pizzas and a bottle of Chianti?"

Mike added. "And the rigatoni with sausage and fennel, plus the bucatini with cherry tomatoes? And, uh"— he consulted the menu—"the whole sea bass?"

Mike was over-ordering to try to make up for the empty tables, which cheered me up a little. He was one of those independent guys who I couldn't quite picture, say, filing a joint tax return with a girl, but he did care about his friends.

"Honey's place is a cottage by the Sandbar Club, on the north end of the island. A little run-down, but a cool old house," Mike told me, adding that the house had its own grove of grapefruits and was a quick walk to the beach.

I gazed into Mike's dreamy brown eyes, not listening to a word he said. I couldn't help noticing that Mike still had his tan from last summer—I guess all that time outside with the cows, even in the winter, meant he'd never lost it. As usual, a dark scruff gave him a slightly dangerous air. That is, if a guy in Gucci loafers can be considered dangerous. Since Mike had on jeans, I guess the navy blazer and his loafers counterbalanced things and made his outfit party-appropriate.

I forced myself to focus on the seven months that John Hall had been an incredible, loyal, and great boyfriend. I mean, John was the kind of guy who'd help you paint your kitchen and take your dog out for a late-night bathroom break in a sleet storm. John was also really handsome with his own brand of preppy, wholesome sexiness. What was wrong with me, anyway?

"I figured I'd get out of the cold and hang out with Channing and Jessica a little, check out their new place," Mike continued. "Then earlier today, I stopped at The Breakers for lunch and bumped into Chef Gianni, who invited me tonight."

The bartender poured the Chianti and appeared minutes later

with the thin-crust fresh-mozzarella-and-basil pizzas, while Channing—who, unfortunately, had time on his hands, since both tables appeared to be winding up dinner—chatted with us.

"How was the drive down with Bootsie?" Mike asked, forking into a cannoli.

"Long. And horrible," I admitted. "It got worse when Waffles howled for all of South Carolina, Georgia, and Florida."

"You brought your dog—to Magnolia Beach?" Mike asked, surprised.

"Definitely. He's in the guesthouse right now, and he's having what Martha's calling a spa weekend. She made him poached chicken and vegetables for dinner, and he's sleeping on six-hundred-thread-count sheets."

"This I need to see," said Mike, throwing some money down on the bar. "Let's go."

Chapter 13

I'D PLANNED TO invite Mike inside to see Waffles, but when he pulled up his rented Toyota at Holly's, a black Mercedes was idling in the driveway.

On Holly's front porch steps, J. D. Alvarez was standing next to Holly as she unlocked the door. I watched as J. D. leaned over and gave Holly a kiss on each cheek. And he lingered way longer than was necessary.

This wasn't okay at all. I mean, there wasn't necessarily anything romantic about a double-cheek kiss—but then again, when you looked like J. D. and Holly, and when one Howard Jones, husband of the kiss-ee, was in Indianapolis and wasn't able to defend himself against allegations of cheating with one Dawnelle Stewart—that was a setup for way more than a friendly good-bye.

I realized I was in no position to feel superior, since I was about to invite Mike inside and potentially cheat on my significant other, too.

"You should go," I told Mike. "You can see Waffles another time. Thanks for the drinks!"

As J. D. WHOOSHED away in the Mercedes, and Mike in the Toyota, I started to tell Holly she should stay away from J. D., but her phone rang: Gerda.

"I called you like six times, Holly!" Gerda complained as Holly put her on speakerphone.

"Sorry, Gerda, I couldn't hear anything at that party," Holly told her.

"What I wanted to tell you is I eavesdropped on Barclay tonight," Gerda said over speakerphone. "He's been drinking since he got back from Miami, and he's pretty loud when he's had a few."

"So what did he say?" asked Holly.

"He spoke to Scooter Simmons on phone around six p.m., and he told him to move up the plan," Gerda told us. "Barclay told Scooter to get his brother out of town tonight, and then get the hell back here tomorrow, before condo plan gets totally ruined."

Chapter 14

I WOKE AT eight the next morning to find Bootsie staring down at me in the guesthouse bedroom, which completely creeped me out.

"Don't stare at me when I'm sleeping!" I told her, having flashbacks to high school sleepovers when I'd been awakened by her in this same staring technique. Waffles, who'd been snoring at the foot of the bed, woke up and gave a startled little bark.

"I already went to Maine Coastal Catch in West Palm Beach," she told me, opening the curtains as I blinked in the bright sunlight. "They open at six a.m. The manager said he personally dropped off the shipment at Gianni's on Saturday because he wanted to see what all the fuss was about, and he saw Gianni's staff put it all into their walk-in fridge. So I don't see how we can link that receipt to what happened to Slavica."

I sat up, threw off the crisp white sheets and duvet, and blinked as Bootsie opened the white linen curtains and sunlight flooded into the room. Bootsie had on the most un-Bootsie-like outfit I'd ever seen her in, consisting of a crisp navy sheath dress—J. Crew, if I wasn't mistaken—with a gorgeous silk Hermès scarf expertly knotted at her neck, and glossy black patent leather pumps. She'd borrowed one of Holly's Hermès handbags and, most surprisingly, had on full makeup, including a very polished coral lipstick. Her blond bob was perfectly blown dry and sprayed into submission.

"What are you wearing?" I asked her blearily. "Isn't that a little dressy for a tennis tournament?"

"I'm taking the day off from the tournament," Bootsie told me, while I got up, let Waffles outside to conduct his morning affairs, and went into the bathroom to brush my teeth. "I'm now one hundred percent focused on finding out who tried to run down Holly and Jessica. Which I'm positive is somehow tied to Scooter and Barclay."

"Oh, really?" I said as I brushed, thinking, *This isn't good news.* Bootsie gone for most of each day watching tennis in Delray would have been a break. Bootsie's like the human equivalent of Stoli—fun to do as a shot sometimes, but it's usually better when diluted, and not on a daily basis. "Er—won't you miss the top players if you miss the last few days of the tournament?" I added lamely.

"I already talked to my editor this morning," Bootsie yelled from the kitchen area, ignoring my tennis query, "and we're going to do a three-part series on my trip down here. It's called 'Drama in Paradise' and starts with Gianni's opening and the healthy competition between his place and Vicino."

"Are you sure that's a good idea?" I asked, grabbing a sundress from the closet and hoping Bootsie would give me three minutes alone to take a shower.

"Well, I'm not a hundred percent sure that 'Drama in Paradise' is actually going to work for the *Gazette,*" Bootsie admitted, surprising me. "It's more in the reporting stage right now, and if I can nail down enough facts, and if we can get Vicino back on track and actually prove that Gianni and Barclay are committing some actual crimes, then it's a go."

"Okay," I said doubtfully. Maybe along the way, she'd uncover a way to help Channing and Jessica, as well as assist Adelia's wish to save the schoolhouse. Plus, there was no way I could stop Bootsie, so I might as well get on board.

"We leave in fifteen minutes," Bootsie told me. "First stop is Scooter's house, next stop the town zoning office."

SCOOTER'S HOUSEKEEPER ANSWERED the door and informed Bootsie that no, Scooter wasn't home, and no, she didn't know where his brother Bingo was. After a somewhat heated exchange (the housekeeper wasn't the friendliest lady, and Bootsie wasn't the most tactful as she continued to grill her), she finally informed us that Scooter had gone away for the night but had told her he was due back in town later this morning and would go right to his office. Then she slammed the door in our faces.

Next, Bootsie parked in front of Magnolia Beach's Mediterranean-style Town Hall and started gathering up her handbag and a clipboard on which she'd placed some important-looking documents. I took a closer look and saw that she'd grabbed the multi-page lease Holly and Howard had signed for the Bahama Lane rental.

I wondered briefly if she'd asked Holly if she could borrow the documents, or if she'd simply rifled through Holly's belongings and pilfered them. The latter, probably.

"I'M BARBIE MCELVOY, and how are *you* this gorgeous day, Brian?" Bootsie asked a weary-looking guy behind the counter in the zoning office of Town Hall. He sat behind a name plate that read, "Brian Connelly, Zoning Assistant." "We've talked on the phone a bunch of times, and you're even handsomer in person than I could have imagined!"

I stifled a giggle at the bizarrely perky persona Bootsie had adopted in the forty seconds between the car and the administrative building. She wore a huge, friendly smile and had taken on what I think was a Bostonian accent, as if possessed by the spirit of one of the Kennedy clan.

Brian was about fifty-five and had a sweet but harried face, as if his daily dose of getting hammered with documents detailing mixed-use permits, non-conforming zones, and allowable routes of ingress and egress had left him with permanent acid reflux and the realization that whatever he did, someone was going to be mad at him. I hoped his job paid well. The guy had a jumbo bottle of Pepcid next to his phone, which was currently ringing. A jumbo 7-Eleven cup of black coffee (which couldn't be good for his reflux) and a donut sat next to his computer, which was insistently pinging with incoming e-mails.

"Hi, Barbie," Brian said politely. "Um, right, you've called before, sure. And that was about . . ." He trailed off, looking at a stack of manila folders next to him, as if one of them might tell him what Bootsie was after.

"I'm Scooter Simmons's new executive assistant!" Bootsie told him. "I'm sure he told you about me. I'm new to Palm Beach County, and let me tell you, I LOVE it here. Brian, we are living the dream, are you with me?!"

Brian gulped some coffee and mustered a smile. "Yeah, you're right, you can't beat the weather here," he said pleasantly. He seemed a truly patient man.

"What do you say next week I take you for mojitos at The

Breakers after work one night," Bootsie told him, giggling vivaciously and giving him a little wink. "On Scooter's tab!"

"Okay," said Brian, looking a little less downcast. "Sure. I love mojitos. But, uh, I'm married."

"Me, too!" Bootsie said, seating herself onto the clerk's counter suggestively. "But that doesn't mean we can't have a little fun! Now, why I'm here. Scooter sent me over to pick up copies of the Seabreeze Lane file. He needs a copy of what you guys have here."

I realized that this was going to be as bad—or worse—than Bootsie's lying spree at The Breakers yesterday.

"But Scooter filed the proposal, and it hasn't gone under review yet," Brian said, puzzled. "Doesn't he have the original?"

"He did," Bootsie said, "but Scooter's cleaning girl here"—she indicated me with a dismissive wave of her muscular arm—"knocked over a whole bottle of Glenlivet on Scooter's desk last night, and it was like a tidal wave sloshing over every single file he had up there. And he was, if you'll excuse the expression, freakin' furious!"

Brian was nodding sympathetically. "I've been on the wrong end of Scooter once or twice myself," he told us, giving me a pitying look. "He does kinda lose it sometimes. But I'll have to have written permission from him to let you make a copy." Brian lowered his voice to a whisper. "Scooter has a special arrangement with the zoning chairperson, who's one of his cousins. We're supposed to call Scooter directly if anyone asks for his files, and then say we don't have them if we can't reach Mr. Simmons. Even though, well, technically they're public record."

Brian looked embarrassed at being complicit in this obviously unethical file-hiding fiasco. "I guess he probably told you about all that, though."

"Oh, he did," Bootsie lied. "But he said in this case to just tell you it's okay to hand me the file."

"Er—maybe I should call him real quick," Brian said, wavering.

"He'll fire her if you bring it up again!" Bootsie told him, her Kennedy accent slipping a little as she pointed at me. "I mean, look at her—she's not the sharpest tool in the shed. And she's supporting a bunch of elderly relatives up in Okeechobee!"

While annoyed that Bootsie had cast me as a brainless goof, I nonetheless assumed the posture of a hopeless klutz—which wasn't hard for me to conjure up, since I'm not all that coordinated. I decided to mingle my slumped shoulders with the sorrowful expression of a girl who'd recently been excoriated by her rich, angry boss. I thought about adding a sob but decided that might be too much.

Brian caved. He slid his desk chair back to the filing cabinets and withdrew a folder. "Just don't let word get out that I let you do this."

"Not a peep!" said Bootsie, making the zip-your-lips-and-throw-away-the-key gesture with her right hand while she grabbed the manila file with her left.

"I'll just make a quick copy, and we'll be out of your hair," Bootsie said, which wasn't the greatest choice of words, given the fact that Brian didn't have all that much on top of his head.

"Okay, and don't forget those mojitos next week!" Brian said hopefully. He popped another Pepcid and finally returned to his dinging e-mails.

I SPENT THE afternoon with Joe at a designer furniture marketplace in Miami, while Bootsie decided she'd go through her purloined zoning papers . . . after a quick trip to watch just one tennis match in Delray. At 2:00 p.m., outside the Donghia fabric showroom, where Joe was debating a pink chintz, I got a text from Mike Woodford, which I ignored.

At 5:00 p.m., Joe and I arrived at Holly's.

"Okay, so it's you, me, Scooter, and J. D. Alvarez for dinner tonight," Holly told me, as Joe and I stared at her. Even Martha stuck her head out of the kitchen to listen in with an alarmed expression.

Chapter 15

"WHAT!" I SHRIEKED. "You shouldn't be going out with Alvarez—you're married! And why would I want to tag along?"

"This is strictly investigative," Holly said coolly, checking her manicure on hands that were still ring-free, I noticed. "J. D. and Scooter will tell us everything about the condos, and we'll find out where Bingo is, mark my words."

"Whaddaya mean—you're seeing Juan Diego tonight?" Sophie said to Holly, clucking disapprovingly. "Holly, ya gotta be careful with those gorgeous Miami types. I mean, that guy could probably snap his fingers and get, like, the entire Victoria's Secret modeling crew to do him backstage at that show they have!"

"Another wonderful image you've shared with us," said Joe.

"Not me, though, Honey Bunny!" said Sophie nervously to Joe, running toward the couch, jumping in next to him, and giving him a hug and kiss. "I mean, if I didn't have you, I *might* be attracted to Juan Diego, but I'm not at all! Because of how much I love you!" she added unconvincingly.

"Well, he's not taking you out to dinner tonight—he's after

Holly," Joe reminded Sophie. "Who I'm pretty sure isn't supposed to be going out on dates, since she's been married for almost three years." We all stared accusingly at Holly, who wore a sunny expression as she poured herself a tumbler of club soda and sipped at it without a care in the world.

The alarm that Sophie, Joe, Bootsie (and, apparently, Martha) were experiencing was centered around Holly and her all-too-close rapport with Juan Diego. That worried me, too.

But why was I being dragged along to occupy Scooter? I was dating John Hall, and even if I wasn't, Scooter and I didn't seem like a match. Me: dog-obsessed girl from small town outside Philadelphia, barely making a living at a rickety antiques store. Scooter: wealthy Magnolia Beach fixture who, if our suspicions were correct, didn't mind scooping up an extra hundred thousand bucks every once in a while by helping shady development plans gain zoning approval. And who had probably kidnapped his own half-brother.

This all did sound a little risky. And—*was* Holly shopping for a new husband? What better revenge could she wreak on Howard than running off with the ridiculously handsome and seemingly very rich J. D.?

"Please," said Holly with a nonchalant wave of her thin hand. "I'm not interested in Juan Diego, except in the matter of finding out more about Barclay and Gianni Mare, and investigating the vandalism of Vicino. This is all in the name of business.

"And, well, justice!" Holly added, a competitive gleam in her sky-blue, almond-shaped eyes. "I mean, someone named Scooter can't be allowed to win out over Adelia."

It's true that Holly can be very competitive, and on the rare occasion when she takes up a cause, she goes all out to see it through. Still, I eyed her warily. I mean, I don't think she'd *see it through* with Juan Diego, if you know what I mean, while married to Howard . . . unless she and Howard were actually on the brink of breaking up.

"Well, I guess it's true that we can't let Scooter and Fuckhead—that's one of my nicknames for Barclay—screw over Channing and Jessica. I mean, I got all that cash sunk in Vicino. And I do like Adelia," said Sophie. "She's a cool lady."

"Obviously, we need to get to the bottom of about four hundred issues concerning Barclay, Gianni, and Scooter," Holly said airily. "And since J. D. said Scooter's back in town and wants to have some fun tonight, that's where you come in," she told me as the doorbell rang.

"About that—I don't want to have fun with anyone, especially Scooter!" I protested, drumming my fingers nervously on the Lucite coffee table. "How exactly did I become Scooter's date?"

Holly opened the front door, where, between two enormous potted jasmine trees, a five-foot-ten-inch blond woman stood, wheeling in a small suitcase and toting a hairdryer and huge make-up case.

"Juan Diego asked me to bring a friend along," Holly said, shrugging. "Bootsie's married, and Sophie and Joe are in love, so that leaves you."

"I have a boyfriend," I reminded Holly.

"Well, he isn't here. And Scooter's date isn't going to be *you,* exactly," Holly said, inviting the blond hairstylist inside and politely relieving her of some of her hair-a-phernalia.

"That's her," Holly told the tall blond hair expert, indicating me with about as much enthusiasm as you'd use when pointing out a shredder at Staples.

"Svetlana here's going to transform you into someone with some actual sex appeal!"

TEN MINUTES LATER, I found myself on an upholstered French bench in Holly's dressing room/bathroom with the hairstylist, whose name was, obviously, Svetlana. She was Holly's favorite hair person at The Breakers Salon, and she was eyeing me critically, while Holly, Joe, and Sophie offered not-very-uplifting commentary.

"The idea, Svetlana," Holly told the hairstylist, "is that Kristin here becomes a bombshell with huge hair and major eyelashes for tonight. I'm thinking of changing her name, too."

"Great idea!" Sophie said enthusiastically. "Call Kristin something hot, like Bambi! I can come tonight, too, if ya need backup!"

"You can't come along—Gianni would tell Barclay if you were there," Holly told her. "Gianni doesn't know who Kristin is. I know he's seen her a bunch of times, but since she doesn't wear much makeup and can't afford to hire him to cater parties, I don't think he's ever noticed her."

This was one hundred percent true, so I didn't bother to correct her.

"Gianni knows you're married," Joe reminded Holly. "Won't he think it's weird if you're on a date with his investor?" Then he paused. "Never mind. That's dumb to think Gianni would care if a married person's out with another guy."

"Obviously, Gianni doesn't care about cheating," Holly said airily. "He's *pro*-cheating. Not that that's what I'm doing, of course. This is all just so I can interrogate Juan Diego and Scooter."

"Kristin can't be a Bambi," Joe said as Svetlana lifted a wavy strand of my long brown hair and shook her head, looking hopeless. "She's too blah to be Bambi."

I felt a surge of resentment but then realized Joe was right.

"We could borrow your name, Svetlana!" Holly told the hairstylist. "I mean, that's totally sexy."

But Svetlana was shaking her head emphatically in the negative.

"This one"—she indicated me with a long index finger, as if I was a ten-year-old Mitsubishi on a used car lot—"can't be Svetlana. But with these"—she pulled out a long tangle of dark-brown hair extensions, a container of enormous hot rollers, and packets of lengthy false eyelashes from her giant rolling bag—"we can make her someone more you, know, attractive."

I felt slightly insulted, but also intrigued as I eyed the mountain of hair and eyelashes, while Holly pulled out a glittery pair of strappy sandals and held them up to my feet. I've sometimes longed to be an exotic, leather-legging-wearing type. It just hasn't panned out for me, since I'm surrounded by antiques and a basset hound.

"I have the spray tan equipment and tanning tent in car, too," noted the beauty expert.

"Perfect, Svetty!" Holly told her. She gazed at me, my hair still in a ponytail, and eyed my shorts and Old Navy sandals. "It's going to take a miracle, though."

"Kristin should stay silent all night," Sophie said. "Men think it's hot when a woman doesn't talk."

"That's true!" confirmed Joe. "Not that I've ever met a woman who doesn't talk incessantly, but it sounds incredible."

"Let's get her slutted up and then pick the name," suggested Sophie. "I went to Vegas a million times with my ex. Something will come to me."

An hour later, Waffles took one look at me and gave a confused bark.

My skin was a dark, glossy, Kardashian tan. My hair had been extended and teased. I literally didn't think it was possible to get this much makeup onto my face, but there it was. In a tiny Dolce & Gabbana mini dress and strappy sandals, I looked nothing like myself. All you could see was hair, lashes, and dark lips.

"I'd go with Alessandra," Sophie said, proving herself surprisingly adroit at coming up with fake sultry names. "That way, Kristin can pretend she doesn't speak English, but nobody knows if she's Brazilian or what."

"I thought I was supposed to get info out of Scooter?" I said desperately through my overly glossed lips.

"Don't talk!" Holly ordered. "That's how you get *him* to start blabbing. I'll ask a few questions, and then open up the floor for him to tell us everything."

"Okay," I agreed dubiously. I could barely move my head to speak anyway, plus too many facial expressions might dislodge the false eyelashes.

"Here," said Svetlana, handing me a tiny bottle of eyelash adhesive remover as we headed toward the door. "You're going to need this tomorrow. If I were you, I'd leave on fake stuff for a while, though. You say you have boyfriend. He will love it."

"He's a veterinarian," I told her. "Very into the natural look, so he won't like all the extensions and lashes."

"Oh, yes, he will," Svetlana informed me.

"SCOOTER, THIS IS Alessandra," Holly said as I held out a spray-tanned hand to greet our dinner companions. I whispered hello, trying for a sexy but unspecific accent as Holly and I stood in the entrance of Gianni Mare. It was 7:30, and the restaurant was packed, a happy buzz filling the space and music flowing through speakers out onto the patio.

"Hellooo," said Scooter as I lowered my glued-on lashes demurely. I would have burst out laughing if my face hadn't been immobilized by makeup. For his part, I noticed J. D. looking at me curiously, as if he thought he recognized me but wasn't sure. Even though I'd met him before—and had talked to him in this very restaurant not twenty-four hours earlier—Holly had been positive J. D. wouldn't place me as the ponytail-wearing, casual girl of the night before.

I wasn't so sure. I looked different, but I also had a feeling that J. D. was a very smart guy who didn't miss much. Then again, he was now focused on Holly, who looked gorgeous in a simple beige dress and no jewelry.

No jewelry! I looked at her left hand and heard an inner alarm bell: She still hadn't picked up her wedding rings?

Holly was definitely taking her "I'm not really married" scenario too far, but there was nothing I could do about it now. The hostess was leading us to a table along the banquette, where Holly and J. D. slid in and sat next to each other.

"Why don't you sit next to me, Miss Alessandra?" Scooter said, politely pulling out a chair for me. We sat, me in my borrowed black dress, and Scooter in a pink checked sport coat, khakis, Ferragamo loafers, and a matching pink oxford.

"Are you a Floridian, Alessandra?" Scooter persisted, while I gave a vague shrug and sipped desperately at a glass of water, hoping my lipstick would stay put. "Wherever did you meet this exotic creature, Ms. Jones?" he asked Holly.

I choked a little on the water, and I noticed Holly couldn't hold back a small giggle. Never in my life have I been anywhere in the exotic spectrum.

"Alessandra goes to my workout class at The Breakers. She doesn't talk much," Holly told him with a merry expression. I nodded mysteriously and looked around the room, desperately hoping Gianni and Olivia were back in the kitchen, and not working the room. I was pretty sure Gianni would have no idea who I was, but Olivia had bitchy-female radar that could definitely see behind all the big hair and fake tan. She'd know exactly who I was and wonder what I was up to.

Juan Diego, meanwhile, had lost interest in Alessandra. He was totally focused on Holly. I got the feeling that in Miami and the other glamorous places in which he spent time, girls like Alessandra were like telephone poles—there was one on every corner. It seemed I didn't need to worry about him placing me as the somewhat drab friend of Holly's he'd previously met.

What was worrying me, though, was Juan Diego's deliciously scented and elegant arm, clad in a stylish pale-gray tropical wool sport coat and crisp white dress shirt. He had immediately draped it over Holly's bare shoulder while he'd ordered wine and a round of oysters.

I had to admit, Holly and Juan Diego looked incredible together. It was like Wealthy Tasteful American Barbie and Gorgeous International Businessman Ken were sitting across from me on the blue banquette. I felt a rising sense of concern as the champagne was poured—waiters were hovering and rushing, given that our table held two of the restaurant's investors. Holly leaned in to listen to something J. D. murmured in her ear, and the sexual tension was such that I was tempted to grab a menu and fan myself with it. *Holly was going way too far with this fake flirting!*

Howard and Holly had always made a nice-looking couple, but Juan Diego was along the lines of Michael Fassbender, with the square jaw and soulful expression of Hugh Jackman thrown in. And now he was actually stroking Holly's shoulder!

"Cheers to your incredible success with this restaurant," said Holly to J. D. and Scooter as we all toasted each other. "I'd love to hear about your next business venture, too," she added, including both men in her wide-eyed interest.

"You own part of Bal Harbour—that's so glamorous!" Holly told J. D. smoothly. "I love Bal Harbour."

It was twenty-five minutes later, and another bottle of champagne was already being poured as Euro-music thumped throughout the dining room, where every table was now filled. J. D. drank at a measured, moderate pace, I noticed, while Scooter was knocking back champagne like it was Gatorade. He'd also ordered a three-olive martini, which he'd quickly drained. "I know J. D. has some banking interests and real estate, but what about you, Scootie?"

Scooter looked flattered to already have a nickname from Holly, and he smiled proudly as he munched an olive. "My family's been down here in Magnolia Beach for decades," he told us, his hand grazing Alessandra's (mine, that is) on the tabletop as he buttered a hunk of ciabatta bread. "We have a lot of property and, of course, invest in real estate all around South Florida. You name it, we own a piece of it!"

"You have a brother, don't you, Scootie?" Holly asked.

"Half-brother," muttered Scooter.

"And he lives here in Magnolia Beach? I'd love to meet him!"

"He's out of town. Went to Maine for a couple of weeks," said Scooter. A server brought him a fresh martini, which he downed by two inches with one large sip. He spoke curtly and changed the subject, asking how long Holly was planning to stay in town.

"I'm thinking of buying a place!" she told him. "Do you have any new properties coming up I should know about?" J. D. solicitously passed her the three-tiered platter of oysters resting on ice and a bed of seaweed. Holly took one, but I knew she'd never eat it. Solid food seldom passes her lips, and when it does, it isn't oysters.

"Actually, yes!" said Scooter, inhaling one of the chilled shellfish, which the waiter had explained were a variety called Apalachicola from the Gulf Coast. I gazed at the fancy seafood staring back at me from my plate, feeling uneasy as I gazed down at the squishy bivalves.

Given my peanut-butter budget, I'm thrilled to eat anything that isn't being served out of a can or a jar, but I honestly didn't think I could down one of these suckers. I mean, I know raw oysters are a delicacy, but all I could think about was Slavica's dead run to the Vicino bathroom after the clams.

"We've got an amazing historic property right here in town that we're developing," Scooter rattled on. "It's something I've been working on for years. It's a piece of land that's been in my family for almost a century, and we're going to build a magnificent custom home on it that will be in the $25 million range," Scooter told us. J. D. shot him a warning look, which Scooter ignored.

"J. D. and I have a partnership with, uh, another investor from out of town," he added tipsily. "And that tree-hugging brother of mine. But I can get anything past him!" he bragged. All of a sudden, though, he noticed J. D.'s frown and began dialing back on his information sharing.

"So we're exploring a lot of different options," Scooter finished vaguely, then stopped talking and started eating, while J. D.

changed the subject, asking Holly whether she'd ever been to the polo matches that were held in nearby Wellington, Florida, where he owned a few horses.

As Alessandra, I merely sipped my drink silently, while as myself, information was zinging around my brain. Scooter had seemingly been about to spill plans for a property that could only be the schoolhouse. I mean, the island we were sitting on wasn't all that large. How many historic family properties could he have?

My fingers inched toward my phone to text Joe. I was also starving. I took a small piece of delicious ciabbata bread, tore off a corner, and quickly buttered it, ignoring Holly's disapproval. Alessandra might not eat, but I needed to.

I realized chewing had possibly de-glossed a corner of my lower lip—and was one of the individually glued-on lashes becoming dislodged? Maybe I needed to go in and yank off said fake lash.

I'd gulp down some more champagne, then make a run to the ladies' room. I was just gulping down a large sip when I froze, swallowed wrong, and choked.

Chef Gianni!

"Holleee Jones!" said the tattooed Gianni, who'd bee-lined out of the kitchen straight for our table, while also managing to triple-kiss several other female diners en route. "You got more gorgeous overnight! How you do it?"

"Excuse me," I whispered to Scooter, getting up and moving toward the restrooms, which were down a little corridor just past the crowded bar. Gianni hadn't even noticed me, or if he had, all he'd seen was the back of a huge head of hair.

It was time to wind up this dinner, I thought.

Holly had basically gotten the information we'd been after—or at least, we now knew that he and J. D., plus a third partner who had to be Barclay, were up to *something*. We could figure out our next move vis-à-vis the Barclay/schoolhouse plan tomorrow.

As for tonight, I'd be back in the guesthouse soon, away from all this craziness, back in my Old Navy pajamas and watching E! News with Waffles by 10:00 p.m. Maybe Alessandra could develop a migraine or something and I could ask Bootsie to come pick me up? That might work, I thought—then suddenly froze.

Mike Woodford was standing at the bar, staring at me. Or rather, at Alessandra.

"NICE DRESS," SAID Mike, eyebrows raised.

"Thanks," I said bitterly. "It's Holly's," I told him. He was in jeans and a white shirt, a fresh vodka tonic in front of him. "A girl named Svetlana who works at The Breakers Salon provided the tan, the hair, and the eyelashes."

"And the reason for this new look?" asked Mike.

I peeked past Mike, around a giant arrangement of flowering tree branches on the bar, to see if Alessandra's absence was causing any disruption of our meal. Apparently not, because Gianni had actually sat down at our table, which both J. D. and Holly herself didn't look too thrilled about. Scooter looked well and truly drunk, supporting himself with both elbows on the table (which I doubted his stepmother would approve of) and appeared to be one vodka away from toppling into the truffled risotto that had just arrived in front of him.

I sighed, and decided to tell Mike the truth.

"We're trying to help Joe's friend and client, Adelia Earle, prevent that guy over there in the pink shirt from building on one of the last pieces of undeveloped land in Magnolia Beach," I explained. "His name's Scooter Simmons, and he and the handsome guy next to Holly are probably partners with Barclay Shields. They also might be trying to sabotage Vicino."

"How does that translate into you looking like a—" Mike paused here. "I mean, wearing that outfit and all that makeup?"

"I'm not entirely sure," I admitted. "Holly basically ordered me to show up here as a Brazilian, or possibly French, girl—someone Scooter wouldn't be able to resist spilling information to. But now poor Scooter's too drunk to talk. And Holly's date is too smart to let any secrets slip."

We looked around the giant tower of flowers again, and I could see Gianni was getting up to continue his tour de dining room. Holly caught my eye and gave me a "Get Back Here Now" glare.

"I need to go," I said to Mike.

"I thought you were pretty serious with John Hall, and isn't Holly still married to Howard?" Mike asked, waving a disapproving finger at me. I couldn't address all his points just now, so I grabbed Alessandra's borrowed Gucci clutch bag.

As I reluctantly turned to head back to the table, a tall, well-dressed man entered Gianni Mare. I realized immediately that it was Holly's husband, Howard.

He gave me one quick glance, but his eye went instantly across the restaurant to where Holly was seated on the banquette . . . very close to J. D.

Holly saw Howard and froze. And Howard merely turned around and left.

DINNER, THANKFULLY, ENDED three minutes after I sat down again. "I think I should take my friend home," J. D. told us, eyeing the slumped form of Scooter across the table.

Scooter's head was listing slightly toward my shoulder, and I tried to gently prop him upright with my left arm. I felt a little bad for Scooter, who was now in the nonverbal stage of overconsumption. He seemed like an experienced drinker, but he probably shouldn't have mixed vodka with champagne. To be honest, while Scooter might be a sneak and a liar, he wasn't the worst date I've ever had. Unless he'd killed his brother Bingo—then he was the worst, hands down.

J. D., who had impeccable manners, refrained from further comment about Scooter's blotto condition. He merely paid the bill, left a generous tip, held both my and Holly's chairs as we exited the table, and retrieved Holly's car from the valet for us.

He then politely scooped up Scooter from the table and inserted him into the passenger side of his own black sedan.

"Thawasdelightful . . . lessalldoagain," Scooter mumbled, giving us what might have been a wink as Holly pulled away from the curb in front of Gianni Mare.

SINCE DINNER ENDED early, we got back just as Bootsie was finishing up her perusal of Scooter's zoning filing, which she had spread out on Holly's living room coffee table along with a half-empty bottle of wine.

Holly refused to talk about Howard on the ride home. In fact, she didn't seem to be *able* to talk. Holly isn't much of a drinker, but she headed straight to the liquor and poured herself a vodka.

"Call Howard!" I urged her. "You can explain about the dinner."

Still frozen in her seat, Holly told me she was thinking over her course of action. "But Howard should have come over to the table and asked me what was going on," she said.

"What's to ask?" Bootsie told her. "You were on a *date* with a guy, and your husband walked in and caught you. What's Howard supposed to do, join you?"

"I never thought Howard would show up unexpectedly," Holly

admitted, taking another gulp of her drink. "He's usually more of the type that sends you his itinerary a week in advance." She checked her phone. "He's at The Breakers," Holly said. "I have him on my iPhone tracker."

"You should have used that tracking app earlier," Bootsie pointed out. "Then you would have noticed he wasn't in Indianapolis and was heading right for you at Gianni's."

"So helpful of you to tell me that," Holly told her. "I was a little busy trying to solve the potential murders of myself and Jessica, plus poor Bingo Simmons."

"Well, you better get over to The Breakers, pronto," Bootsie told her. I noticed she seemed a little tipsy. Maybe this wasn't her first bottle of wine tonight.

"I'm not going over there! If Howard doesn't trust me, he can deal with my lawyers!" Holly said.

I sighed and sat down to look at the Simmons condo papers.

"This isn't what Scooter described to Holly," I said as Bootsie handed me drawings and documents requesting that zoning rights be waived for a new condo development on Seabreeze Lane. While some of the legalese was tough to decipher, the gist of the proposed plan was clear.

Scooter et al were going to build a mid-rise, eight-story structure that would include two enormous condos per floor, plus a huge shared pool, tennis courts, and a separate clubhouse and gym. An architect's rendering showed two bulky, columned structures that took up every square inch of beach frontage.

Demolition of the schoolhouse was noted as having been approved in a private zoning hearing.

As soon as a permit was issued, probably by Friday, the teardown could begin. And no one could get in touch with either Bingo or Susie Simmons to try to stop the schoolhouse deal.

Chapter 16

We called Adelia to tell her about the secret condo plan early the next morning, and she promised to try to reach Susie Simmons again via her dog-sitter.

As for Bingo—no one had heard from him. Adelia said that Scooter had to be lying about his brother being in Maine, since no Magnolia Beacher would go that far north this time of year.

"Maine?" Adelia asked. "In January? That can't be right."

Sophie called to check in with Gerda, who said she'd work the Internet to track Bingo in Maine—if that's where he was.

Holly flatly refused to discuss the Howard situation, insisting that *he* needed to contact *her.* After twenty minutes of begging her and offering to call Howard myself, I dropped the subject for the moment.

After that, we decided to take Tuesday off from anything to do with Vicino, Gianni Mare, Gerda, and the Colketts. Even Bootsie agreed that a break from snooping was in order, and we agreed to spend the day doing actual Florida-style activities.

Since we all had different ideas about what constituted a relaxing day, everyone got to pick one activity.

"Lunch at Captain Harry's Sea Shanty," said Bootsie. "It's right on the water in Deerfield Beach. Everything's fried, and there's buttery corn on the cob and pitchers of beer. Newspaper instead of tablecloths and peanut shells on the floor."

"Let's go to the beach!" I said. "There *is* a beach in Magnolia Beach, right?"

"I pick Bal Harbour," said Holly. "And don't worry, I won't bring any credit cards." I'd heard of Bal Harbour, in north Miami Beach, about an hour south of us. Its reputation was a mecca of the most glittering and expensive shops the world has ever dreamed up. But since Bootsie was getting her beer, and I was pushing for the beach, it seemed fair to let Holly do her retail thing.

"Calypso St. Barth's!" Sophie shrieked. "It's a store with the mother lode of caftans! We're talking silk chiffon embroidered ones!"

"Sophie, are you wearing Lilly Pulitzer?" I asked, suddenly noticing that Sophie was wearing a full-length, brightly patterned cotton frock. Where were the Versace and the Cavalli?

"You bet," she told me. "Bootsie and I hit a couple of shops yesterday. I figured, I might as well get into the whole Palm Beach look since we're hanging out near there."

Joe looked alarmed, and I, too, wondered about Sophie's interest in a Lilly caftan. Sophie is one of the smallest girls around, topping out at four foot eleven. Her tiny frame was swimming in the flowered caftan.

"Adelia's look is great for *her*," Joe told Sophie, "but on you—you're too, uh, young and beautiful!"

"I'm getting at least four more caftans today," Sophie said. "You're gonna love it, Honey Bunny. But maybe that's not really a day off, since caftans are becoming kind of part-time job for me. What about . . . um . . . miniature golf?"

Bootsie perked up at this. "There's mini-golf right by Captain Harry's!"

"La Tente," said Joe. "I want look at some Colefax and Fowler they just got in."

"How is going to La Tente a day off?" Bootsie demanded.

"I don't like downtime," Joe admitted. "There's always something annoying about it. Look at the schedule you four cooked up. Sand, messy food, an hour drive to the same stores they have right here in Magnolia Beach, and then probably a bunch of crying kids at a mini-golf joint. But"—he paused—"let's do this!"

After some minor arguing about how to organize the day, plus gathering beach towels and sunscreen, we all piled into Bootsie's Range Rover at 9:45 a.m. and headed south. Waffles was set for a special day with Martha, who would walk him, sauté some chicken for his lunch, and watch his favorite show (*Ellen*) in the guesthouse with him later in the afternoon.

La Tente was first, where Sophie got Joe to agree that they could tent the ceiling of at least one of her rooms in Bryn Mawr. Sophie was still pushing for her living room, while Joe, who'd taken an unlikely frugal stance, was pushing for the front entry hall, which was relatively small and would cost about one-twentieth of the living room.

Next, Bootsie sped down 95 to Bal Harbour, where between the Gucci, Lanvin, and Tiffany & Co. stores, I hugged my arms close to my sides, terrified I'd somehow topple a two-thousand-dollar handbag or bump into a shelf of hand-painted dinner plates. But the shopping district was seriously gorgeous, all glossy marble and gleaming chandeliers. We breezed in and out in under forty-five minutes, since Holly decided it was "not worth it" to be at Bal Harbour without her credit cards.

By 2:00 p.m., we were at Captain Harry's. Sea grapes and dunes and indigo sea were just beyond the outdoor deck, where Jimmy Buffett blasted over the speakers and a balmy breeze wafted through the festive bar, decorated with faded beer signs and fishing nets. Two pitchers of frosty Heineken sat on the table, and Sophie and Bootsie had gamely tied on lobster bibs, while I was working my way through a plastic basket of spicy shrimp. Joe was midway through a drippy and awesome cheeseburger. (Holly had a salad and some white wine.)

"This is fun!" shrieked Sophie, cracking a claw.

"Can we have some more butter, please?" Bootsie asked the waiter.

"And some Perrier?" Holly added.

"We got seltzer," the waiter told her.

After lunch, we all used the free sanitizing wipes provided by Captain Harry, then did eighteen holes of putt-putt, with Holly's competitive streak emerging and prompting a somewhat heated battle between her and Bootsie. Holly won by one stroke.

Finally, at 4:00, we hit the beach in Delray. The ocean water was a little chilly, but I jumped in, if only to silence Joe, who was taunting me. Finally, wrapped in towels and covered with sand, we got back to Holly's at 5:30 p.m.

"That was a freakin' awesome day!" Sophie proclaimed.

"It was the best!" I agreed, hugging Waffles, who wore a blissful, pampered look and was slightly damp from an outdoor bath that Martha had administered using fragrant coconut shampoo.

"It was sixty-seven percent not horrible," said Holly, sounding surprised.

Sophie's phone rang. "Should I get it?" she asked. "It's Gerda. I know we said we weren't going to do any restaurant or divorce stuff today." She hesitated for a second. "I can't resist picking up! Hi, Gerda!" she said into the phone.

She listened for a few minutes, adding an occasional "Uh-huh" or "You're shitting me" to the conversation, then ended the call.

"My ex got nailed again," she told us, popping some gum into her mouth. "Attacked at his rental house while Gerda was out jogging."

IT TURNED OUT that around the same time we'd been hitting the miniature golf course, Gerda had returned from a five-mile run to Barclay's rented house and found the real estate mogul facedown in his backyard near the pool. A meatball sandwich that Barclay had been halfway through had been found next to his prone form, a few bites gone from the mass of meatballs and provolone cheese.

He'd been knocked out cold. A sizable and growing bump had been visible on the back of Barclay's head, and Gerda had called for an ambulance. It had arrived minutes later. With some effort, a couple of EMTs had transported the developer to Palm Beach Gardens Medical Center, with Gerda along for the ride. Barclay had regained consciousness in the ER and told the staff there that he had no idea what, or who, had knocked him flat. He hadn't been all that coherent, but he'd conveyed that he'd been about to head to his pool house to chow down on the meatballs before Gerda got back, when boom! He'd blacked out.

The police had been summoned to the hospital to interview Gerda and Barclay, and had then visited Barclay's house with Gerda in tow. There, on the white marble kitchen island, they'd found the receipt for the hoagie, delivered from a pizza place in West Palm, and gone to visit the shop. The delivery guy had told the police he'd dropped off the sandwich without incident at around 4:30 (as soon as Gerda had left for her run—apparently Barclay hadn't wanted her to know about his unhealthy snack). Since there didn't seem to be any reason why a twenty-three-year-old part-time college student/delivery man would have gone after Barclay, the meatball hoagie guy hadn't been a suspect.

Gerda, though not a woman who rattles easily, had decided she'd been slightly uneasy at Barclay's house after the police left, so she'd walked the block and a half to Adelia's.

"Gerda and Adelia want us to come over," Sophie told us.

By 6:30, hastily showered, we were all in Adelia's living room, where Gerda was sipping some spring water to calm her nerves.

"I call up to Palm Beach Gardens. They said Barclay staying overnight in hospital, but he's okay. He's got a hard head," Gerda informed us.

"They should've gone after a different body part," Sophie opined. "This is the second time he's gotten whacked in the head and lived to tell about it."

Unsurprisingly, Sophie wasn't too upset about her once-beloved's latest injury. When he'd gotten bashed in the head with a bookend the previous spring, she'd shrugged it off. Sophie explained that people were always getting mad at Barclay. Just in case someone successfully killed him before their divorce was final (Barclay had once had mafia ties, so it wasn't impossible), she'd made sure her lawyers had an airtight agreement that gave her a hefty payday if Barclay died.

"I had something else I was gonna call you about before this happened," Gerda said. "I got on Barclay's computer this morning while he was in the hot tub, and he had e-mail from that guy Scooter. Scooter told Barclay he's heading to the old schoolhouse tonight around 8:30 with a surveyor."

"Who surveys a property at night?" asked Joe, who was working his way quickly through a margarita. "It's dark by seven-thirty."

"Scooter knows the neighbors will kick up a storm if they see surveyors around the schoolhouse," Adelia told us, sounding surprisingly sober for a tiny woman who'd been sipping tequila since lunchtime. "There's quite a few rules in town about what can be torn down, as well as what can be built." She sipped for a minute. "Though Scooter certainly knows all the right people to get the most favorable zoning. Especially if he blindsides the neighbors and starts demolition quickly enough."

"We'll follow Scooter over there later," Bootsie announced, nodding her blond bob decisively. "In the meantime, I can't stop thinking about that meatball sub Barclay was eating when he got nailed. Gerda, do you know the name of the place the sub came from? And did it look good?"

"Yeah, it's called Broadway Pizza," Gerda said, shaking her head disapprovingly. "But you don't want that food. Meatballs sit in your gut. Shorten your life by like twenty years."

"I sure do want it!" said Bootsie, Googling the pizza place on her phone. "I can't eat any more seafood. I need meatballs. I'll order some pizzas, too."

The meatball sandwiches honestly did sound pretty good, even if Gerda was now muttering darkly about colonic clogs and genetically modified beef.

"I don't think we want to follow Scooter over to the schoolhouse," I said, since no one else seemed to have noticed the first part of Bootsie's plan. "That sounds like a bad idea."

"I'm up for it," Joe announced.

"This sounds fun!" Adelia said, excited. "We'll trail that little sneak over to the schoolhouse and nail his ass. And pizza would be fun!" Apparently, pizza wasn't something Adelia had ever ordered. She didn't seem like the pepperoni type.

"I'll take care of ordering the food," Ozzy said, who also looked pleased as Bootsie suggested he get three large pies and eight meatball hoagies. I guess a night off from cooking was a break for him, too.

A COUPLE OF margaritas later, sneaking over to the schoolhouse was sounding better to me.

Ozzy had gone to pick up the pizza and sandwiches. The delivery guy from Broadway Pizza, traumatized after being interviewed by the police, had told his bosses he was taking the night off.

At this, Bootsie, Joe, and I exchanged glances.

"We need to find this delivery guy tomorrow," Bootsie announced. "Find him, tip him, and grill him. A college kid moonlighting as a delivery guy needs cash, and that's how we can get info the police can't."

I noticed Bootsie wasn't drinking margaritas but instead was sucking down some club soda, having appointed herself the designated driver for tonight's detecting activities. She had a telltale investigative gleam in her sky-blue eyes, too. Maybe she'd tired of her tennis obsession and gotten back to the core of her being—which is information gathering.

"Let's do it," said Joe tipsily. He crunched noisily on his sandwich, then grabbed a slice of pizza. Joe is usually a really healthy eater, but when he's stressed out or drinking, he throws caution to the wind and really chows down.

"Trust me, hand this kid a few twenties, and he'll give us every bit of information we need to know," Bootsie said. She paused for a moment and stopped chewing, her decisive chin frozen in thought. "You don't think Barclay's old mafia connections have tracked him down here to Florida, do you?"

"I'm pretty sure Barclay's all good with the mafia," Sophie told him. "He paid up everything he owes years ago. I mean, I guess ya never know, but I think all of Barclay's uncles from Jersey don't want him involved anymore. Ya know what a pain he is! Even the mafia doesn't want him."

While we feasted on junk food on Adelia's handpainted Herend china, the mood at Adelia's became quite festive.

Adelia told us she'd given Slavica d'Aranville a call and informed the unlucky realtor that she was counting on her to be at the Reptile Luncheon at Vicino *no matter what.* Slavica would have to get over her bad experience and attend, given Adelia's standing as leading town doyenne.

"I knew Slavica before she was Slavica," Adelia told us. "She's an okay girl, but she needs to stop whining about the other night. I mean, who hasn't puked in a public restroom? I know I have!"

By 8:15, we were folding up the empty pizza boxes, getting ready to head out. Except for Holly—she'd taken out her makeup case and was expertly touching up her lip gloss, having ignored the food fest around her.

"I'm not coming along to the schoolhouse," she announced. "I have my own plan. First, I'm going to stop at Vicino and Gianna Mare. I feel like we're not doing enough to help Channing and Jessica, and I'm pretty sure Gianni's the one who's sabotaging them.

"And then," Holly added, "I'm going to meet Scooter for a drink." She began texting as we all began protesting her plan, then she held up a cautionary hand. "I know what I'm doing. Scooter will be all juiced up after his meeting with the engineers, and I'll be able to find out everything about the project if I get him alone. J. D.'s way too discreet—I need the four-one-one from Scootie."

Holly punched at her phone and looked up triumphantly a moment later. "I'm on with The Scoot. Nine-forty-five at Tiki Joe's."

"That's a horrible idea," Joe told her. "That guy's going to maul you like a bear in a campground. I mean, he even went after Kristin, so just imagine what he'll do when he sees you."

While I shot Joe a pissy look, I couldn't help wondering what would happen if Howard were to wander into Tiki Joe's and discover his wife with yet another man, but I didn't raise the issue. Holly seemed a bit defensive on the topic.

"I can handle Scooter no problem, but I'm taking Gerda with me," Holly told us. "Just in case. She can sit at the bar while Scooter and I take a booth."

Having Holly arrive with an Austrian Pilates instructor in tow couldn't be Scooter's idea of a fun date, I thought to myself happily.

"This is good idea," Gerda added, looking pleased. "This Scooter sounds like a real weasel. Maybe I get to toss him out onto Palm Avenue tonight."

TWENTY MINUTES LATER, we parked Bootsie's SUV on North Ocean Boulevard around the corner from Seabreeze Lane, pulling as far over into a bougainvillea thicket as possible. We'd decided to arrive shortly after Scooter and company's scheduled meeting and approach in secret. It was close to 8:45 p.m. now, and even in Florida's mild climate, it was quite dark at this time of night, with only a half-moon and a streetlight halfway down the block lighting our way. Bootsie, ever prepared, pulled a tiny flashlight the size of a Bic lighter out of her glove compartment.

The tequila was wearing off, and I felt fear clenching my stomach. It was hard to picture the polo-wearing Scooter as scary, but then again, he had a lot riding on this project. And he'd probably kidnapped his own brother.

"This is a terrible idea," Joe hissed as he climbed out of the front passenger seat.

"I know," I said miserably. "You wanted to do this, not me!"

"I was drunk then," Joe told me. "I'm sober now."

Beside me, Sophie and Adelia had scrambled out of the car, Adelia's sunglasses still firmly in place. It was uncanny to see them both standing there in full-length caftans, both under five feet tall and tiny-framed. How Adelia could see though the huge dark lenses at 8:45 at night, I wasn't sure.

"Why did we let Adelia come?" hissed Joe.

"She told you she'd cancel the dining hut job if you didn't," I reminded him.

"Now, this is what I call action," announced Adelia. "Sneaking around in the dark is just plain good times. Reminds me of all the men who tried to take me out to Daddy's stables back when I was a debutante. You wouldn't believe what Virginia men will try in a barn!"

She and Sophie took off behind Bootsie, who'd turned the corner and was scampering down Seabreeze Lane.

"This freakin' caftan is slowing me down big-time!" squeaked Sophie. "I shoulda worn my Versace jeans."

As Joe and I followed, a light came on in an upstairs room in a Mediterranean mansion a hundred yards down North Ocean. A window went up, and a head poked out to see what was causing a ruckus on the otherwise tranquil street.

Joe and I froze. A moment later, the light clicked off again, and no attack dog or spotlight appeared on us. Hopefully, the home-owner had gone back to watching TV or whatever he did at night and hadn't called 911.

Scooter's property was next door, and a tasteful black and white sign proclaimed the driveway as "Magnolia Beach Schoolhouse, Built 1901." The entranceway wound back toward the ocean, and in the moonlight, I could see that the tiny wood and stone structure was surrounded by at least a dozen acres of slightly overgrown palms, grasses, and dunes. The view of the beach, even in this dim light, was absolutely beautiful.

To be honest, if I was a developer, I'd love to get my hands on the property and put up some pricey condos, too—anyone would want to live on this gorgeous parcel of land. Then again, Adelia's point about the property functioning as a park with birds, frogs, turtles, and other wildlife enjoying an undisturbed beachfront lifestyle made a lot of sense. In fact, I could hear tree frogs having an absolute ball all around us.

We paused behind a dense grove of hickory trees, the chirping, grunting amphibians creating enough noise to drown out the twigs that crunched under our feet.

Armed with flashlights, three men were pacing off the property. One—in profile, given the beaky nose and golf shirt, it had to be Scooter—was typing notes on a tablet. They spoke in hushed voices. And they were heading our way.

"The driveway and parking will need to be set back at least sixty-five feet from Seabreeze Lane," said a voice, presumably the surveyor's. We all froze as they continued their approach toward the hickory thicket. Then the three men paused to talk. "You have nearly seven hundred feet of oceanfront here," said the surveyor, sounding impressed. "I'll get an exact measurement tonight, but if you can get around the preservationist groups and get zoning pushed through quickly enough, you're looking at a couple of very lucrative options. Land like this just doesn't become available anymore."

"Can there be two separate structures built on a lot this size?" asked the third member of their group in a familiar deep and very masculine voice.

Guy #3, briefly illuminated by Scooter's flashlight beam as he trained it upward on a grouping of gorgeous old live oak trees, was, of course, J. D. Alvarez. Too bad he was involved, but the schoolhouse project was just business to J. D. Developers, especially ones like Alvarez, who had no emotional ties to the island and tend to look at land and see dollar signs. Birds, turtles, palm trees, and dunes are obstacles just waiting to be bulldozed.

Scooter, though a native Magnolia Beacher, didn't seem too attached to the natural beauty of this oasis, either. He peered at some graceful live oaks dripping with Spanish moss and announced that was where he would situate a gatehouse on the newly developed tract.

"These oaks will have to come down fast," Scooter hooted. "Once they're gone, it's too late for tree-huggers like my brother to get their knickers in a twist. Preservationists will have a hard time protesting a pile of mulch!" He glanced at his watch. "Let's pace off the beachfront measurements real fast, and I'll look at zoning in the morning and give you a call, J. D. I got a little appointment set up in forty-five minutes."

"Who's your appointment with?" asked J. D., shooting Scooter an appraising look. At least, from what I could see in the dim light, it seemed as if J. D. wasn't thrilled about Scooter's plans for the evening. I wondered if he'd somehow found out that Scooter was meeting up with Holly—or maybe he thought Scooter was planning to try to go around him and cut him out of the deal on this land. Clearly, no one—not even his own business partners—thought Scooter was all that trustworthy.

"Oh, just a friend," Scooter said, sounding pleased with himself as he headed at a trot toward the beach.

Chapter 17

SCOOTER LEFT A few minutes later, zooming away in his BMW toward Tiki Joe's, while J. D. and the engineer finished up a whispered discussion about zoning, given the nesting turtles and protected sand dunes. With Joe lending a supportive arm to Adelia, we crept down Seabreeze Lane and climbed back into the Range Rover, where I implored Bootsie to take me back to Holly's. Instead, she headed for West Palm Beach, where, she'd decided, we were going to get hand-churned organic ice cream at a place she'd read about in the *Palm Beach Post*.

Sophie and Adelia thought this "sounded like fun!" while Joe and I looked at each other unhappily. I could tell he felt the same as I did: Going home and instantly falling asleep under crisp white cotton sheets "sounded like fun."

By 10:00 p.m., we were all digging into some mint chip with hot fudge (except for Adelia, who'd fallen asleep in the front passenger seat). We were parked outside Two Scoops with the Jimmy Buffett on low volume, when Sophie's phone rang. After a few "Uh-huh's" and "You're kidding's," Sophie hung up.

"We need to go to Jessica and Channing's house. Jessica's freaking out," Sophie said. "She got some kind of package delivered that she's screaming and crying about."

"Where do they live?" said Bootsie, intrigued. She two-pointed the remains of her ice cream out the driver side window into a trash can, then called up her navigation system, ready to keep the night rolling. While I personally felt bad that Jessica was sobbing at her cottage, I also felt like I'd love to go home.

Sophie told her the address of Jessica and Channing's rented cottage, which was the gatehouse of a larger property past Palm Avenue.

"I couldn't understand what Jessica was so upset about!" Sophie said. "I think she said this weird package was from Hermès. I mean, how could you get upset about anything from that awesome store? Anyway, she's got the police there already."

Joe's phone dinged as Bootsie pulled out of the Two Scoops parking lot.

"We need to stop at Tiki Joe's and pick up Holly and Gerda," he said. "Something happened to Holly's car keys. She said she'd tell us when we get there."

"Everything was going perfectly," Holly said. We found her sitting with Gerda at one of the little tables by the bar at Tiki Joe's. "Scooter was in a talkative mood, while Gerda was sitting over by the piano, looking relatively inconspicuous."

"This is a nice place," Gerda said. "I like the look—very classic."

"Anyway, Scooter and I had some champagne, and he told me he'd just been over to his property on Seabreeze Lane, which is the single most desirable piece of undeveloped land in all of South Florida," Holly said. "Then he ordered a double Scotch. After that, he started bragging about how he had so many connections around town that he could do anything he wanted with the piece of land. Then he put his sneaky little arm around me."

Holly gave herself a little shake, as if to rid herself of the memory of Scooter's unwarranted groping.

"Now you know how I felt the other night!" I pointed out to Holly.

"Scooter looked at Holly like she was lunch," Gerda offered.

"So at this point, Scooter was pretty tipsy, but he pulled himself together and told me again that he'd decided to go with a single house on Seabreeze Lane, since that was what his stepmother wanted. He said he loved her and respected her wishes, and that she didn't want anything more than one beautiful, tasteful house built there," Holly said. "So then I brought up Bingo, but he got a little annoyed and said he didn't want to talk about his brother.

"Luckily, he ordered more drinks, and he kept talking, saying that Gianni's restaurant was going to put Vicino under by the end of the week," Holly continued.

"He laughed about Slavica getting sick, and then he said he knew for a fact that Vicino's air-conditioning wasn't going to get fixed anytime soon—he didn't elaborate on *how* he knew that, but he seemed positive about it. He mentioned that he knows all the right people in Licenses and Inspections, and could get the place shut down anytime he feels like it. But he said Vicino will probably just go out of business on its own.

"I was just getting him back on the topic of the schoolhouse, since I know he's lying to us about that, when a little problem happened."

"Not so little," Gerda put in. "Holly's husband walked in. Took one look at Scooter with his arm around Holly, and left."

Howard had caught Holly again on a date?

"It probably looked bad to Howard," Holly admitted. "And then about two minutes after that," she summed up, "things got worse when Scooter's wife showed up."

"Scooter has a *wife*?" I was horrified. I would never have agreed to pose as Alessandra if I'd known that.

"I didn't know about the wife," Holly admitted. "She wasn't all that happy to meet me. And she didn't seem to believe Scooter when he told her I was just a business contact, and a potential investor in his Seabreeze Lane project."

"I forgot about her!" Adelia said vaguely. "Mary Simmons. I'm not sure if they're still married or not," Adelia added. "She took off for Sanibel Island a while back. I guess she got tired of Scooter's lying and cheating."

"When she came in and grabbed Scooter, she announced herself as 'wife,'" Gerda told us grimly. "I told Holly it's not good to date married man. Plus, Holly herself has a husband."

Holly laughed merrily. "Gerda, you're too literal," she told the fitness instructor. "What you just witnessed between me and Scooter was nothing like a date. That was merely information-gathering." Holly indicated me with a wave of her tanned hand.

"Now, what Kristin had last night with Scooter was an actual date!" she said airily.

"That's completely untrue!" I shrieked. "First of all, no one ever said anything about him having a wife. And second, I went against my will!"

"Whatever you say," Holly told me soothingly. "Plus with Mike Woodford in town, you're at risk for cheating on John Hall pretty much every time you walk out the door. I just hope that amazing boyfriend of yours doesn't find out."

"I haven't been anywhere close to cheating, and I won't be!" I protested, then paused to consider Holly's assessment of the situation. There *had* been that kiss with Mike by the Windex and mops in the back room of The Striped Awning in Bryn Mawr last week, but that had been a surprise, and I'd cut it off as soon as I'd realized it was happening.

Plus, John and I weren't married or engaged or anything. But I still wouldn't treat John that way. I was probably in love with John, and I was ninety-eight percent over Mike.

I was exhausted from the day, the schoolhouse sleuthing, the trip for ice cream, and the incessant chatter from Sophie and Adelia (when Adelia was awake). But I forced myself to think for a second: *How would I feel if John Hall was having drinks with another girl while he was out of town?* I'd feel terrible. I squared my shoulders, resolved to avoid Mike at all costs.

"Hi, Mrs. Earle!" said the bartender, not looking all that surprised to see the tobacco heiress arriving at 11:00 p.m. for a cocktail. I felt like yelling at Holly about her Scooter comment, but that would draw even more attention to our already odd group, including Sophie and Adelia in their caftans and Gerda in her workout garb.

"The usual, Mrs. E.?" asked the bartender, who was already pouring Patrón Silver into a shaker.

"Just a quick one!" Adelia said, seating herself on a zebra-print bar stool. "We'll need seven margaritas, actually, Henry," she told the aproned barman, making a quick and surprisingly accurate head count of our group.

"Er, we should probably head to Channing's place!" Joe told her, aiming for a breezy tone. "It sounds like they have a situation over there."

"Put these on my tab," Adelia told the bartender, ignoring Joe.

"So what happened to your car keys?" Bootsie asked, cutting to the chase.

"Scooter's wife saw Holly's keys on top of her handbag here," Gerda told us, indicating a small tortoise-shell clutch in front of Holly. "She was pissed. She take keys, walked outside, and threw them up on roof there."

We looked through the front window, where Gerda was indicating the heights of the Gucci store across the street.

"I climb up and get them tomorrow," Gerda said. "Too dark right now."

Just then, Adelia's houseman, Ozzy, walked in. "I understand one of your friends lost her car keys, so I'm here to give you a ride home, Mrs. Earle," he said politely, offering his arm to the tobacco heiress, who seemed ready to go.

"I come along, too, you can drop me!" Gerda said, jumping up and following Adelia and Ozzy.

I made a move to follow them and hitch a ride with Ozzy, but Joe grabbed my bag, effectively blocking my escape. "If I'm stuck going to the Chessica cottage, so are you," he told me. He found a twenty-dollar bill in his back pocket, left it as a tip for the bartender, and sighed. "Let's do this," he said, heading out behind Bootsie and Sophie as Holly and I followed.

"I like Scooter's wife," Holly said, apropos of nothing. "I'm minus one set of keys, but I think I'd like to get to know Mrs. Scooter Simmons."

CHANNING AND JESSICA's rented cottage turned out to be a white stucco carriage house on a grand property down by the old Sandbar Club. We parked on a side alley near the pricey private golf course, since a police car, lit up like a Christmas tree, was in the driveway outside their place.

"Zack!" called out Sophie to her detective ex. "Yoo-hoo!"

"Hey, Sophie," he said, waving to all of us. "Better if you all stay back. In fact, you shouldn't be here. We're going to do some fingerprinting, even though this doesn't seem to be technically a crime. It's more like a prank."

"It's not exactly funny," said Jessica bitterly. She was seated on a little bench in front of her rented cottage, shivering in the late-night air. Jessica was composed, but her eyes were puffy, and she looked especially downcast.

"We closed Vicino early, because, well, business stinks right now," Channing said, his arm around his girlfriend. "Jessica got here a couple minutes before I did, and there was a delivery on the front porch."

"It was an Hermès shopping bag, the signature orange one with the brown ribbons at the top," Jessica said. "I figured Channing had bought me a present to cheer me up and had it delivered here."

But when Jessica had opened the bag and pulled out some tissue paper and a small square Hermès gift box, she said, a baby alligator had popped out.

"Like, a live one?" Sophie squeaked.

"Yes, a freakin' scaly-looking, prehistoric, monster baby reptile!" Jessica said, her voice rising to a scream.

"Are you sure about that?" Joe asked skeptically.

"Absolutely!" Jessica said. "It ran away into the bushes, but not before Channing got here, and he took a picture of the little fucker." Channing produced a pic of what indeed looked like a very tiny alligator.

"You can order them over the Internet for about a hundred

bucks," Safina explained. "Kinda horrible, but people get them as pets."

"Then a bunch of lizards jumped out, too," Channing told us. "Pretty gross." He gave his shaky girlfriend a reassuring squeeze.

"You mean those little tiny lizards you see everywhere in Florida?" Bootsie asked. "What's scary about them? They're harmless."

"It doesn't seem that way when they jump out of an Hermès bag at you," Jessica told her. "You try it sometime!"

Channing had shaken out the bag and decided after some debate to open the orange Hermès box. Inside had been a man's silk pocket square in a vivid red and yellow pattern that included the striking image of a snake. In the box, too, had been the invitation to the Reptile Foundation party at Vicino, which had been ripped in half.

"The text message is what really upset her," Channing added calmly. "Jessica and I got the same message from a private number about thirty minutes ago. It said, 'Consider the reptiles a warning: Cancel the fund-raiser and get out of Florida.' "

Chapter 18

"WE'LL START AT Hermès, because my theory is that the little pocket square was bought recently—in the last day or two," Bootsie told me on Wednesday morning, after she'd stared me awake at 7:45 a.m. "Then we're going to find the pizza guy who delivered to Barclay yesterday and see what he knows."

"Why are you so sure the Hermès square was bought so recently?" I asked.

"Mummy buys a lot of Hermès scarves. I texted her, and she said that most patterns are only around for a few months, or just weeks if they're popular. I described the square to her, and she knew it immediately—it's called Baiser du Serpent, and it came out this week."

"She knows that much about Hermès?" I said, impressed. Kitty Delaney, like Bootsie, was mostly a Lilly Pulitzer and L.L.Bean type, but come to think of it, I had seen her wear Hermès scarves at the country club back home.

"Absolutely," Bootsie told me. "Mummy's wired in with Hermès on Facebook and Twitter, and gets their e-mails every week, plus the saleswomen call her all the time.

"Anyway, I'm taking you and Joe with me. Holly said she's going to work out, plus I think she needs to work on her Howard issues, and Sophie's spending quality time with Gerda today."

"WE'RE WONDERING IF you can help us," Joe said in his most charming tones to an elegant young saleswoman standing behind the glossy counter at Hermès.

Joe is good at ingratiating himself with women, so, before entering the sumptuous store, the three of us had deemed him the best person to cajole the Hermès staff into dispensing information. We'd sat in the car, sucking down mochas picked up at the little coffee place near the drugstore on Ocean Drive, until Hermès' perfectly polished doors had been unlocked at 10:00 a.m.

"How may I assist you?" said the salesperson, who was about twenty-three but wore her blond hair in a topknot that evoked a cool, supermodelish vibe that called to mind Catherine Deneuve circa 1967. She had also mastered a bright red lipstick that somehow looked amazing on her. She faced us down with an impressive display of politeness mingled with an unspoken *Are you going to buy something?* as she assessed the three of us.

Joe looked good in a handsome pink Lacoste shirt and crisp seersucker trousers—not to mention an Hermès belt. Bootsie wasn't bad herself today—she'd abandoned the caftans and was back in a more user-friendly Lilly Pulitzer shift dress and a pair of Jack Rogers sandals, which, she'd told me, was her go-to outfit for reporting in warm weather climates.

I realized I should have gone with one of Holly's loaner outfits. My Target dress, which I'd thought looked fine back at the guesthouse, didn't cut it in Hermès. I looked to my left, where a simply magnificent beige suede skirt hung gorgeously on a rack. I'd peered at the price tag and almost choked up some of my mocha: *$4,700.*

"Thanks so much," Joe told the topknot girl. "We're wondering if you remember anyone buying the Baiser du Serpent pocket square over the past few days. You know, the red silk with the winding snake motif that just came into stores this week."

I had to stifle a laugh at this. Joe has near perfect memory for this kind of thing. Bootsie had downloaded the details about the snake scarf on the ride over, and, true to form, he'd remembered every single one.

The girl looked somewhat reluctant as she appeared to think this over.

"Forty-two centimeters square, retails for two-seventy-five?" prompted Joe in his sweetest tone, leaning over the counter winsomely. The blonde hesitated, clearly somewhat taken in by Joe, who's pretty cute when he wants to be.

"I can't give out that kind of information," she said finally. "I would, but Corporate doesn't allow us to discuss customers. I mean, some of these ladies will literally bribe us to find out when the next handbags will be in, and we can get in a lot of trouble."

"Oh, come on!" wheedled Joe. "It's just a little man-scarf. Who's gonna care?" He added a small wink.

"I can't," said the girl.

"Oh, really?" Bootsie said loudly, having lost patience and forgetting she was supposed to stay in the background while Joe talked. "Our best friend is Holly Jones. And you don't want us to tell her to take her Hermès business over to Palm Beach or down to Bal Harbour. Because, and I'm not threatening, just telling—she will."

"Please don't do that!" said the saleswoman, abandoning her frosty stance. "I really need Holly's commissions. She's got two bags being hand-stitched as we speak. That commission covers my rent for three months. You have no idea how expensive it is to live in Magnolia Beach!"

She looked over nervously at the store's other salesperson, a pretty woman in her forties who was over in the shoe department helping a mother and daughter team-dressed in what looked like head-to-toe Hermès. The mom and daughter were determined as they slipped their pedicured feet into pricey footwear. I'd seen the same look on Holly's face too many times to count. These two were buyers, not browsers.

I felt a bit bad for the young girl who'd gotten stuck with us. She was getting browbeaten by Bootsie, while the other salesperson was about to rack up a huge sale.

"Snake-print pocket square," prompted Bootsie. "Who bought it?"

"A guy came in Sunday," said the topknot, leaning on her elbows now, ready to spill all she knew. "I remember him really well, because even though our customers are always well dressed"—I noticed she averted her eyes from me as she spoke—"they're usually not all that dressed up for shopping during the day. This guy was wearing a navy sport coat and a tie, sunglasses, and a Panama hat."

"So what did he look like?" Bootsie hammered the question at her.

"Well, he was pretty tall and thin, but he looked like he was in good shape," mused the blonde. "I couldn't see his hair under the hat, and his face was really pretty much blocked by the sunglasses and the brim of his hat. He had kind of regular features. And he was tan!" she added hopefully, searching Bootsie's face, clearly terrified that she'd lose the windfall from Holly if she didn't come up with more details.

"Wedding ring?" asked Bootsie.

"I don't *think* so," frowned the salesperson.

"How old?" asked Joe.

The girl considered this. I guessed it was hard for her to calculate ages of those who weren't glossy and fabulous twenty-somethings like herself. She looked like she was of a mind-set that placed everyone between thirty and sixty into the same category: on the lumpy downward spiral of life.

"I'm going to say, like, forty?" she guessed. "Maybe a little younger?"

"So he was tan, forty-ish, well-dressed, and had on sunglasses?" Bootsie prompted.

"That's it!" the girl nodded enthusiastically.

"That only describes about half of the male population of South Florida," Bootsie told the girl, which didn't seem to endear her to the saleswoman.

"Carly"—I had no idea how Joe had gleaned this girl's name, but he's quite skilled at surreptitiously gathering that kind of information—"isn't there a security tape from Sunday? We could come back later, after store hours, and look at it really quickly?"

"The security cameras are on the blink," Carly whispered, looking around nervously. The older saleswoman appeared to be finishing up with the mother and daughter, who'd now each tried on about seventy-five pairs of shoes and had amassed a hefty pile they were preparing to purchase.

"Please don't tell anyone I told you the cameras are down!" Carly added desperately. "No one's supposed to know. We can't get anyone out to fix them til Friday, and Corporate would freak!"

I noticed that her colleague, though still smiling pleasantly at the moneybags mother, who was slipping on one more pair of suede flats, was giving us a curious glance that contained the same *Aren't you going to buy anything?* query we'd gotten earlier from Carly.

Joe, defeated, shrugged at the girl, but Bootsie wasn't quite finished.

"Here's the single most important thing I'm going to ask you," Bootsie informed her. "Did the guy have an accent?"

"That's so weird that you're asking that!" said Carly. "The guy who bought the snake item didn't speak. Not a single word. He just pointed at the pocket square, nodded when I asked him if he'd like to have it gift-wrapped, and handed me the cash for it."

"You're just telling us this now?!" Bootsie said, in a very un-Hermès shout, as the other saleswoman began carrying stacks of orange shoeboxes toward the checkout counter.

"Well, sometimes people just shop, pay, and don't talk," said the girl defensively. "This isn't the kind of store where there's always a lot of chitchat. I mean, when you're paying a thousand bucks for a pair of shoes, that's no time to, like, get into last night's episode of *The Bachelor*."

"GIANNI BOUGHT THE silk square," Bootsie said as we piled back into the car. "Why else would the guy be completely silent? He was hiding his accent!"

"Gianni in a sport coat and straw hat?" I mused. "I'm not sure I see him buttoning himself into a navy blazer—even if it was in the pursuit of screwing over Jessica. I mean, it's true that Gianni's pretty tan, and he's in good shape and about the same age as the guy Carly described. But he's got all those tattoos, which Carly definitely would have noticed."

"Gianni's tattoos don't extend as far as his wrists," Bootsie told me, firing up the Range Rover and heading toward Royal Palm Way in the center of town. "Carly wouldn't have seen them, since he was wearing a tie and blazer." She paused. "I didn't find an Hermès receipt in his desk yesterday, but he probably tossed it at his restaurant or in a trash can on the street as soon as he bought the pocket square."

"I guess," I said doubtfully.

I could imagine Gianni dreaming up the reptile theme and the overly dramatic Hermès "gift" for Channing and Jessica. But the idea of Gianni being able to keep his mouth shut during an entire five-minute shopping errand struck me as nearly impossible. The man couldn't stop insulting people for any period longer than sixty seconds.

"Do you think it could have been Scooter?" I wondered aloud. "He's a navy blazer kind of guy."

"Scooter isn't six feet tall, and he's not in good shape," Bootsie said. "He's the right age, but I don't think he's the one. Plus, he doesn't seem like the type to make an effort with the whole Hermès bag and the Reptile Party invitation and the crazy live lizard. Scooter's a dealmaker on a bigger scale, not a guy who leaves little notes around."

"And they probably know Scooter at Hermès," I agreed. "He's pretty much a fixture in this town."

"Maybe Gianni sent one of the Colketts in to buy the snake thingy, and then did the lizard delivery himself?" Joe said. "Gianni loves to screw those guys over. The Colketts wouldn't have known what Gianni was up to, and they'd be the ones looking guilty if one of them had gotten caught on security cameras—if the cameras had been working, that is."

I agreed that I could easily picture Gianni doing this. Both the

Colketts are very nice guys and would definitely agree to do the chef a favor.

Bootsie, meanwhile, had parked in front of Gianni Mare. "I'll ask the Colketts about that the next time I see them. You know, it's always possible that Gianni's somehow hired them as hit men, and *they're* the ones trashing Vicino!"

"The Colketts wouldn't do that," I told her.

"They might, if Gianni paid them enough! They said themselves business is slow."

"That's ridiculous," Joe told her. "They might be scared of Gianni, but they're not exactly going to turn into Paulie and Silvio from *The Sopranos* anytime soon."

"You never know! Meanwhile, wait here," Bootsie said. "I need to snap a quick pic with my phone. Joe, you make some calls. We need to know what's up with Channing and Jessica, and get an update on Barclay's head injury. Maybe Adelia tracked down Susie and Bingo Simmons, too."

"It's hot out here," said Joe grumpily. "At least leave the motor running and the air on."

"I'm risking my life here!" Bootsie yelled, while Joe cranked up the air to full arctic. "Fine—sit in the car and run the air conditioner if you really need to!"

"How is taking a fucking picture risking your life?" Joe screamed back at her.

"Because I need the picture of *Gianni* to go back and show Carly at Hermès! Maybe she'll recognize him. And I'm taking a big scary risk because the guy's probably in a homicidal rage and unleashing deadly baby gators on people!"

She hopped out of the Range Rover and crouched behind a hibiscus bush to snap a few pics. Gianni was visible inside the large open windows of Gianni Mare, where he was yelling, red-faced, at a hapless teenager who was mopping the expensively tiled floor.

"By the way, we just missed Olivia," Joe retorted when Bootsie got back in the SUV a moment later. "She was in the passenger seat of that beat-up pickup truck that pulled out while you were screaming at me. The truck hung a left toward the mainland."

I looked up from texting John Hall that I was about to kill myself if I spent one more hour with Bootsie and Joe. I hadn't noticed Olivia in the truck.

"We should have followed her! Now you tell me?" Bootsie said, her face bright red. "She was probably going to run some evil errand for Gianni. You ruined the whole investigation."

"Shut up, Bootsie!" Joe screamed. "I'm a decorator, not freaking Hercule Poirot! Olivia's a girlfriend-slash-assistant who Gianni orders around, not some criminal mastermind. She's probably headed to the airport again to pick up a bunch of heirloom tomatoes or something."

"You should stick to trying to hustle old ladies into spending thirty-six thousand bucks on ceiling tents!"

"Um, guys, let's breathe for a second," I said. I was still kind of mad at Bootsie for casting me in the role of not-very-bright minion to Scooter Simmons, but I was determined to get this day over with as quickly and efficiently as possible.

Also, I had the sense that against all odds, we were actually making progress and uncovering a few clues about the Vicino incidents and even, at the same time, possibly figuring out what exactly Barclay and Scooter were up to.

"We had a long day yesterday, and it's only natural that we're all a little tired. And, Bootsie, have you had your protein bar yet this morning?" I asked her calmly.

"No," she said grumpily.

"Okay, let's get you a snack," I told her in my best kindergarten teacher voice. "I think there are a couple of Clif Bars left in the glove compartment. Joe, do you need something to eat, too?"

"I guess so," he whined.

"How about some water, too?" I suggested, handing around some bottles of Poland Spring that Martha had thoughtfully placed in the car as we were leaving. We all munched and sipped for a few minutes, listening to the Escape spa music channel on Bootsie's Sirius radio.

"Everyone okay now?" I asked. Joe and Bootsie nodded.

Sugar, salt, chocolate, and whatever the heck else is in a Clif Bar coursed through my veins, and I felt somehow renewed myself. At the same time, I had a sudden realization: *I need to go home to Bryn Mawr.* If we could just figure out who was wreaking havoc around Magnolia Beach, I'd head home to the frosty, sleety weather and not have to referee these bullshit arguments or listen to Sophie's legal woes and Holly's Howard problems.

I summoned every ounce of patience I had left and tried to think of how best to rally the troops, such as they were. I leaned and spoke in encouraging tones into the front seat.

"Okay, Bootsie, do you still think we should try to find the pizza delivery guy who took the sandwich to Barclay?"

"Of course I do," Bootsie said, balling up her Clif Bar wrapper, grabbing mine and Joe's, and dunking the little bundle into a trash can just outside her car window. She even did a little fist pump, so I knew she was back in peak form. "I've got a few twenties ready to get this guy talking. Unlike the police, who aren't supposed to pay for information, I have no such restrictions. We'll bribe him and find out everything he knows."

"I've always wanted to bribe somebody," said Joe, who perked up, chugged some Poland Spring, and started entering the address of Broadway Pizza into Bootsie's navigation system. "There isn't much bribery in decorating," he told us. "I mean, you might get your fabric order in a little sooner if you take the rep out for drinks, but that's about it."

He pondered the pizza guy scenario for a minute as the nav ordered Bootsie to turn left and head over the Intercoastal bridge.

"Maybe we can get him to talk by threatening to get him in trouble with his boss, too," Joe said hopefully. "Or, know, tell him we're going to follow him home and tell his mom he's in big trouble? That could be fun."

"Let's find this pizza kid and scare the crap out of him!" shrieked Bootsie.

"I SWEAR ON my grandma's life—all I did was drop off a hoagie to the dude," said Andy the pizza guy.

We'd found Andy outside his workplace heading for the Broadway Pizza van, toting three large pies in a special insulated pizza carrier.

Bootsie had ordered Andy over to one of Broadway Pizza's few outdoor tables, where the unlucky target of her investigation had looked nervously inside to make sure his boss didn't see him dawdling instead of delivering.

"Er, I really need to get these pizzas to the Jaguar dealership," he told us. "They have a standing order." Andy was a tanned surfer type, wearing flip-flops, long shorts, and a ball cap on backward. Mafia hit man was a hard role to imagine Andy playing.

"This will just take five minutes," Bootsie said. "And hold on a sec, I need to place a quick order." She dashed inside Broadway Pizza and was back in under a minute.

"I already told the police everything," Andy told us, squirming. "All I did was get handed a sandwich yesterday afternoon by my manager, and the order ticket with the address over on Seagrape Lane on the island."

"Had you ever been to that house before?" asked Joe.

"Naw, man, people in Magnolia Beach almost never order from us," Andy told him.

Joe looked at Bootsie and made a hand gesture that indicated it was time to peel off some bills, so Bootsie shrugged and handed Andy a twenty. He looked intrigued, but unsure if he should take it.

"Did anyone ask you to go attack the guy—Barclay Shields is his name?" Bootsie asked. "You know—maybe someone paid you to hit him in the head?"

"Absolutely not!" Andy said, holding up both hands in protest. "Seriously, I'm getting a degree in marine biology at Florida Atlantic. I'm not some hit man, lady. I literally rang the doorbell, handed the guy the meatball hoagie, extra cheese, and took his money. Guy was a good tipper. He handed me twelve bucks, and the sandwich was seven."

"Did you see anyone else at the house on Seagrape?"

"No one," Andy said. "Except there was a really tall, muscular woman with a blond braid jogging past me when I got there, but she was already out on the street and heading toward Ocean Boulevard." *Gerda.*

"No scary guys, no one parked in the driveway, no hookers waiting outside in their cars?"

Andy again held up both hands. "No one, and definitely no scary dudes . . . or hookers," he said. "I mean, I don't know if I could tell a girl was a hooker, but there weren't any women there at all."

Bootsie held up a couple more twenties and dangled them in front of Andy. "Andy, this is my last question, because I'm getting hungry, and I don't want your boss to get mad at you for letting those pies get cold. Is there *anything else at all* you want to tell us about yesterday?"

Andy's blue eyes darted around nervously for a second, then he jumped up and jogged to the van. "Naw, sorry, that's it!" he shouted, jumping in and peeling out toward his delivery van.

"Uh, ma'am, you with the flowered outfit? Your calzones are ready," said a girl who leaned out of the pizza place's front door to Bootsie. "One pepperoni, one spinach, one cheesesteak filled, and the plain mozzarella-ricotta. That'll be twenty-two bucks."

Chapter 19

"Andy's lying," Bootsie said in the car a minute later, biting into a gooey spinach calzone as cheese dripped down onto a paper plate and a pile of paper napkins in which she'd mummified her lap. Joe handed around the Diet Cokes, grabbed a plastic knife from the bag, cut the three other calzones in half, and offered me my choice of cheese-filled mound of dough. I went for half of the plain, though I'd secretly wanted to try the spinach one. Too late—Bootsie had almost finished inhaling it.

"He's leaving something out," Joe said, chewing on his half of the cheesesteak calzone. "I'm not getting mafia vibes from this kid. It's more like he got caught up in something stupid, and now he's too scared to tell anyone."

For once, I was on the same page as Joe and Bootsie.

"Should we follow him?" Bootsie asked hopefully.

"No," I said firmly. "Bootsie, please. You've lied to everyone in Magnolia Beach and most of Palm Beach at this point, and I don't want you to start stalking."

"I need to get over to Adelia's and check on how the sconces look," sighed Joe. "The bribing was fun, though."

Bootsie was looking wistfully in the direction that Andy had zoomed off toward, but she sighed as she put the Range Rover into gear. "We need to finish going through Scooter's zoning papers anyway," she agreed, swinging out of Broadway Pizza. "I'm actually running out of lies at this point."

"Head back to Hermès first," Joe told her. "I'll show the pic of Gianni to Carly and see if she thinks he's the guy who bought the man-scarf. Bootsie, you stay in the car. No offense, but Carly hates you."

"I NEED TO go to The Breakers, find Holly, and get her to apologize to Howard," I told Bootsie. "Can you drop me there?"

Joe had reported that Carly was pretty sure Gianni wasn't her customer from earlier in the week. After Hermes, we tried in vain to think of other suspects as we crossed the bridge toward The Breakers. I'd texted Holly to meet me in the lobby of the hotel, and as we approached the palm-lined driveway, Joe's phone pinged, too.

"It's Channing," he told us. "He and Jessica decided to shut down Vicino for a couple of weeks."

THE HOLLY WHO was waiting outside the hotel was a shell of her usual upbeat self. Not only was her marriage on the rocks but the restaurant she and Sophie had put so much money into was closing down as well, even if it was supposedly just a temporary shuttering. She looked miserable, but she was channeling her low mood into obsessive exercise.

"You're just in time for the afternoon Glutenator class," she told me. "I got you some workout clothes and sneakers at the hotel shop. Let's go!"

We zoomed through the gorgeous hotel toward the ocean and the pool—make that pools, since I could count at least three separate bodies of water, including one with fabulous people lunching and cocktailing around it. Palm trees and umbrellas shaded these lucky folks, and a gorgeous breeze wafted in from the ocean. I gazed longingly at the mojito-sipping crowd, but Holly sternly ushered me into the spa and fitness area, where she quickly signed us in at the front desk.

An hour later, thighs screaming in pain and hair soaked, I emerged into the sunlight. Other than my few sessions at Booty Camp, a horrible fitness program Holly sometimes drags me to when we're home in Bryn Mawr, and one tennis lesson I'd taken from Bootsie last year, I'd never experienced such physical agony in my life.

"Please don't ever ask me to do that—wait," I interrupted myself, pausing beside a majestic pillar and indicating a table hidden over near the outdoor bar.

Olivia from Gianni Mare was eating a salad as she talked animatedly with an attractive older woman and a guy in his late twenties. While the guy wasn't sitting close to Olivia—he was across from her and the older woman—the three clearly knew each other well. They sat with informal posture, heads together as they talked and ate.

"We need to know who's sitting with Olivia," Holly said, appearing to have been perked up a little by the class. "I'll be right back." She returned a moment later with Stefan the concierge in tow.

"Who's that guy in the green polo shirt?" Holly asked Stefan. "And the other woman, do you know her?"

"That's Daniel Ainsley," Stefan said. "Good guy, very ambitious. Lives down in Gulfstream and runs a few businesses. He's in construction and owns part of a marina. A local guy, and self-made."

"And the woman in the yellow dress? Not Olivia—the other one."

"Ah, yes, Olivia," said Stefan wearily. "Keeps showing up at the salon last minute without an appointment and throws a fit until one of the stylists agrees to blow-dry her hair. She also likes to order room service, but she's a terrible tipper." He looked more closely at the woman with Olivia and Daniel.

"Will take me five minutes or less to find out who she is, where she lives, and what she does for a living," he told us, disappearing inside the hotel again.

"That lady is Olivia's mother," Stefan said a minute later. "She's been a fifth-grade teacher in West Palm Beach for more than thirty years. One of my parking valets was her student some years back. She's a well-respected lady, he says."

I hadn't known that Olivia was a Palm Beach native, and thought it must be helpful to Gianni to have a girlfriend who knew the area so well. She looked happy sitting with her mom and Daniel—which was a big change from her usual expression when she was with Gianni. I was just surprised she'd been able to get away from Gianni to spend time with her mom.

"Can you find out what the relationship is with Daniel Ainsley and Olivia?" Holly asked in a very Bootsie-like manner. Stefan nodded, stepped back into the lobby, and returned within moments.

"High school sweethearts," he said. "About ten years ago. I guess they've stayed friends."

Holly and I exchanged significant glances. Once again, it seemed one of Gianni's younger girlfriends might have found herself an outside love interest or, in Olivia's case, reunited with an old flame.

We followed Stefan back to the lobby, and I was just about to start begging Holly to call Howard's hotel room when I noticed the Colketts were at the bar.

"We think Gianni might have asked one of the Colketts to buy that Hermès scarf," I told Holly.

She headed the designers' way, and they rose and greeted her happily. Somehow, I noticed, Holly still looked flawless after the horrible workout class. Her hair was perfect, and she didn't seem to have perspired.

As Holly chatted with Tim and Tom, I couldn't stop thinking about Bootsie's theory that they'd somehow gotten entangled with Gianni. If the pair really was having financial troubles, maybe they were desperate enough to have gotten on Gianni's payroll, and had delivered the bad clams and sabotaged the air-conditioning.

The Colketts are good guys, though! Tom and Tim had helped us during last spring's crime spree back at home, dishing up information about Channing, Jessica, and Gianni that hadn't turned out to be all that important but had at least been true. They'd had nothing to do with the attacks on Sophie's ex and on Gianni, even though Gianni had given them reason to want to go after him. Meanwhile, Holly had seated herself next to Tim, who had his iPad out and a pitcher of Bloody Marys at the ready.

"Hi, doll, have a seat," he said, politely pulling out a chair for me. "Bloody?"

"Sure!" I said, wanting to go with the flow and also thinking that the cocktail looked quite refreshing. "By the way, I really love your design for the Gianni Mare. The chef and Olivia must be so happy with the way things turned out."

"So far, Gianni's only screamed at us once this week," Tom told us. "Now Olivia . . ." He looked around to make sure she wasn't anywhere in the bar. "Her temper is actually making Gianni look good."

"Olivia's really a pain," Tim Colkett said. "We're honestly just in this project for the exposure and for our design portfolio. And, well, the money. Not to brag, but the restaurant is a total career-maker."

"We've been on the phone a few times with *Elle Decor*, and they'll be sending down a team next week to photograph the restaurant," Tom said. "Unfortunately, we have to share credit with Sienna for this job"—here, he made a face that indicated he had less than full respect for the *Restaurant in a Weekend* star—"but that's just because of the HGTV angle. After this job, we're rebranding ourselves as Colkett Interior and Landscape Design."

"Plus," Tom added, "not to sound conceited or anything, but Tom and I are both pretty darn handsome, and HGTV is all about looks. They love remodelers who work as a duo, too."

I momentarily forgot my suspicions that the Colketts might have tried to run down Holly and the Vicino management team the week before. If they got their own show, it would put Joe in the kind of spiral that often leads to spending several months in a quiet sanitarium.

"That was weird that the realtor got sick on Saturday at Vicino, wasn't it?" I said. I felt horrible bringing up the incident again, not to mention implying that it was Channing and Jessica's fault.

But since I wanted the Colketts to start talking, I went one step further. "I mean, Channing allowing bad clams in his restaurant was the first nail in the Vicino coffin!" I said bitchily. "Sorry, Holly."

"That's okay!" she said, throwing the young chef under the bus. "I'm not too happy that Channing let that happen. And now the restaurant's temporarily closed."

"Yeah, we heard about that," said Tim, nodding. "But Gianni's such a star. Poor Channing isn't in his league."

"We don't have any malice toward Chan, of course," Tom said, shrugging. "The guy's nice. It's just that Gianni's star power, combined with our blue-and-white design, is unstoppable."

I considered this for a moment as we sipped and nodded assent. Maybe the Colketts really were as unconcerned with Vicino as they seemed to be. They didn't seem like running-people-over-in-an-alley types, either, but since I was already channeling Bootsie's nosiness, I decided to find out if they'd been anywhere near Magnolia Beach on the night of the trash can incident of the week before.

"So you two have been down here for a week or so, right?" I said, aiming for a casual tone. "Putting together the restaurant had to have taken some time."

"I don't think it's been a full week," Tim said blandly, seeming blasé about the length of their visit, probably because (like myself) he had someone else footing the bill. "I guess we've been here about six days now? We did all the buying for this place while we were still up in Pennsylvania, so it was basically just overseeing painting, tiling, and installation once we got down here."

If they'd arrived Thursday or Friday, that was too late to have run down Jessica and Holly in the alley on Tuesday night.

"The days get away from you down here, don't they?" Tom added happily, pouring himself more of the Bloody Mary from the frosty pitcher in front of us. "Island time!"

We thanked them for the drinks and rose to leave. I honestly couldn't imagine the Colketts running down Jessica and Holly. Maybe Bootsie was right and Gianni had wielded the Chevy and personally tried to scare Jessica out of town. I followed Holly, who was zooming out of the lobby.

"Why don't you call Howard and see if he's here at the hotel?" I said as Holly handed the valet parker a couple of twenties. "You two really need to talk. We could explain about the whole situation with J. D. and Scooter. I'm sure he'd understand!"

"If he doesn't trust me implicitly, I don't see the point of talking to him," Holly said stubbornly.

I wanted to point out that she didn't trust Howard, either, but I knew it was pointless.

"But if you just told him you were trying to help Jessica and stop a sneaky developer, I'm sure Howard would get over the whole thing!" *Well, probably he would.*

Holly shook her head. "You don't understand." She scrolled on her iPhone for a moment and handed it to me.

"Howard has no room to talk," she said, affecting a serene expression in her almond-shaped blue eyes. "Look at the lead photo of *Indianapolis Social Life*, from a party that was given Sunday night. Then we'll talk."

Truthfully, it looked bad. Headlined "Saving Presidential Park—in Style!" the posting detailed a black-tie fund-raiser held at a private home in a suburb of the Midwestern city. There was a huge heated tent and dance floor. More pics showed guests lounging on white modern sofas in a temporary "Selfie Lounge" under the tent. NFL and NBA players mingled with local businesspeople, and, of course, Dawnelle and her family. And Howard, who was twice pictured with Dawnelle.

"But you really love Howard," I reminded her. "Just ask him about Dawnelle."

"Of course I love Howard," Holly said. "But right now, I need to help Channing reopen Vicino."

Chapter 20

WHEN WE GOT back to Holly's house from The Breakers, two enormous flower arrangements were on the table in the living room. I was hoping they were from Howard, although I couldn't think of a reason why he'd send his wife flowers after catching her out with two other men.

"The white roses and orchids are from Scooter, and the other one is from J. D. Alvarez," Bootsie said, holding up the cards, which she'd opened.

"And J. D. wants to take you to Prime 112 in Miami for dinner tonight," she told Holly.

"Forget it," Holly told us. "I'm not going. Just because J. D. looks like Michael Fassbender and lives in Miami and California doesn't mean I'm going to have an affair with him."

"Great!" I told her, relieved.

"So what are you going to do?" Bootsie asked.

Just then, Sophie and Joe walked in carrying huge bags that smelled awesome and bore the inscription of Captain Harry's Sea Shanty.

"We figured since your whole life's a disaster, we should stay in and have takeout!" Sophie told Holly.

WAFFLES WAS SITTING at my feet, drooling, while we sat at the dining room table in Holly's house and ate fried shrimp, beer-battered fish, corn on the cob, and curly fries from Captain Harry's.

I'd noticed that Holly, who'd changed out of her workout outfit, was sitting up straighter as the meal progressed. She appeared lost in thought for about five minutes, then a determined gleam appeared in her expression as she nibbled Captain Harry's slightly limp side salad and did some quick texting.

"I might have made a few mistakes this week," Holly told us. "First of all, J. D. is too smart to spill information, and it turns out Scooter is way more discreet than I figured he would be."

"Ya fucked up, big-time," Sophie told her. "Both of those guys are liars, even if J. D. is really good looking."

"They're both trickier than I realized," Holly admitted. "We still don't know who did the damage at Vicino, or where Bingo is. Which is why I'm going to go over in about ten minutes to visit Chef Gianni at his suite. Gianni's the loose cannon in that group! He'll tell me everything he knows."

"Holly, let me give you a piece of advice," Sophie told her, nibbling a shrimp. "There aren't a lot of guys out there like my Honey Bunny and your Howard. Get your crap together and go apologize to your hubby."

"I just texted Chef Gianni to meet me at The Breakers. He's leaving his restaurant right now," Holly said, getting up and heading for her front door. "After I get everything I need from Gianni, I'm going to take Sophie's advice, find Howard, and make up with him," she added over her shoulder.

"I'll drive you!" Bootsie told her.

Chapter 21

NATURALLY, I WENT along too, and minutes later Bootsie and I sat in The Breakers' Tapestry Bar sipping Diet Cokes after Holly headed up to Gianni's suite.

"It's eight-thirty-five. Holly was supposed to text us at eight-twenty," I said, worried. "Gianni's so creepy!"

"Even worse, I just saw his girlfriend walk into the hotel," said Bootsie, who was facing the hotel lobby. She held up her huge tote bag. "My Breakers uniform is still in here. I think it's time for Housekeeping to head up to Gianni's suite."

Two minutes later, Bootsie emerged from the ladies' room in her maid's outfit, and we headed down a corridor to the elevators that led up to the guest rooms. A twenty-something girl with a blond ponytail in a Breakers uniform and nametag that read "Britney" was dusting the crown moldings outside the now-closed gift shop as we passed. She gave Bootsie a curious glance and rueful half smile, communicating that (A) Bootsie must be a new employee, and (B) it sucked to be working the evening shift, didn't it?

Just then, Bootsie grabbed my arm and turned toward Britney. "Hi, Britney! I'm new on staff here. Barbie McElvoy!"

Three minutes and forty dollars later, I was in Britney's uniform and had her Swiffer in hand, while Britney waited in the restroom wearing my Old Navy sundress. Bootsie had launched into an explanation that we were surprising a friend and it was all a practical joke, but Britney interrupted her, saying she didn't care, and she was clocking out at 9:00 p.m., so hurry up.

"Turndown service!" Bootsie hollered outside the door to Gianni's suite.

"HOLLEEEE, IGNORE THAT!" we could hear Gianni yelling over thumping music as Holly opened the door.

She looked fine, if a little frazzled.

"I know where Bingo is," she whispered to us. "I just need to grab my handbag, then I'm out of here." She beckoned us in, and Bootsie and I came in behind her.

"Hollee, get rid of the maids," Gianni said, turning up the Euro music to full volume and throwing open the balcony door.

I Swiffered the suite's baseboards, thinking that Gianni's neighbors couldn't have been too happy about all the noise, and that Olivia was going to wonder what all the commotion was in her boyfriend's room. Gianni was now doing his trademark shimmying dance, manic energy pulsating from him, trying to get Holly to join in and have another drink.

"This has been fun!" Holly told him, heading for the door.

Unfortunately, Bootsie decided at that moment to go off-script. She pulled a rumpled piece of paper from her apron pocket and waved it in Gianni's face. "This invoice is for clams from Maine Coastal Catch!" Bootsie yelled at the chef over the music. "Did you tamper with the clams that got Slavica d'Aranville sick last weekend?"

"Hey, baby, fuck you," Gianni told her. "I don't need to screw around with Channing's place. And who the fuck are you?" He stared at Bootsie for a minute, recognition dawning. "Hey, I know you! You that annoying reporter from home, the one with the flowered outfits. Get outta my suite!"

"I'm an investigative reporter!" Bootsie told him.

"Investigate this!" Gianni said with a rude gesture south of his waistline.

"So you're saying you didn't have anything to do with the bad clams?" Bootsie shot back. "Or the damaged air-conditioning?"

"No, you crazy flowered pants chick!" Gianni said, his earrings jangling and his bald dome taking on a sweaty sheen. "I didn't do nothing to fuck Channing over! And guess what—if I did, you'd never find out!"

"Gianni, I am so sorry," Holly said, staring at Bootsie, eyes wide in fake shock. "Bootsie here has been off her meds for the past few weeks. We'll leave now."

"You don't need to go, Holleee! You got some weird friends, but that's okay!" Gianni told her. "These two gotta leave!" he shouted rudely to me and Bootsie, then he clutched at Holly and tried to get her to join him while he started dancing again.

Just then, the door from Olivia's connecting room opened, and Olivia—wearing leather leggings and a black silk tank—walked into the suite. She didn't look too happy as she took in her boyfriend in mid-shimmy with Holly.

"Thanks so much, Gianni, but I better go," Holly said breezily. "Bye!"

We all hustled out of the room toward the hallway and onto the elevator, and when the elevator doors opened on the ground floor, Howard was standing there. He looked at Holly, then at me and Bootsie in our maid outfits, then back at Holly.

"We need to talk," he told her.

Holly and Howard headed for the Tapestry Bar, and within a few minutes, Holly texted us that (A) she wouldn't be home for a while, and (B) Gianni had bragged to her that Scooter Simmons had sent his half-brother to a wilderness retreat in Arizona, a remote lodge in the desert outside Tucson for technology addicts. Naturally, the lodge didn't have phones or e-mail, since its residents were supposed to be on lockdown as they went cold turkey on their need to communicate 24/7. From what Gianni had drunkenly told Holly, Bingo was due back on Saturday, the day after the schoolhouse was due to be torn down.

Chapter 22

THE NEXT MORNING, Holly still hadn't come home, and she'd stopped returning texts.

Sophie had given Zack Safina the news about Bingo's whereabouts, and the detective was tracking down the younger Simmons brother at the wilderness retreat.

Adelia's Reptile Foundation lunch was scheduled to start at 12:30 at Vicino—which was going to be the last meal served for a while at the restaurant. After the luncheon, Channing would post a "Closed for Remodeling" sign and inform the staff about the temporary shutdown at Vicino.

At eight-forty-five a.m., Channing called Sophie to tell her that except for his sous-chef, Rob, every single staff member had either called in sick or left a message that they quit. They'd all heard about the place closing down and were out looking for new jobs. That's how we ended up serving lunch to Adelia, Slavica, and two dozen other Magnolia Beach ladies.

I FELT BAD for Channing and Jessica as I gazed around at our assembled selves in the kitchen: We were honestly a pretty terrible staff. None of us are decent cooks, except for Joe, who can put together a passable lasagna and grill a steak.

By 11:00 a.m., Bootsie started drinking and wasn't all that much help. Sophie and Joe turned out to be the best of us: I tried to help serve the salads, but Joe took one look at my attempt at balancing plates and ordered me behind the bar to pour Moët and chardonnay, which I served to the ladies when they arrived.

The last guest to arrive was Slavica, who had on a somewhat funereal sleeveless black dress, an impressive Chanel necklace with a lot of gold double Cs on it, and a wide-brimmed black straw hat. She honestly looked pretty fabulous, if a bit on the scary side.

"Slavica, you look absolutely beautiful," Adelia told her. "And so thin!"

"Well, there's a reason why I lost some weight," Slavica told her. "And let's just say, this restaurant was part of the reason."

"Let's talk about you coming over to see my new dining pavilion," Adelia told her. "You're sitting right next to me, dear."

Luckily, Channing had made something called individual morel galettes. None of us knew what a galette was, including Joe, who eats at a lot of fancy restaurants, but it seemed to be a small quiche filled with a lot of delicious-looking mushrooms and herbs. Thankfully, the dish was served cold, since there was no way our "staff" could have gotten thirty plates onto tables quickly enough to keep anything warm.

The lunch flew by with even Slavica seeming to enjoy herself, once she'd made sure the lunch contained no seafood. The vibe was upbeat, except for when a University of Florida professor gave a short lecture about how pollution in the Everglades was decimating the snake population, during which Adelia fell asleep.

Meanwhile, Bootsie continued to drink more wine than she served. We finally sent her home at three o'clock after she told one lady to "forget it" when she complained about the cheese and eggs in the galettes and asked for a vegan lunch.

"Walk back to Holly's," Joe told Bootsie. "You can't drive. It's less than a mile. And stay on the sidewalk."

"Bye!" said Bootsie, handing over her car keys and taking off out the back kitchen door.

"I really like the Chanel necklace Slavica's wearing," Sophie mused aloud. "I think I might start collecting Chanel. Maybe vintage *and* new. This could be great—caftans and Chanel!"

"Why don't you two go out to dinner?" Sophie told Channing and Jessica when the ladies finally left at 4:00 p.m. "There's a bunch of cute places down in Delray Beach. We can finish the cleanup here, plus you two probably want to head home and get some lovin' after such a crazy week!"

Channing and Jessica protested that they couldn't leave us with all the cleanup work, but they finally relented and took off, looking relieved.

By 6:00, we'd gotten all the dishes, pans, and wineglasses cleaned and sanitized, so I borrowed Joe's car and went home to check on Waffles and take him for a quick stroll.

Then I headed back to Vicino to help with the final cleanup of the dining room and bar. We figured we'd be done by 7:30. As I parked yet again around the corner from Vicino, all I could think about was finishing up, rushing home, and finally cannonballing into Holly's rented pool.

Then, I'd insert myself into the fluffy white robe hanging in the guesthouse bathroom. *Fluffy white robe! Fluffy white robe!* flashed happily in my cortex as I pushed open the front door to Vicino and beheld a sight I honestly could never have imagined: Sophie and Joe yielding a broom and a mop.

Joe was cursing, while Sophie had rolled up her caftan and was discreetly perspiring, looking as morose as I'd ever seen her.

"This mop is kinda heavy!" she told me. "Channing told us the whole kitchen needs to be Cloroxed nine ways til Sunday, too!"

"You guys should leave," I told them. "Seriously, I'll finish up. Go to Tiki Joe's! Show off your new caftan, Sophie!"

"We couldn't stick you with that crappy Cloroxing," Sophie protested, while Joe's expression telegraphed joy at the prospect of a drink at a stylish bar, served to him by someone who was actually skilled at making cocktails.

"I'll finish up in the kitchen. I'll be out of here in, like, twenty minutes. Then I'm going to walk home, get in my bikini, and jump in the pool!" I assured them. After a couple more minutes during which Sophie said she felt bad leaving me, and Joe kept telling her that I had an antiques shop and was used to cleaning, they finally took off in Joe's car for Tiki Joe's.

"Remind me never to do anything nice again," Joe told me. "I hate helping people."

I was exhausted as I locked Vicino's front door behind them. I'd leave via the kitchen, then use the key Jessica had given us to secure the back door when I left.

And at least I had the image of Holly's shimmering pool to keep me motivated as I closed and secured the dining room's French doors to the patio, pulled down the shades, and shut off all the lights except for the required EXIT lighting.

I checked to make sure the patio lighting was down and the music turned off.

Along with the bossa nova music, somehow there had been an upbeat vibe again at Vicino today. Channing had done his best hunky-chef table-hopping with the ladies, and Jessica had booked several tables for the following weekend. The current plan, she'd told us earlier, while we'd plated molten chocolate cupcakes topped with tiny spun-sugar "lizards," was that she and Channing would hire back a few employees and reopen for dinner Thursdays through Sundays. They were positive they could be up and running again, full-time, in a few months—as long as no more incidents plagued Vicino.

I'd nodded, refraining from pointing out that we still didn't know who'd been sabotaging Vicino. Gianni had insisted it wasn't him, and oddly, I kind of believed him. I also couldn't see why Scooter, who was busy trying to tear down a historic building, would be after Jessica, and Barclay wasn't the type who would sneak bad clams into a kitchen.

Anyway, I'd Clorox, lock up, and be home within thirty minutes, I thought, as I pushed through the double doors into the darkened kitchen.

"WHAT THE HELL are you doing here?"

The question came at me in an angry hiss from Olivia, Gianni's girlfriend, who was holding a large and shiny chef's knife up against Jessica's throat over by the walk-in refrigerator.

I froze. The kitchen lights were turned off, but as my eyes adjusted to the dim light I could see that next to Olivia stood the young guy we'd seen with her at The Breakers the day before: Daniel Ainsley.

Daniel looked confused and upset but remained quiet while Olivia, for her part, displayed a surprisingly icy froideur as she stood in four-inch heels and skinny black leggings, looking like the evil dark-haired twin of the blond, bony Jessica—who's not all that warm and fuzzy herself.

"Uh, Olivia, not to upset you, but what's going on here?" I asked her, my voice quavering. "Did Jessica do something to offend you? Can I help?"

Olivia looked annoyed. "Seriously, what the fuck are you doing here!" she snarled. "Get over here. Daniel, tie this girl's hands behind her back."

I frantically looked around the kitchen for some kind of way to disarm Olivia. Not a single knife was visible anywhere, and I remembered that Channing took his expensive knives home with him at night.

There were large heavy cooking pans that could serve as weapons. . . . The fire extinguisher might work to blast this crazy girl and her accomplice. . . . But given the glinting blade up against Jessica's jugular, I couldn't risk a single move toward any of these potentially helpful objects. It could be fatal to further set Olivia off, and while Daniel had looked like a mild-mannered guy the other day at The Breakers, maybe he was a dangerous nut job, too. I began walking toward him on wobbly legs.

"I'm not a part of this," said Daniel. "Olivia, come on—you're getting in over your head," he told his high school girlfriend. Who, I guessed, was also his current inamorata, since why else would he be here helping with the knife-wielding Olivia?

"Shut up!" Olivia told him. "I'm doing this for you! Well, sort of," she added with an evil little smile on her beautiful face. "And you've been involved all along, so don't try to weasel out of this now. Grab that butcher's string Channing uses for his tenderloin and tie this girl up. Now!"

"I was okay with planting the old clams and tampering with the air conditioner," protested Daniel, who reluctantly cut off a couple of lengths of string as directed and began to secure my wrists. "You never said anything about knives and, you know, holding people against their will." I noticed that he wasn't making the twine tight enough to hurt me—but, given his sailing background, the knots felt unbreakable, and I had no chance of freeing myself. I shivered as I stood next to the frozen-in-place Jessica.

"What are you doing back here, Jessica?" I asked her desperately, whispering so as to hopefully not set Olivia off even further. "I thought you and Channing had dinner plans."

"I left my wallet in the office, and after Channing and I had a quick drink, I came back to get it," she said desperately.

"And I followed her in, thinking I'd finally have my chance to get rid of this blond bitch!" screamed Olivia. "Until you messed everything up!"

"I'm sorry," I said, a tear dripping down my cheek. "I apologize. For both of us." I wasn't sure what Jessica had done, but trying to make amends—fast—seemed like the only plan.

"I'll just have to take care of both of you," shrugged Olivia coldly.

"Olivia, Channing will wonder where his girlfriend is, and he'll show up here any minute," I told Gianni's girlfriend with more assurance than I actually felt.

Where *was* Channing, anyway? He and Jessica weren't called Janning and Chessica for nothing. The two were inseparable.

"No, he won't," Olivia told me smugly. "Channing's halfway to Tampa right now, in the middle of the Florida swamp on Highway 60. I made a fake call an hour ago inviting him to meet with the manager of the Hard Rock Hotel for a Monday-through-Wednesday chef job. I told him I was the dining manager, and that he had to come over and interview on the spot. The guy was just desperate enough to jump at the chance."

I looked at Jessica, who nodded miserably. "It's true," she mumbled. "Channing hates not working, and he was ecstatic when he thought he could do the Hard Rock job for part of the week until we get this place open full-time again."

"That's not going to happen," Olivia told her. "After tonight, you'll be dead, and so will his restaurant. No one's ever going to want to eat at Vicino after I kill you here."

"But why are you after Jessica?" I whispered, another tear dripping onto the white apron I still wore.

"She's done nothing but screw up every opportunity I've ever had!" Olivia, enraged again. "When we worked together five years ago at a steak house in Philly, Jessica got all the best shifts. Then she met Gianni and started posting on Facebook about the trips to Italy. She wore Louboutins and lived in a fancy house with Gianni. What did you ever do to deserve that life, anyway?" Olivia screamed this in Jessica's direction, and we both shrank back as Olivia waved her shiny knife.

"But Gianni's awful," Jessica whispered. "I mean, you know how he is."

"You bet I do," Olivia told her. "But I'm not as lucky as you—of course, you met Channing and ran off down here to open your own fabulous place, while I ended up taking over as Gianni's manager. And girlfriend," she added bitterly.

"Gianni was talking last summer about opening a place in Beverly Hills, which is why I decided to date him," Olivia told us. "All

I've ever wanted my whole life is to live in California! And I finally had my chance! We were days away from signing a lease on a place out there, and I had an audition for *The Voice* set up.

"Then Gianni got the offer in November from HGTV to do a pop-up restaurant down here, and everything fell apart. He canceled plans for California. And he started obsessing about you again. Every fucking word out of his mouth was 'Jessica'!" Olivia screamed at the quaking Louboutin-wearing blonde.

"Even before we got here, I realized I needed to put Vicino out of business. Gianni's so crazy-competitive that if Vicino flopped, I knew he'd get bored of Gianni Mare. If he didn't have you as competition, I knew I could get him to close the place here and go to California!"

Daniel looked flummoxed. "You told me Gianni was forcing you to plant the bad clams! You said Gianni would hurt your mom and her Cavalier King Charles spaniel if we didn't do what he said!"

"I lied," Olivia told her old flame.

I HONESTLY DON'T remember the next few minutes all that well, but the gist of the ensuing heated argument between Daniel and Olivia was that Daniel had believed that his high school girlfriend was back for good, just waiting for her asshole boyfriend Gianni to get tired of Magnolia Beach.

Olivia had promised Daniel that Gianni had the attention span of a chipmunk (true), and once Jessica was no longer across the street at Vicino, Gianni would get bored in Florida. Olivia and Daniel could take over the daily operations of Gianni Mare, and eventually buy the place from the chef.

Gianni, Barclay, and the Colketts had set up a top-notch restaurant, which Gianni would sell to Olivia for next to nothing once Jessica was gone.

"Once I got down here and had to see you every day, I realized again how much I hate you," Olivia told Jessica. "And since Daniel and I haven't been able to scare you into leaving town, I'll just have to kill you."

"But you said we were going to terrorize Jessica," Daniel argued. "Not, you know, stab her."

"I can't wait anymore," Olivia told her hapless ex. "I gave you a week to run over Jessica, plant the bad clams, and send her the live fucking alligator—and you see her! She's still here!"

"I'll leave town," Jessica promised, her voice trembling.

"Feet-first is the way you'll be leaving," Olivia told her. "Get in the walk-in freezer. You, too," she told me.

"Oh my God! I hate the freezer," screamed Jessica, finally losing her cool (so to speak). "Please don't make us go in there!"

"That sounds pretty bad," Daniel agreed.

"Shut up!" Olivia told him. "You were in this with me the whole time, and there's no way you're getting out of it now. And stop screaming!" she hissed at Jessica.

Olivia opened the walk-in freezer door, which was of heavy galvanized steel, and gestured to me and Jessica to get inside. I knew the freezer had an interior safety release to make sure nothing except food got locked inside, but Olivia had worked in enough restaurants to have planned for this. She was just reaching into an expensive tote bag and pulling out a length of chain when the kitchen door suddenly burst open. It was dark outside by now, but there was just enough light from a corner lamppost that

I could make out a tiny form in a caftan—and Joe, who had what appeared to be a tire iron in hand.

"Drop everything," Joe told Olivia. "Put that knife down, Olivia."

"Are you kidding me?" she said scornfully. "You don't scare me."

"He might not, but I definitely do," said Detective Zack Safina, who walked in after Joe and Sophie and flicked on the overhead kitchen lights.

Chapter 23

THE MORNING AFTER Olivia tried to turn us into human Popsicles, I slept 'til 10:00 a.m. Holly was still at The Breakers with Howard, which I took as a good sign.

As for myself—I was packing up my Old Navy and Target dresses, and Waffles's kibbles and food bowl. It was definitely time to head home, since I couldn't keep up the Magnolia Beach pace. The dinners, the late nights, and Gianni's nutty girlfriend almost freezing us to death had given me a new appreciation for the non-eventful month of January at home. I mean, it was cold in Pennsylvania, but it wasn't as scary as being locked in the walk-in at Vicino.

I knew Bootsie wasn't ready to leave yet, but I could work around that. I'd rent a car, and Waffles and I could make the trek north tomorrow. We could leave at 3:00 a.m.

John Hall, horrified by last night's events, was taking a few days off from his bovine project out west and was heading home. And so were Waffles and I!

"It makes no sense that you're leaving now, when no one's trying to kill you," Bootsie informed me as I tossed an unworn bargain bikini into my suitcase. Luckily, I'd only worn two of Holly's fancy outfits, so hopefully she'd change her mind and return the stuff that still had tags on them.

"That's okay!" I told her. "Honestly, I need to get back to work."

The work excuse was true, but mostly I just wanted to go home. And get away from crazy leather-pants-wearing killers.

"Okay," Bootsie shrugged. "If you've made up your mind, you can take the Range Rover home. I talked my editor into letting me do a travel story on the Keys, and I'm trying to convince Joe and Sophie to come along. I'm renting a Mustang convertible."

"Thanks!" I told her. *Maybe I should leave right now!* Then again, it would be scary driving once it got into the middle of the night, and I needed to find Holly and say good-bye. . . .

"Ya should say good-bye to Mrs. Earle, too," Sophie pointed out. She was in a great mood this morning, given that she was taking a large share of credit for saving my life, and Jessica's, last night.

She and Joe had just started sipping their drinks at Tiki Joe's when Sophie, overcome by guilt, had insisted they come back and help me finish up the kitchen. As they'd approached the kitchen door to Vicino, they'd overheard the shouted argument between Daniel and Olivia. Sophie had immediately texted Zack Safina.

What was even better, though, was Sophie's pride in Joe.

"My Honey Bunny was so manly when he grabbed that tire iron out of his rental car!" Sophie told us about three thousand times this morning. "I'm still turned on!

"Let's go into town, get some lattes, and stop over at Adelia's place," she added. "We can tell her all about that cuckoo Olivia!"

WE STOPPED AT the espresso place, got coffees for ourselves, Joe, Adelia, and Ozzy, and turned toward Adelia's.

I couldn't bear to look at Vicino. I shivered just thinking about that walk-in freezer. I averted my eyes, gazing instead at Gianni Mare, where I figured we might see the Colketts futzing around with the patio plantings or sipping their morning cocktails. At least we knew Olivia wouldn't be there.

She'd gone on an ugly rant to us as we'd waited for more police to arrive. And she'd thrown Daniel even further under the bus than he'd already been, revealing that he'd been a complete pawn.

Olivia had bitterly told us she'd been working behind the scenes to get the Food Network to give her and Gianni their own show—based in Beverly Hills, this time.

Her real plan hadn't included Daniel at all. She'd just been using him to get rid of Jessica, and once she and Gianni got the TV deal to open a restaurant in L.A., Daniel would be history. In her crazy world, Olivia even thought she could get *Channing*—once he was done mourning Jessica—to move out to California and fall in love with her. So basically, she'd steal everything Jessica had once had.

"Hello! Paging *Single White Female*!" Bootsie had remarked when we'd told her Olivia's nutty scheme.

Right now, in the bright light of day inside Bootsie's car, I shivered again. Then I noticed that the Gianni Mare sign was being pried from the lintel above the restaurant's elegant white frame-and-batten front door, and an enormous moving truck was parked around the corner.

Bootsie, similarly intrigued, two-wheeled it into a parallel parking space, and I noticed two well-tailored, sport-coated backs visible just inside the open French windows of Gianni's place. They were bubble-wrapping the expensive Chinese blue-and-white vases that decorated Gianni Mare. Or what had been Gianni Mare.

"Hey, Tom and Tim," Bootsie shouted, jumping out of the Range Rover as Sophie and I trailed her. "What's going on?"

"Moving!" Tom told us. "To . . . drumroll please . . . Beverly Hills! Gianni got the Food Network gig, so he's closing this place and opening up a new restaurant in L.A."

"It turns out this really *was* a pop-up restaurant," Tim added. "And Olivia had been pitching the Food Network like crazy. Last night, right after they arrested Olivia, Gianni got a call that the Food Network was sending movers here to close up this place and take everything to California.

"The network doesn't want Gianni trying to run a place here in Florida as well as his places in Philly *and* in California, so Gianni's bagging Magnolia Beach! We're packing up and taking all the furniture, the window treatments, the Ralph Lauren plates, everything that isn't nailed down—and a few things that are, like the banquettes and the antique mahogany bar."

"We're flying to California today to oversee design and installation for the new restaurant, which is right around the corner from the Beverly Wilshire Hotel," said Tom, as Bootsie's fingers flew over her phone, furiously texting her editor. "And not to brag, but we'll be making a pile of cash as recurring characters on Gianni's show!"

"That's great," I told the Colketts, happy to hear about their good fortune. "That sounds really fun! Will you guys still have the florist business in Bryn Mawr, though?"

"Oh, sure," said Tom. "We figure we'll help Gianni get the new place up and running, and then jet back and forth to work at both Colkett Florists and our new interior design business."

I blinked, taking in the implications of this surprise development. Gianni was abandoning Magnolia Beach and heading for California—just as poor, crazy Olivia had wanted all along. And

Channing and Jessica could proceed with running Vicino without Olivia, Daniel, and Gianni sabotaging their every move. With the help of Adelia and her rich friends, Vicino would soon be filled with moneyed diners again.

"What about Barclay and Scooter, not to mention J. D.?" asked Bootsie. "Didn't they sink a few hundred grand into Gianni Mare here in Florida?"

"Fuck Barclay! And Scooter, too!"

Naturally, these words came from Gianni, who'd suddenly appeared from the restaurant's interior.

He popped through a French door and began yelling at the workmen to be careful with the handmade zinc sign, then turned back to us, his gold earrings glinting and intricate tattoos visible on his bulging biceps.

Gianni looked good with his Florida tan, much as I hated to admit it. In anticipation of his new West Coast lifestyle, the chef had added a bandanna tied in a sort of '90s-rapper style over his bald dome, and he'd switched up his trademark orange Crocs for a new pair in black.

I couldn't really explain it, but I couldn't deny it: *There was something weirdly attractive about Gianni.* He was the tattooed, muscled-up Vitamix of every guy you'd ever gone out with against all your better instincts, and who then hit on your friends and cheated with your coworkers. TV would be the perfect medium for his undeniable charisma, not to mention a good showcase for his Emmy-worthy tantrums.

"Barclay gonna lose like three hundred grand on this place, but who cares? He can afford it! Plus, he signed papers that said he understood restaurant is a big investment risk!" Gianni told us, looking happy as he recounted how he was sticking it to Sophie's ex. "And Scooter and Alvarez, they only put in like five thousand each. I tell them they can invest in my new Gianni Mare if they want to—maybe they get a couple minutes on my TV show. Probably not, though!"

He gave an evil little laugh and consulted his watch.

"Hey, flowered pants woman, I forgive you for harassing me at my hotel," Gianni told my nosy friend. "You can take quick picture of me as I leave town for your paper," he added. "Hurry up though, I got *Esquire* and *Food & Wine* coming out later, then I leave on six p.m. flight from Miami. I see all of you back in Bryn Mawr—if I don't sell my restaurant there. I might be too famous to come back!"

While Bootsie snapped a few pics and took some notes to e-mail back to the *Bryn Mawr Gazette,* I considered the fact that Gianni had once again come out on top.

It was official. The guy was unstoppable. He'd been named one of America's rising-star chefs last year. He'd told his staff, his customers, and anyone else who would listen that he'd have his own TV show by the time he was forty—and now he'd actually done it.

And I had no doubt he'd be mingling with celebrities within a few weeks of landing in Beverly Hills. He'd probably spend next summer doing cannonballs into the Mediterranean from the deck of Leonardo DiCaprio's yacht.

Unfortunately for Olivia, she wouldn't be going to Beverly Hills, too.

Chapter 24

"THIS DAY IS turning out awesome!" Sophie shrieked when we got to Adelia's, handed around the cappuccinos, and relayed the tale of Gianni's imminent adventures in Hollywood.

"First of all, we're not dead," Sophie said, giving Joe a squeeze as he came in from the dining hut, where he'd been overseeing the La Tente installation.

"Also," Sophie ticked off her mental list, "Barclay lost a truckload of cash on the restaurant *and* he got whacked in the head again. And with Gianni gone, and Olivia not trying to fuck everything up at Vicino, Channing and Jessica will get Vicino back as the number-one spot in town."

"I have some good news, too," Adelia told her, sipping a cappuccino, though she looked like she'd rather have had something stronger. "Bingo and Susie both got back in town late last night, and Susie already filed an injunction this morning against anything being torn down, sawed down, or even a blade of grass being cut at the old schoolhouse."

A FEW MINUTES later, all members of the Simmons clan arrived at Adelia's, summoned by Susie to this neutral location. Bingo greeted the tobacco heiress with a big hug, and Susie wafted an air kiss to Adelia, while Scooter and his wife, Mary Simmons, came in wearing sour expressions. Soon, the family meeting devolved into a verbal brawl.

Scooter began a three-minute monologue during which he explained that Chef Gianni had gathered his investors in Gianni Mare for a guys' weekend in Miami back in November, soon after he'd signed on to do the HGTV pop-up place.

Gianni had known he couldn't put together the kind of place he wanted for fifty grand, and he'd lured Barclay down with the prospect of screwing over Sophie vis-à-vis her investment in Vicino. Scooter and Barclay were introduced at a boozy group dinner, where Scooter had tipsily bragged to Barclay about the prime piece of real estate that his family held. Barclay had at once jumped at the chance to get in on a high-end condo development in such a ritzy town.

Poor Scooter realized he'd been manipulated and forced into the deal to build the condos, now that he really thought about it. At least, that was the version he was now serving up to his stepmother.

"It was all her husband's idea!" said Scooter, pointing at Sophie.

Susie Simmons seemed immune to her stepson's woeful tale.

"Scott, what did I tell you and your brother about tattling?" said Mrs. Simmons.

"That it's bad," Scooter mumbled.

"That's right," said his stepmother. "And one other thing. Remember how we used to ground you when you lied to us as a teenager?"

Scooter nodded.

"Well, it's happening again," Mrs. Simmons told him.

"You can't ground me, Susie! I'm forty-one years old!" screamed the hapless lawyer-slash-developer.

"Oh, yes, I can, because I still have control over your allowance," said Susie Simmons, who seemed rested and energetic after her classic-film cruise. "And as of an hour ago, the accounts are all under my control, and I'm giving your former monthly stipend to Mary."

She nodded at Scooter's estranged wife, who couldn't help a small triumphant smile. Scooter, for his part, looked pretty upset as he reached for a decanter and sloshed brown liquor into a glass.

"Mary and I will be in charge of the money, and you're not to go to restaurants. Or drink." She gave a pointed look at Scooter's drink as he gulped it.

"Susie, please," said Scooter hoarsely.

"All right," Mrs. Simmons said, relenting. "You can drink with me, since Mary and I have decided you should stay over at my house for a while, until she decides if she wants you back. We'll have a two-drink maximum, though, and I'll consider adding a glass of wine for you at dinner if you behave yourself."

"Okay," Scooter whined.

"If you want to come hang out at the yurt, you're welcome anytime," Bingo told his brother forgivingly. "You might want to start meditating with me."

Scooter didn't look too interested in this idea as he sipped his cocktail, but I thought it was remarkably nice of Bingo.

"Aren't ya mad at this jerk?" Sophie demanded of Bingo, pointing at Scooter. "And why the heck didn't you bust out of that spa you were in?"

"Scooter's on his own path in life," Bingo told her serenely, while the rest of us tried not to roll our eyes. "He may still become a man who's connected with the earth at a deep level."

"I doubt that," Scooter told him.

"Anyway, I love my brother no matter what!" Bingo told us. "As for the technology addiction lodge, it's a very interesting place," he added. "It's filled to capacity with really stressed-out people who haven't put down their iPads or phones or computers for years, so when I begged to make a call to my lawyers to try to stop the schoolhouse project, they locked me in an isolation room."

Bingo explained that all the tech addicts at the spa eventually freaked out and claimed they'd been kidnapped and were being held there against their will—which, of course, Bingo actually *had* been. But none of the staff had believed him, so he'd eventually just decided to wait it out until his weeklong stay was over. Then Arizona state troopers, alerted by Zack Safina, had come to pick up Bingo and take him to the airport.

Bingo said he didn't hold a grudge against the tech-rehab staff, or against Scooter. "I just knew that somehow that schoolhouse would still be here," Bingo said serenely.

"Ya know, I like your style," Sophie told him admiringly. "Maybe I'll try to work on forgiving Barclay, too. Well, probably not, but ya got a good attitude!"

AFTER THE SIMMONS family left, Sophie had another thought.

"If Barclay had money in this condo deal, he ain't going to give up so easily," she told us. "He'll sue Scooter, not to mention Bingo and his mom. My ex loves stuff like that."

"Mr. Shields waived legal action," Adelia said. She picked up a folder and waved it. "All four of the condo partners agreed. That Gianni person only had a few thousand dollars invested, so he was easy to get rid of. And Scooter, Mr. Alvarez, and Mr. Shields—your ex," she said, nodding to Sophie, "signed this dissolution of partnership. There's also a letter here that the property stays untouched until at least 2025."

We all took in this surprise development for a moment.

"Why's Barclay giving up so easily on the schoolhouse?" Joe wondered, voicing my own thoughts. "It seems weird that he'd let the condo deal go just because Scooter dropped out. Even a head injury and a hospital stay wouldn't usually stop Barclay."

"Yeah, I could see Barclay trying to sue Scooter for breach of contract," Bootsie said. "He'd love to find some loophole and force the Simmons family to sell the property."

"Ya got that right," Sophie said. "Are you sure he signed this non-suing agreement?" she asked Adelia.

"I'm positive," Adelia said, a little note of triumph in her voice. "Because I went over to the hospital with my lawyer, and I bribed him."

We all stared at her as she sipped at a frosty glass, smiling happily in her lemon-yellow Oscar de la Renta silk caftan and hot-pink lipstick.

"I don't know Barclay, but I don't appreciate him helping Scooter with his schoolhouse plans," Adelia told us.

We all nodded, having overheard Adelia regaling the Reptile ladies the day before with how bad the traffic and construction noise would be if the condo deal went through. "I'd expect it from Scooter, and that Mr. Alvarez is so good looking that it's hard to get mad at him, but I decided we needed to take care of Mr. Shields, once and for all.

"Of course, I didn't know that you three were being almost-murdered at the same time, but, anyway, Ozzy and I packed up a little suitcase with some cash I had in the safe, met my lawyer, and drove over to the hospital. I told Mr. Shields that the best thing he could possibly do in this situation was take the money and leave the schoolhouse alone," finished Adelia. "I explained that my lady friends and I may look elegant and have good manners, but we don't screw around."

"Mrs. Earle brought her gun, too," commented Ozzy.

"That's so Jersey of you!" Bootsie shrieked admiringly.

"So, this suitcase you gave Barclay: How much cash are we talking about?" asked Joe.

"It was about two hundred and fifty thousand," Adelia said. "He could have made a lot more on the condos, but if the whole town turns against him, it wouldn't be worth it. I like to deal in cash, and I think Mr. Shields respected that. He told me he was packing it in and heading to Miami for a couple months. He might do some condos down there."

We all nodded, thinking Barclay might enjoy Miami more, honestly.

"That still doesn't explain who knocked Barclay on the head the other day," mused Bootsie. "Olivia confessed to everything else, but she swears she and Daniel had nothing to do with that."

"Oh, that was me and Ozzy, too," Adelia said, nibbling a cashew from a Sevres bowl on the coffee table.

Adelia told us she and Ozzy had picked up an extremely heavy, three-arm Christofle candelabra from her dining room sideboard, waited for Gerda to go jogging, and done the deed. The meatball hoagie delivery had just been a coincidence. "When Gerda told me how poorly he's been treating Sophie here, I got so mad I decided he needed a little Southern-style justice."

Ozzy nodded, a note of pride in his eyes. "The guy went down like a bowling pin," he said.

Chapter 25

HOLLY WAS HOME, packing to spend the rest of the weekend at The Breakers, when we got back to her house.

"Everything's perfect with Howard!" she told us. "And look at this." She pulled up the Indianapolis society column on her phone, on which the top story was Dawnelle Stewart's engagement to a twenty-five-year-old backup quarterback for the Green Bay Packers.

"Dawnelle's totally out of the picture, and Howard completely understands about J. D. and Scooter," she said happily, grabbing her Celine handbag. "And everyone's invited for dinner at the steak house at The Breakers tonight. Seven p.m.!"

I looked longingly at the pool, wondering whether I'd finally be able to jump in this afternoon.

"Holly, do you think I could come back down in March . . . just for a long weekend?" I asked Holly. "Maybe without Bootsie, Joe, and Sophie? No offense," I added to Bootsie.

"I already got you a ticket," Holly told me, waving away my

protests that I'd pay my own way. "Don't get upset, I have about four million frequent flyer miles.

"Plus," she added, "I don't want to be all alone down here in March, especially since I'll be spending three weeks in February with Howard in Indianapolis. Dawnelle might be engaged to an NFL player, but that doesn't mean I'm taking any chances."

AT 4:00 P.M., I dove into the pool, while Waffles lounged on a chaise nearby. At 5:00, Bootsie waved good-bye.

"I'm meeting Brian the Zoning Guy for mojitos!" she told me. "After all, I did promise him. See you at the steakhouse!"

THE FLAGLER STEAKHOUSE was paneled with lots of candles and gorgeous ocean views, perfect for a perfect-last-night-in-Florida dinner.

"I'll have the artichoke hearts, the crab Louis, the dumplings—actually, we'll have two of all the starters," Bootsie told the waitress.

She looked around the table, which included Brian the Zoning Guy, who she'd brought along to dinner, and who was currently talking to Sophie about why there wasn't a Versace boutique right in Magnolia Beach.

Adelia and Gerda were to my right, hatching a plan for Gerda to stay on in Adelia's guest room through April. Gerda would help Adelia and Ozzy with odd jobs and some light Pilates classes. "Then I move back to Pennsylvania in the spring," Gerda told her new employer. "I think Sophie needs me. I probably move back in with her, maybe get her boyfriend to work out more, too." My eyebrows shot up at this news. A summer with Gerda was probably not what Joe had been envisioning in the farmhouse he and Sophie were renovating so beautifully.

"Should I order for everyone?" Bootsie asked and, without waiting for an answer, started listing what seemed to be most of the contents of the menu to the aproned server. "Okay, steaks. We'll have the strip, the T-bone, the tomahawk, and a couple of filets. Let's do some veal Milanese and a couple of lobsters, too—maybe two three-pounders?"

After adding about seven different side dishes and three orders of creamed spinach, Bootsie paused, while Howard (who'd be footing the massive bill) paused to order two bottles of a fancy-sounding French wine.

For my part, I began to calculate the total cost of just the steaks Bootsie had ordered. The total was so colossal that I gave up and tried not to think about it. Howard is one of the most generous guys around, and he loves steak houses. I knew he'd sign the dinner to his room charge and forget the whole thing.

"Hey, isn't that the pizza kid?" I said to Bootsie, snapping out of my reverie about tomahawk steaks.

"That's totally him!" Bootsie said. "Hey, Andy!" she shrieked. "Get over here!"

Andy the pizza delivery guy was in a Flagler Steakhouse busboy uniform. He came to our table, looking scared he'd get in trouble with his bosses for lingering at our table, but more scared that Bootsie would go ballistic on him again.

"I got a new job here," he whispered. "Please don't screw this up for me."

"Okay," Bootsie told him, "but I still think you lied to us the other day. There was more to the story about the meatball sandwich delivery."

"That part was true," Andy insisted. "I just dropped off the sub. I had nothing to do with hitting that dude in the head."

"We know who did that," I assured him. "Was there something else you didn't tell us, though?"

"Yeah," he said, squirming. "I did another weird errand that night. I stopped to get a beer after the police interrogated me, and I was sitting at a bar in West Palm feeling all depressed, when this hot girl in leather pants and her boyfriend came up to me and offered me two hundred bucks to drop off this fancy Hermès shopping bag at a cottage in Magnolia Beach."

He paused for a second, embarrassed. "I really needed the money for tuition, and the girl was kinda scary, too. She told me if I didn't drop off the bag, she'd hunt me down and make me regret it. She said not to look in the bag, either, which, by the way, had something alive in it. So I did it! I just hope it wasn't a kitten or something in that bag!"

"It was a baby alligator," Bootsie told him.

"Oh, okay, that's cool," said Andy. "Can I get you guys some more butter?"

Love *Killer Getaway*?

Then keep reading for a sneak peek
at the first book in the Killer WASPs Series

KILLER WASPs

Available from Witness Impulse

"*You* FOUND BARCLAY Shields after someone tried to kill him last night?"

I didn't have all that much information about what had happened to Barclay Shields, local builder of shoddy mini-mansions that are about as well constructed as your average game-show set. But I knew from long experience that Bootsie McElvoy would never leave until she had put me through a Guantanamo-style interrogation that would stop just short of waterboarding.

"I did find him." I sighed as Bootsie flung open the screen door to my antiques store, The Striped Awning, and charged toward a little French chair in front of my desk. "How did you hear?"

"More like, how would I *not* hear?" responded Bootsie, her sky-blue eyes bulging with intensity. "Let's start with the police report," she said, rummaging in her canvas tote bag, and emerging with a sheaf of papers, which she brandished triumphantly. "I have a lot of questions."

I sat down at my in-the-style-of-Chippendale desk, pushing aside a stack of paperwork—actually, a pile of unpaid bills—resigned to being grilled like a rib-eye.

What a waste of a gorgeous, sunny May morning. All around Bryn Mawr, lilacs were blooming in front yards, drivers were tooling by in convertibles, and women were happily pulling out their summer clothes—which in Bootsie's case meant a pair of flowered Talbots shorts, a Lacoste shirt, and pink sandals embroidered with whales. My dog Waffles, a freckled, drooling basset hound with an oversize belly, a permanently soulful expression, and an addiction to Beggin' Strips, wagged happily at Bootsie from his bed in the front of the store. He likes to sit up there, close to the tall front windows, where he can chew his rawhide bones and check out passing poodles.

Bootsie ignored Waffles—she doesn't believe in any dogs that aren't Labs, which are the preferred breed of her L.L. Bean–catalog family. Bootsie *defines* preppy: Even her marriage is preppy, with her two adorable toddlers, a chintz-filled brick Colonial, and tennis matches galore.

Bootsie, who graduated from high school with me fifteen years ago, is six feet tall, has chin-length blond hair and a permanent tennis tan, and is married to a former Duke lacrosse star named Will, whom she met through her equally bronzed, blond brothers. Bootsie and I don't have much in common, but we've stayed friends over the years—she works just down the street from my store, at the *Bryn Mawr Gazette*, the local newspaper in our small town outside of Philadelphia, where she covers both real estate and charity events. Basically, she writes about gossip.

Working at the newspaper is perfect for Bootsie, because she's incredibly nosy. She has a network of family members and friends placed around the suburbs of Philly who funnel her information each day. When she's not on her cell phone, she's working the aisles of the Publix, the liquor store, and the post office. She's honestly pretty talented at intelligence gathering: Bootsie once called me in the middle of the night to tell me that our friend Holly Jones was getting divorced, which Holly herself didn't even know until the next morning.

"You probably remember Will's cousin Louis from our Christmas party," Bootsie went on. "Tall? Blond? Big on golf and skiing?" This described every member of the McElvoy clan, but I nodded agreement.

"Louis is a lawyer, and he's defending Barclay in a lawsuit about those town houses Barclay built that fell into the giant sinkhole. And Louis got a call from Barclay's wife at one-thirty this morning about the attack on Barclay," said Bootsie triumphantly, pleased that her husband had such a useful person for a cousin. "Of course, the police called Barclay's wife to let her know about him being attacked, even though Barclay and his wife are in the middle of an epic divorce. So, anyway, Louis got the police report faxed over, which said that a Kristin Clark—*you*, that is"—with this, Bootsie pointed a tennis-tanned finger at me—"found Barclay after he'd been bashed in the head with something heavy. Like a hammer."

I nodded glumly, and shuddered at the memory of the inert mass of real estate developer, prone under a hydrangea. It all seemed unreal, and the memory was especially blurry given that it had been made late at night, in the dark, after three glasses of Barolo wine at a party. Waffles, sensing my discomfort, gave a sympathetic whine.

"Obviously, this is going to be big news," Bootsie continued happily, not looking upset in the least at the thought of Mr. Shields's recent head injury, "because Barclay Shields is loathed by pretty much everyone in Bryn Mawr, the entire Philadelphia area, and even as far as Wilmington, Atlantic City, and Lancaster County. Even Amish people hate Barclay! And it's not like people are whacked in the head with blunt objects around here very often."

True on both counts, I thought to myself. Thanks to his habit of cramming as many townhomes as possible onto tiny plots and his zestful overcharging of unsuspecting buyers, Barclay was one of the biggest and least popular builders around Philly. (And I do mean big: Even in the dark last night, I could see that the man weighed a good two hundred and seventy-five pounds.) In addition to the man's real estate notoriety, a violent attack in Bryn Mawr is unheard of: In downtown Philly, people get beaten to a pulp all the time, but things are pretty quiet in the suburbs. Bryn Mawr is where people live in charming old stone houses, play tennis, and break out the vodka tonics at five-thirty every night. A dog show or a restaurant opening constitutes big news. For instance, a new place called Restaurant Gianni had been front-page fodder this week for Bootsie's newspaper. Actually, Wednesday's entire front page had been devoted to the chef, the fabulous decor, the chef's girlfriend—who happened to be a decorator and had designed the place—the wine list, and his recipe for cappellini con vongole.

Bootsie and I had both been at Restaurant Gianni's opening party the night before, and it was after the party that I had found Barclay, right across the street from my house, while I'd been taking Waffles for a quick late-night stroll. Barclay had been bleeding from the head when I'd last seen him, but definitely alive when police and medics had arrived and whisked him into an ambulance headed for Bryn Mawr Hospital, if you can use the word "whisk" to describe hoisting a man the size of a vending machine.

"I called the hospital an hour ago, and as luck would have it, our old babysitter Jeannie was at the nurses' station"—Bootsie has a seemingly endless supply of nursing-student nannies—"and she told me that not only did Barclay make it through the night, he's awake. Awake and eating—he ordered in a salami-and-egg hoagie from the diner this morning.

"But none of that is important," Bootsie finished. "What matters is: Who do you think hit him?"

"You must be talking about my husband," squeaked a petite blond woman from the doorway, in an accent that rang with the unmistakable tones of South Jersey. "Can you believe the police had the nerve"—in Jersey, that's pronounced "noive"—"to ask me where I was last night? Like I have the upper-body strength to knock Barclay out!"

She had on four-inch heels, purple jeans, and a swoopy Roberto Cavalli multicolored silk blouse that retailed for seven hundred dollars. I knew this only because I'd seen the same blouse in my friend Holly's closet, with the Neiman Marcus tags still dangling from it. Behind her, a massive Cadillac Escalade was idling in the no-parking zone in front of my shop.

Clearly, this apparition was Sophie Shields, aka Mrs. Barclay Shields. Bootsie stared at her, her mouth agape and her eyes registering gossip nirvana.

"Besides, I was with my Pilates instructor all night last night—Gerda's from Austria, and she lives in our guest room—and then before that I was at Restaurant Gianni's party, so I've got an alibi," Sophie Shields chattered on. "You two were at the party, too, right?" Sophie said to us, a gleam of recognition in her puppylike brown eyes. I could only nod back at her, too stunned to speak. Her voice had the timbre of Fran Drescher mixed with the intonation of Tony Soprano, all in a package the size of your average fourth-grader.

"I thought ya looked familiar! Anyway, the police told me you found him, and then I tracked you down to this place. So I wanted to come by and thank you for finding him," she continued. "You saved me a bundle. If he dies before the divorce is finalized, I'm screwed. I need him alive! He hasn't signed anything yet, except some papers that cut me out of his will if he croaks before the divorce is done."

"That's too bad," I said weakly.

"Cute store," she said, looking around at the pieces in my shop, which range from little French sofas to English dining tables to mid-century lamps. "This is like a museum of, you know, *old stuff*!"

"Thank you," I said uncertainly, getting up to make sure Waffles didn't tackle Mrs. Shields in his overly friendly way, since he definitely outweighed her, and was already huffing over toward her happily. I took hold of his collar before he could drool on her shoes.

"My ex hates antiques," squawked Sophie. Looking around again, her small face broke out in a smile. "And you know what, since we're splitting up, I can buy as many as I want! And this junk—I mean, these things—really would add an old Philly feel to the place. I gotta bring my decorator back here. Well, when I hire a decorator, I'll bring him here."

"Thank you," I said again, hoping I could show her around the shop a little. Sophie was clearly the Holy Grail of Retail: the Revenge Shopper. Just then, though, incessant honking erupted from the Escalade waiting at the curb, and a woman with incredibly muscular shoulders in the passenger's seat gestured sternly at Mrs. Shields to hurry it up and get back in the car.

"That's Gerda," whispered Sophie, looking scared and waving at her passenger in an attempt to placate her. "But anyway, I really do like your store." She teetered indecisively on her heels for a second, while Gerda gave another thunderous blast on the Cadillac's horn.

"What the hell!" Sophie finally shrieked. "I'll take all of it. I have to meet with my lawyers in five minutes, and then I got Pilates at eleven-thirty, so I can't dick around looking through all this stuff. Just wrap up the whole store, all the tchotchkes and the furniture—the whole nine yards. Here's my Visa card. I'll have a truck pick it up tomorrow!"

AFTER I'D DULY recorded Sophie's Visa number, she, Gerda, and the SUV whooshed away, Bootsie and I high-fived each other, and I did an impromptu happy dance for a few seconds. Bootsie knows I've been struggling to make rent on The Striped Awning (and, well, pay my AmEx bill, too), since I inherited the store from my grandparents last year. The contents of the whole store—sold! I started calculating in my head how much money I'd make, and took out a notepad to start listing my inventory and totaling the bill. I turned over the sign on the door to read "Closed."

Unfortunately, though, Bootsie didn't take the hint.

"Well, now we know that Barclay Shields's wife claims she didn't attack her husband, and she has reason to want him alive. Why were you wandering around across the street at midnight, anyway?" she asked.

This was a good question, because I'm not really a midnight kind of person, and Bootsie knows it. I'm more of a pajamas-at-8:30-p.m. kind of person. "It also says here in the report that you were with someone, the guy who made the emergency call when the body turned up. Named"—she consulted her paperwork—"Mike Woodford. Who is *that*?"

"Is Woodford his last name?" I blurted out. I had never met this guy Mike before last night, and had only been in his company for about thirty minutes before we'd stumbled onto Barclay Shields. And I really didn't want to talk about said person with Bootsie, because, truth be told, I had been slightly drunk when I'd met him last night, but if memory served, he was very cute. Bootsie was tapping her foot while I considered all this; I could feel my face turning fuchsia, and I started hedging.

"Mike works across the street from my house at the Potts estate," I told Bootsie. "Waffles needed to go out, and then we bumped into this guy Mike, and then the three of us found Barclay Shields," I said, heading into the back storeroom to grab some newspaper and boxes to begin wrapping up my entire store.

"Well, I better start packing all the silver and china!" I yelled cheerfully over my shoulder. "Thanks for coming by!"

"You took the dog for a walk that late?" demanded Bootsie.

"Well, I don't think it was *that* late," I said, returning with my boxes and resisting an urge to scream.

"Yes, it was. It was 12:04 a.m. when Mike Woodford called 911 and said he'd found a body at Sanderson," she sang back at me, brandishing her fax, which I was tempted to grab and rip to shreds. "It's on the police report." Bootsie's a good person at heart, but her persistence was taking on the quality of Barbara Walters during an Oscar night interview. "And why were you walking that mutt over at Sanderson, anyway?" she prompted.

Sanderson, an estate in Bryn Mawr, is home to the blue-blooded Potts family, which has, amazingly, kept three hundred acres of valuable real estate intact as an exceptionally lush farm around their 1920s stone manor house. There's a barn, a ballroom, a greenhouse filled with rare orchids, and a library that holds thousands of rare books, and all of this happens to be across the street from my tiny, slightly creaky old cottage, which is, no doubt, a blot on the landscape in the eyes of the Potts family.

Waffles, sensing that he was part of this story, went around my desk to Bootsie and pawed at her leg, then unleashed a pint of drool on her knee. Bootsie glared at him, and rose to leave.

I love that dog.

"Why were we at Sanderson?" I repeated. "Well, Waffles really had to go. You know him—he bolts sometimes, and I can barely hang on to the leash. He took off for the bushes at Sanderson last night. Sometimes he just wants to, um, do his business there!" This was mostly true. Waffles does sprint to Sanderson sometimes, but he doesn't do his business just anywhere. He's partial to a certain bush in my backyard where he enjoys complete privacy, and if desperate during the workday, he'll make use of a grassy nook behind the store. He'd never sully the gorgeous lawns of Sanderson.

Waffles whined, then went over to his dog bed to lie down. He knew he had just been dissed.

Bootsie laughed, picked up her tote, and strode in her whale-print sandals toward the door—finally. She even acknowledged Waffles by nodding at him on the way out. "That dog's got good taste. I love that he likes to take a crap at Sanderson!"

About the Author

AMY KORMAN is the author of *Killer WASPs* and *Frommer's Philadelphia and the Amish Country,* and is a former senior editor and staff writer for *Philadelphia Magazine*. She has written for *Town & Country, House Beautiful, Men's Health,* and *Cosmopolitan.* She lives in Pennsylvania with her family and their basset hound, Murphy.